Tell me the rest of the story that goes with the picture.

The Brood (1979)

SEMIOTEXT(E) NATIVE AGENTS SERIES

"The Truth about Noses," was published in *Five Fingers Review*, February 2007 and *Monkey Bicycle*, issue 6, spring 2006. An excerpt of "Who's Afraid of Virginia Woolf (The Reception Climate)" appeared in *Unpleasant Event Schedule*, June 2006. "Peter & Pictures," was published in *Fence*, winter–spring 2007, vol. 10, no. 2. "Houses (Or the Uncanny Glows in the Dark)," was published in *Drunken Boat*, issue 8, 2006 and *How2*, vol. 2, no. 4, spring–summer 2006.

Special Thanks to Maximus Kim for copyediting.

Published by Semiotext(e)
2007 Wilshire Blvd., Suite 427
Los Angeles, CA 90057
www.semiotexte.com

Cover Art by Marilyn Minter
"Gap" C-print (photo) 36" x 50", 2004.
Back Cover Photography: Masha Tupitsyn
Design: Hedi El Kholti

ISBN-10: 1-58435-044-X
ISBN-13: 978-1-58435-044-6
Distributed by The MIT Press, Cambridge, MA. and London, England
Printed in the United States of America

BEAUTY TALK & MONSTERS

Masha Tupitsyn

To Wesley, The One who got away and then came back.

And to my mother and father, as always,
with everlasting love & gratitude.

CONTENTS

1

Diegesis (World of the Fiction)

*Up until the 1970s the ancient world, the world which is daily life
and thinking and loving, existed—but it was swept away. From the
age of innocence we've passed to the age of corruption.*

— Kathy Acker

I WALK DOWN the hill on Law Street like it's the beginning or the
end of the world and the world and the end are a movie. I ride my
bike like I'm a kid with no parents and I'm opening the frame and
things happen to me that you wouldn't expect. Not Japanese POW
camp things like in *The Empire of the Sun* or the dream-loss in *The
City of Lost Children*. But there's a spiritual trajectory, this thing
about kids who are loners, fighters—prophets—and it started at a
young age. You wouldn't notice me anywhere but in a movie
because movies are these fake ideal spaces. These wishful places.
These possibilities. Someone like me would have a chance in a
movie. But not an American one.

A prescription with side effects, this movie gives me a language I
can't get anywhere else, except my brain. And it's my brain that's
welling up with emotion. I'm interesting the way a kid, a girl in
a movie can be interesting, and I understand things like sex and

sensuality and boys and myself and destiny as if someone had written it all down for me and shot it because they want me to be special in this story and cinematic at age 9. At age 10. My heart shoots a million miles a minute and I know I have a heart, a big one, which is already a head start. This place is my shot at being real. At being a future. In the *mise-en-scene*.

This place is the perfect production and set. And I have all these people in this tiny town who want me to be exciting to look at and know. Who are rooting for me. I want everyone I know and don't know to sit down and watch, think about me the way they'd think about a character in a movie. Think about me as though I have a chance. I want to collect my viewers and seat them all in a theater. At the very least, I'm interesting. So I film myself. Whenever I've watched the apocalypse on screen, I've wanted to be a part of it. I've wanted to be left behind. Freed of the world, which was only ever a movie.

There is no longer a world to matter to. So I walk around and swim around and bike around as if I've got a steady cam on me, or more precisely, since I'm the one filming, a snorricam (a camera device that gets rigged to the body of the actor) that I wheel with me like Stanley Kubrick in *The Shining* whenever he's following little Danny. It's attached to me, or in me, or behind me, and I know I'm being watched, but by whom? I'm half-seer/half-seen. I'd rather be a steady wide-shot, a deep-focus, than a cheesy close-up. Most American movies exploit the close-up, going from distant to close, over and over again. Zooming tighter and tighter, until the face in question has been drilled into your head and everything else just disappears. You're left feeling stuck with this either/or feeling. Before and after. Close and far away. There is nothing in between. A cropped view gets rid of all the meaning and percentage and shuts it down, leaving only the lowest factor. If I'm going to be larger-than life, it'll have to be subtle in the frame, like a little bird flying around in the background. Everything can go in that way. If I mattered on my own, I wouldn't need movies.

I have this ocean, this exciting, sexy ocean that everyone here rattles and uses for different reasons. To swim in, to fuck by, to sail through, to look at, to tan on, to walk on. Nan Goldin photographed this ocean. It's in a lot of pictures at the Whitney and the Pompidou, along with her newer people-less nature shots. But museums and galleries are more interested in exhibiting her sex diary stuff, which takes place mainly in bedrooms for obvious reasons. What I'm in is a movie. What I am is a movie.

This place is a place you want to look at, with a camera, or with just your eyes. Most people think that unless you use a camera, you're not seeing anything. But that's a 20th century disease. I like looking at it with my brain, where the language and the I/eye are in total cahoots. I pretend I'm a mermaid with hair all over my breasts. I want to be oxygen savvy, taking or leaving the shore. Because I'm little and haven't been breathing for that long, I think I can stay underwater forever. I test my limits. Most of the time my hair is sandy. Proof that I've been down as far as I can go. I want to go underneath. I think that's partly what movies are trying to do—get underneath the skin by using the skin. But it's the skin that's fucked everyone up so badly. When we get out of the car, after landing there for the very first time, I go straight to the water and swim until I freeze and I really do feel like me and this place, me and this movie, are the only two things that exist.

WE RUN INTO EACH other in front of the only movie theater in town. The rest died off like an animal by the time I meet you. You live in New York, and that's where I first saw you sitting at a dinner table, so I'm absolutely blown away to find you here, in the middle of my summer. You register me as fast as I register you. This half-smile takes place. I have a lot of pride, even at that age, so I notice something important like *how a boy reacts*. I don't want to be drooling if you're going to be ambivalent the whole time. But I learn that you're never as sweet as when you're surprised.

You're dark, like me, except I've been polished off by the sun like a sea pebble. You've just gotten there, you say, as if you've made the trip all by yourself. Two characters meet all over again. I want to burst from the serendipity. At nine, I know what that is. I feel it. "It's just like a movie!" I tell my English friend Chloé, who doesn't get the picture until I set it up for her. Movies are really into serendipity, but I don't know if real people are. There's a big gap between what people will let themselves experience in a theater and what they're willing to feel in real life. I run through the plot. He's the love-object, or the one I want to call *destiny*, I say. Except I don't how I would have said something like that at that age. I'm pursuing him. Afterwards, he slips away into the theater with his dad, his really fat dad, even though he's so skinny, skinny like his mother, skinny like me, into one of the movies that's playing that night— there are two showing everyday at 7 & 10pm. Two different ones, until they switch them. Take them off the board that just stands there in the middle of town like a road sign or a compass. Except in order to do that someone has to literally open up the glass case, stand on a ladder, and tack on new letters that spell out *Dirty Dancing, Blue Velvet, Platoon, Ruthless People, Aliens,* or *Jean de Florette*. When the switch happens, everyone in town goes crazy. I go crazy. I plan my night according to movie. I go alone or I go with my mother. She teaches me that movies are ideological vehicles and she teaches me why and we talk about it. Chloé cares less about the movies. I wonder if it's because she's English? She spends the summer yelling at her mother in front of me.

My own mother is there when this thing with him happens. I think it's a movie by John Hughes, but as an adult looking for more complicated renditions of emotion, I think it's like the movie *Lovers of The Arctic Circle* or *Amantes del Círculo Polar* by Julio Medem, and he looks just like Fele Martínez and I, with my short dark hair back then, just happen to look like Najwa Nimri. Their characters meet and fall in love when they're both really little —kids—and his father ends up marrying her mother, and they try to find their way around the incest thing and have sex anyway while the leaves on the trees vibrate outside. At first, it means more to the boy. The boy is the one who sees into the future. But in real life, I'm the one who does that. He just lives. Their names are palindromes, our names aren't, but the whole situation feels like a palindrome. Like it could go backwards or forwards and the same thing would happen. Does happen.

From the moment I sat down with you at the dinner table, I am so affected by the way you look. The way you look is the myth that's going around about you. And it's the myth that drains me. The first time I actually come face to face with you is in a freight elevator I have to operate at my best friend's house—your building—in Soho. You are with a bunch of other boys and I have bare feet and pajamas on. I'm only nine years old. And I can't look at you and I can't get the elevator to line up with your floor, so you grab the wheel out of my hands. And you're mean about it. And for years, I obsess about that industrial room bumping and grinding somewhere between the third and fourth floor. I'm rattling the metal cage and we're stuck in limbo until you push me out of the way and land it perfectly. That means you're off, and your door closes on the other side of the fence. All those cute boys, hanging around you like groupies, puppies, multiply my desire times ten. I wouldn't mind every single one of you.

At dinner, I stare the way children stare at things they don't understand but feel strongly about. In this case, it's the physical beauty of a boy. Your face and how I feel about it, runs over my childhood and what comes after it like a car. You've been dead for years. What have I been? I think your inside is as good as your surface. But I'm wrong and it makes me think critically about beauty and many other things for the rest of my life.

If I were a boy I'd look like you. I wish. I pretend. I pretend I'm you or something in the middle. I pretend I'm you wanting me. I pretend you're me wanting me, or you wanting you. A flower self-pollinating. I pretend I've got everything I want and I'm feeling it from all angles and sides. I pretend that my hand is your hand and I'm using it. I think I would feel more beautiful if I were a beautiful boy rather than a beautiful girl. If we were both in the seawater floating, would it matter what our bodies did on their own? In the water the body is so easy going. What strikes me the most about *The Lover's of The Arctic Circle* is this idea, modeled after Freud's *Theory of Sexuality*, that children are capable of sexual devotion and passion. Of a sustaining desire. That I am. Like the sun in my eyes, it's hard for me to think when your face is around, looking so much like what I know. A pocket mirror. Together, we're two look-a-likes and it feels like you're the bad side of me, the part I'm not allowed to be, my Hyde. My monster. My boy. In my head I could have your face around all the time, doing things I couldn't otherwise do. Being cocky, being oblivious. Forgetting. I don't think about your body because at this point I really don't know what I'd do with it—how to include it in this whole myth. So I think about kissing, or being kissed, or watching myself kiss you. I think about our faces coming together, and looking alike and being filmed. Revolving pieces in a kaleidoscope. I think about your heart plummeting like mine. In my fiction my thoughts are diegetic, but your thoughts aren't. You're a soundtrack I can't hear from the outside. But once you've said something, and I have it in my head to rewind, it's diegetic again. Part of the story. "Is everything an O," I ask myself? But I don't know when I ask that.

We're all standing in front of the movie theater—my mother, me, and Chloé. I honestly can't remember the name of the theater. Maybe New Cinemas, but really does it matter? Someone else might say something else. About something else. For some people, some writers, these details make such a big difference. Such a contribution to the Story. They want to string their stories along like perfect pearls on a thread. But I'm not trying to pretend that any of this is the complete line up. Or package. But it is wearable, maybe even beautiful. I feel a lust for him that I must have picked up off some movie like a scent. Some movie woman. Or adult women in general. The stink of movie perfume is everywhere. Always. It skunks you, stays on. Me and Chloé are not just two children hanging out together.

My mother just watched me light up. She's a stage light for me. I'm in the spotlight or my life is. She's sweet and cool and laid back about it for me like a girlfriend of a much older girl. I think she tells me I should "definitely meet up with him while he's in town." Go somewhere with him. I think I try to sink out of it due to nerves and that's something I'll retain as I get older. Blocking men out, or making the path one of determination, not in a *The Rules* kind of way, or in an Oedipal conquer kind of way, but in a kind of don't waste my fucking time because I'm no wall flower kind of way. I'm defensive even at 10. I have the mouth of a sailor, some Depression-era kid who uses language to overcome the scarcity of basic gender supplies. In particular, I swear at boys. He either tosses his head back with laughter, or winces when I yell at the "Lemonade Boys" in front of him as we cycle past them on our bikes. I've been fighting with them for weeks. They freeze up when they see that I'm with another boy. An older one. I feel them get jealous, so I use hostile language to show off. I think I do it on purpose to seduce him. I just assume that toughness and honesty are the way to succeed. Are the sexiest qualities. *I'm as tough as you are.*

When he swings by the next day, I'm in a tube-top bathing suit (my mother's) and I'm wearing jeans over it (my mother's). He didn't waste a second. My shoulders are two dark peaches. They're fuzzy, pinkish brown circles from where the sun hit them. I'm in the yard with Chloé making seashell & bead necklaces, which I think I throw over my head and into a tree like a slapstick comedian when I see him ride up to me. Chloé looks outraged that I've just thrown three hours (a movie ticket) of work out the window because of a boy. I don't know why looking preoccupied in front of him seemed embarrassing or detrimental, but it did. I make the date, come up with it, arrange it, schedule it, pick him up, take him to the place— the horse stables—the whole nine yards. I take charge. He's fine with it. He's into it. We walk downhill and along things that have flowers, that are sandy and low key, and we talk about what we want to do with our lives. I'm serious—we actually talk about that. He's snotty and arrogant about it. He got worse with age. Says he knows without a doubt that he's going to be a musician, and makes fun of me because my list is somewhat longer. I say, "I'm either going to be a musician (which I am anyway), a marine biologist (I catch and read about things I find in the water all summer), or a writer." I've been doing that for years. And he's been doing his one thing for years too. It just counts more. It ends up putting us into the same school, into the same department, much later and that's where we play out our sequel. The things I've been dreaming about and plotting. Then we go to the movies. We go to the Swedish maudlin talking picture *My Life As A Dog*, We get one popcorn and I get incredibly embarrassed when, in the dark, which is already pretty connotative, the little girl in the movie, who's been taping her breasts down to look like a boy, appears topless on screen.

Her nipples are so tender and emblematic, right on the hormonal cusp—like mine. I can't stand it. She's burning with the same kind of shame that I'm full of because the female body always gets so tossed around. I feel that what's on screen is a mirror of my arousal around him. Not just for him, but for everything in my life. And I think, he doesn't understand or know, and that really turns me off and makes me nauseous. And of course I feel like I'm secretly looking at my own tits, because girls are always supposed to see themselves in each other, especially on a movie screen. Besides, there's a part of me that's trying to be a boy too—with my short hair disguise, my jean jacket, my walkman, my big 10 speed bike, my sense of direction. All the time I spend in the water by myself.

When I look over at him in the dark, he's smiling like he's so used to it, to topless girls, that I think, "I'm out of my league," or he's out of his. What does he have to lose? It's not his risky prepubescent-boy dick that's up their on the screen. I know he's gonna fuck everything that moves later. I can feel it. See it in his smile. He does, but I don't fuck him back. I don't fuck him because promiscuity, in the larger cultural sense, really fucking bores me. It's like any mass-production/consumption. I don't want to do what every (body) does, do it the way every (body) does it. I want to be abstemious and wean myself off the cynical IV drip. I don't think that context always saves the meaning, but if anything did, it would be context. Years later, when we finally do make out, he still makes my insides curdle and stink like milk. One night, after we get back together for the third time, I lick his dick in the dark, but pull away fast because it tastes like crushed aspirin and a pin-prick. Like he never washes it or whatever's inside is bitter. I pretend I'm kissing the twelve-year old him, his mouth, to get through it. Or to like it more. That he doesn't know what he's doing and I'm showing him how to do it. That he follows direction. Sometimes it's only me that's older.

I'm really attracted, maybe because I'm an only child, to the idea of twins meeting. Not literal twins, but symbolic ones. Of two mirrors facing each other. What happens to people when they become symbiotic? Mesh. No one wants to deal with the fact that if people can be a source of suffering and destruction, then the opposite must also be true. That a relationship can be a space for transgression and enlightenment. A personal case of cultural revolution. Something no one wants to imagine women experiencing, in case they disrupt some boundaries they couldn't otherwise overstep. The kind of female passion Michael Douglas beats-up, then destroys, when it rears its *wild*, curly blonde head in *Fatal Attraction* in the form of Alex. It's Alex's *persistent* desire that really terrified America in the 1980s. The idea of women who just won't be shut down, who just won't go away after you've fucked them, who aren't disposable or a temporary supplement for patriarchy. I know the entire culture is obsessed these days with writing-off anything that has the slightest whiff of codependence. That is, badly needing someone you love in a world where there's no love. Where there's no one. But everyone needs some kind of emotional catharsis. Some kind of collectivity, even the puny collectivity of two. That's where the power of movies, and the success of collective fascist bonding comes into the picture. I think it's a lot more fucked up to obsess about and pine for a system of celebrity that doesn't even know you're alive. Who will never know. Who on principle don't know. Who are in place for that very reason. I want badly for someone to need me, to see me, the way I see the big screen and everything on it. I think I need everything a lot more than it needs me. I deal with this by branching off and doing the most painful things on my own. I carry my desires like stains all over my body—countries on a map—as if I'd spilt them like coffee.

I think of him as a Rochester figurine, moody and dark. But unlike Rochester, he isn't the least bit devoted and could never show me that he loved me until it was already too late. The whole thing could be a Victorian novel in its convolution, its Byzantine treatment of time. In its tragic regrets. "No love can be expressed between us. Love doesn't exist between us. We know only the varied musculature which has developed out of pain," Kathy Acker writes in *Lust* about her own murder, which is her suicide, and all women are partly suicidal around men. He was such an asshole half of the time, a *little* asshole, that I don't know what I was doing besides resisting it. "At least I am resisting it," I think. If this is what it's going to be like, I will learn to resist it. When this proves impossible, even in the face of knowing how to do to it, I begin to think more about The End. About the apocalypse of most things and how good it would be for them to just *stop* and turn off completely. Every movie ends with "The End." As far as an audience is concerned, after the eighty minutes are up, nothing else is ever going to happen. Watching movies is like dying and I want to stop breathing. "I hate most of all being shut up or bored. Say that I hate everyone and every social thing," Acker goes on to say about her murder. But I'm not there yet. I'm still straddling away on the male edifice thinking I can triumph what I can fight and understand. Or I can make it love me. Or I can make myself not love it. I start thinking about all this as soon as I see its shadow show up. It's signs. The sun rising. This means I get tired by the time most people start waking up. *"Me: I believe in*

Romanticism. Romanticism is the word. Why? Because there's got to be something. There has to be something for we who are and know that we're homeless."

He looks so inviting and so is this perfect town, which makes me feel at home when he doesn't. It's why I keep going there. I stare through his windows even when the lights are off and the place is predictably cold. Or I dream this. A house of horrors, a house in a horror movie, but a house nonetheless, and I go up the stairs or down them. Or he goes up and down me. We're always sitting on stairs together. We'll later do this for real and we'll do it when I dream years after that. I imagine that he has his own place to live in town somewhere. And that he's all by himself in it. A twelve year-old boy living on his own like Jim in J.G. Ballard's *Empire of The Sun*. He invites me over and we are children playing out adult plots. I'm turned on by the idea that he will let me in perfectly. I dream his suffering stops as soon as I show up.

Most of what I say on our date, and I say a lot for a lot of different reasons, goes unregistered by him. He's not trying at all, and I don't know if that's a personal quality of his, or a quality that boys take on with girls. *How could I be more interesting? And would it make any difference to him, to me?* He is so many versions of earth tones I mistake him for some beautiful russet-tailed fox. *Oh, those eyes. Oh, mine.* Maybe he's a fire I can toss a log into or wrap around myself like a coat. I believe early on that love gives me something that sharpens who I am. But people are such wimps when it comes to desire it makes love really complicated. He doesn't do anything that's surprising or fun. He never stops to look at me. Our walk is always side-by-side. Neither of us ever turns around. Does he say anything? He never asks to go swimming with me. He never asks me anything. So I ask him, "Do you swim?" and he just says "Yeah." I want him to say how and why and where, and to describe what he does in the water. But he doesn't. I'm tossing bones and he ignores them. The way he swims sounds so mandatory and routine, I forget all about it. I give up. All I know is that he knows how. So what? Later, I learn that so many brilliant men are still such dicks to women. So if it's not being smart that frees you, what frees you? In the tiny note that comes with the Myth of Cupid and Psyche in *The Golden Ass*, it says, "the writer is entertained by what he writes; he believes none of it."

After we say goodbye and make plans to meet "some time," maybe even the next day, he walks away with his fat father, in a dark summer sweater I want to be in, and into one of the movies that's playing. I want to follow him in, already an obsessive unsatisfied with the cliff-hangers of fragments, the kind Roland Barthes says you historically get when it comes to love narratives. What would finishing something look like? "He's either in *Dirty Dancing* or *Jean de Florette*," I tell Chloé and my mother, like a detective. I think I have to be one. I think it's because I know that when it comes to really intense feelings of interest, girls have to keep their feelings all plugged up like a tampon in their cunt, pretending they don't have them, and leave the real desiring to boys. Any fuck-ups count so much more with girls. They're rarely allowed to recover or move beyond their recovery. Besides, I lament, the *available* part is historically the least interesting.

After I'm done talking to him, either Chloé and I have just come out of a movie, or we were planning on seeing one ourselves. We've already seen *Dirty Dancing* two or three times—we love it like maniacs—and I saw *Jean de Florette* in French class at school. The French teacher often plays French movies for us thinking it'll help with the language if we see famous people speaking it. Turning language into a famous performance you spy on and copy. "Maybe they've gone to see *Jean de Florette*," I whisper to Chloé under the movie theater awning, already suspicious and guarding my passion in case someone overhears it and reports me. It's the same awning under which I'll experience at least another ten years of sexual infatuation/heartache.

Slipping into the singular, well-known theater over and over again, like a reoccurring dream. Chloé gets excited by the mystery I've just thrown into the picture as if it were another cheesy summer block-buster she wants to see. My mother goes home and gives us, what seems like, a giant slice of freedom and opportunity to pursue the cosmic role of a lifetime. "He probably went to see Jean de Florette after all," I say disappointed. The line to *Dirty Dancing* still collecting outside without him. His fat, arrogant father probably has a lot in common with the fat, arrogant male lead—Gérard Depardieu. Chloé laughs at this. Or maybe I just laugh at this in my head and don't say it out loud. But I get this sense of *life is political* from my mother, so maybe my mother said it. Men don't make arbitrary choices. That means we can't spy on him, Chloé notes. Shit, I say. Since we've already seen *Dirty Dancing*, it's fine if we don't pay attention to the actual movie. We'd be going again to watch *him*, I fantasize, turned on.

It reminds me of the scene in *The Night Porter* where Dirk Bogarde —a fascist in a fascist movie about fascist desire—is sitting in the opera house watching Charlotte Rampling from behind as if it were a sexual position. Bogarde stares at the back of Rampling obsessively and she feels him doing it and turns around to look over and over again. Sometimes he's not there when she looks back. Sometimes he is because desire is a ghost. She's confused by memo-ries. She's confused about what's real. It's memories we have lifelong affairs with, not bodies. And Bogarde knows this. A sadist, he uses memory against her. Fucks her with it. Patiently watches Rampling like the grim reaper, wanting to take her back to a hell she got off on with him. Would he feel me if I were to watch *him*? In this case, he's Jewish and I'm not and it's forty years after the Holocaust. So I don't know what kind of power is involved. Chloé doesn't ask, "watch him do what?" because desire is so communal. Girls are always sharing it. She's interested because I am, so it makes us split him in half like a sandwich. Does sharing him also make us lovers? He'd be out there sitting in the theater, a dark silhouette, a boy on the screen pulled into whatever action was playing. When I think of Chloé, whom I've never seen since that summer, I think, children are great because they're totally willing to get on board something that doesn't technically *belong* to them.

After the line outside is let in and both movies have been turned on for the night, Chloé and I go inside to ask questions. I look for someone to ask. I want to know which movie he's in? I say, "he's perfect." I say I need to find him. I don't think about the fact that I'm describing a little boy, a child to the adults working there. I jump cut any subjectivity from the construction of beauty. Everyone should see what I see, should like what I like. I pass him around like a picture and enforce him in words because he's my movie star and that's what happens when you want to know one in person. I pray he has no idea how I feel. Some woman says she doesn't know anything. She doesn't know *who* I'm talking about. But the next night, on our way into *My Life As A Dog*, the same woman, who's now selling the popcorn & soda, instead of ripping tickets, remembers my crime-sketch right in front of him, in front of me. And humiliated, I'll want to know: How come you didn't *understand* anything yesterday? How come you didn't pick it up then? And he'll laugh peripherally like a deadly weapon.

I don't watch him, I watch the movie. I don't watch the movie, I watch him.

Before him and after him I'm different. He's a model for years. I keep coming back to him in this cinematic way. Pressing play, wearing the tape out. I think I see him all over the place. Chloé and I first see *Dirty Dancing* in July. The retro 50-60s soundtrack is the movie's big allure. For us and for the female lead "Baby." We can dance even when we don't understand what's going on. We can act like everything is a romance plot and we'll get through it. We've been through it all. High '80s, bathetic decadence. Even if you don't like the movie, you'll love the songs because most of them are classics. And like all classics, we're seduced by the nostalgia for History even when it's not history yet. When I learn that he went to see *Jean de Florette*, another historical recreation, instead of *Dirty Dancing*, I get embarrassed about my taste and my age. Suddenly he feels a lot older and a lot more discriminating. He feels fake. I listen to Philip Glass on my walkman while I ride my bike to the beach. That summer, I saw Laurie Anderson's *Home of The Brave* by myself—a movie record of her "Mister Heartbreak" tour—but I also have a propensity to want to fit in sometimes, or at least to understand what fitting means. So I listen to Madonna too. "Who's That Girl?" and "Everybody" on my walkman. I may go to popular movies, but what I derive from them are the politics behind the films. He doesn't think anything when he watches a movie. He doesn't have to. Later, I'll listen to him tell me *No Way Out* is the best movie he's ever seen, without thinking twice about its cold-war nationalism. I'll remind him about it six years later while we're renting *9 1/2 Weeks* on a date. He'll deny it or say he doesn't remember. He'll call me an elephant or some other animal with eyes in the back of its head. A two-year age gap is everything at that age. It's between us. Or he always brings it up. But at sixteen and eighteen, two years will be all I'll need to outsmart him. Outgrow him. When I ask him that summer, he says he wouldn't go near *Dirty Dancing* with a ten-foot pole. He says it sucks and I wince. He's used to expressing himself. He's a musician after all and a boy. He must know what he's talking about. His mother adores him in all the wrong ways.

In *Home of The Brave*, William Burroughs, long and ropey like a white crane, does the waltz. I may like *Dirty Dancing*, I think to myself, but he wouldn't go anywhere near Laurie Anderson either. *Dirty Dancing* is delivered like a kind of kiddie-porn. It isn't the dancing that's dirty, it's the poor working class politics that it exposes. People dance in dives no upstanding, white citizen would frequent, unless they wanted to slum it, like "Baby" does. But Baby also wants to change the World. "Baby" is a virgin in all ways: she doesn't dance, she's a paternalistic wet dream, she isn't poor or jaded, she doesn't know her body, and she's never had sex. "Baby" is what her father calls her. Baby has a chance, a future. For the first time in her life, she wants to get her father's political 1950s stench off of her. The movie, unlike it's earlier and more conservative pre-decessors *American Graffiti* and *The Big Chill*, was written and produced by two women, Eleanor Bergstein and Linda Gottlieb. In it, music is a form of protest, and goes back to the transgressive roots of rock 'n' roll. Up until her initiation into the sexual under-belly of dirty dancing, or just dancing period—cause she doesn't know how to do either one—Baby's never thought twice about social injustice and how her summers at the Catskill resort every year are built on the socioeconomic oppression of other people. The seedy wooden dance shack of the movie is the moral and aes-thetic counterculture to the white middle-class, adult culture of the Catskills resort. It's an anti-hell hell. When Baby walks in, she walks into her own sexual emancipation. All the dancing behind the door is a primal scene she happens in on. Music is used to define the working-class and to distinguish it from middle-class America. All of this appeals to me, my parents being immigrants, my parents being true-lovers, no matter how lamely it's presented. The movie is told from a woman's point of view. *No Way Out* is all about a man's world and the rehabilitation of an America that's otherwise always been strong & perfect. This makes *No Way Out* a million times more nostalgic than *Dirty Dancing*. When he rejects my movie, he rejects me.

[MICKEY:]
Silvia...

[SILVIA:]
Yes Mickey?

[MICKEY:]
How do you call your loverboy?
[SILVIA:]
Come 'ere loverboy!!

[MICKEY:]
And if he doesn't answer?
[SILVIA:]
Ohh loverboy!

[MICKEY:]
And if he STILL doesn't answer?

[SILVIA:]
I simply say:
Baby,

Oohh baby
My sweet baby
You're the one

When they're not training for a dance competition that signifies universal freedom, Baby and Johnny act out their love through a song called "Love is Strange." "Love is Strange" is what they sing when Johnny's not teaching Baby how to move. When he lets her just do her own thing. The number is a lunch break, maybe even a sex break. It's an unrehearsed schtick for them. The song is meant to illustrate how close Baby and Johnny are, how when you're *really* close, a couple knows the same songs and can read each other's minds and spontaneously break into any song. The movie is not quite a musical, but has musical roots, so instead of a full-on "performance," Baby and Johnny lip-synch "Love is Strange" together. Musicals are about people being on the same wavelength. About multiple perspectives. About language being spontaneously shareable. About people being able to perfectly synchronize and express themselves. I wonder how someone like Jean-Francois Lyotard would feel about the idea that people can speak to each other without misunderstanding, after stating that there'd be no need for speech in the first place if there weren't all these gaps in phrasing? Humans, writes Lyotard, "Learn through the feeling of pain which accompanies silence (and of pleasure which accompanies the invention of a new idiom) that they are summoned by language." Musical renditions, like the one's Judy Garland performs in *A Star is Born*, are a way of righting a wrong, of compensating for a lack. I wish I could remember what we talked about, but mostly I remember what we didn't say. What I wanted him to.

Years later when he said I love you, I stayed awake because of it and replayed it over and over again like a song. Not just because I liked the sound of it or how catchy it was. Or because after so many years, it all lead to that. *Was it the things you said, and you saying them, or was it just those things?* But because it was a perfect phrase— I didn't reciprocate. Hanging on to the moment he got it right and the position he was in when he did. How I didn't plan it, but how it wedged itself into the story anyway. Usually either I didn't say what I needed to, or he interrupted me, or didn't let me, or we chose to talk about something else instead. We always spoke in code. And whatever else he didn't fuck up, or bury, but said with kindness, with me in mind, I remembered because it never worked out.

Years later Gina and I would comb the streets looking for you. I was rummaging through time and space, thinking you'd be there in that area of chance. On city terms, we lived close by. I could count on finding you and you could count on being found. But we never talked about it that way. In the way of the "pact." Too honest and to the point. We didn't really talk period, just sniffed at each other like twin animals. Antithetical, equivalent. Whenever it did happen, running into you, I'd get shocked by a thousand pins & needles. Or what felt like forcing my entire body into an electric socket. A torture device was underneath my hide all along, installed by the secret police like a wire, and it would split my anatomy at the rumor of you. That's just how my body reacted.

Either before he arrived or after he left, I spent some time hanging out with Joanie and her diabetic cousin Becky down on the West End. I live on Law Street, which is in the East End. As West Ends usually are, the West End here is more upper-class and conservative. The houses boring to look at, with overbearing gardens, and lots of fat roses. The East End is full of purple lilac. It's where Anais Nin and Gertrude Stein and Eugene O'Neill and Miles Davis and

Cookie Mueller and John Waters and Nan Goldin have all stayed. It's where everyone I like dead or alive has lived. It's where I live. The houses on this side are falling apart, sea whipped and weather torn. The shingles are gray and vary from house to house. Nothing looks the same. And I think there are more houses on the water in the East End than on the West End. The light is different there too. On the East End, the trees are older, sometimes even old, and the crowd is younger. It's where the *artists* have always lived and stayed. I had a boyfriend who grew up on the East End and, as a Halloween night-time prank, him and all the other East End boys would switch the East End cats with the West End cats.

I think Becky, Joanie's Cousin, was a year or two older. A tomboy, she'd swing by on her bike and ask Joanie to inject insulin into her arm. Or she'd just sit on Joanie's bed and do it herself. They were both blonde, but Joanie was blonder. Becky had tan stringy hair, while Joanie's turned to cream in the sun. I'd watch the needle going into Becky's arm, uncomfortable and transfixed. I was the same way about seeing other kids get naked. I just couldn't understand their comfort. How being naked didn't matter to them, but mattered so much to me. Whenever I got naked, the whole world stood still. I hated needles and was afraid of them, so it was hard to believe Becky would voluntarily push a syringe into herself. I'd rather die of diabetes. I hadn't met Chloé yet. Chloé lived on the East End of town, where I felt at home. Like Chloé, when it came to her mom, Joanie was drawn to any hint of pain, liked being on its unstable borders, and often offered to administer the shots herself—insisting that I watch carefully while she did it.

Joanie might have been a year older than me too. But maybe not. She had big teeth and a whiff of breasts. She always wore baggy shorts and big tee shirts. Her sprawling, New England house, part barn, part *Meet Me in Saint Louis*, belonged to her grandma and grandpa, who practically didn't exist. I never saw them. I think I heard her grandpa's voice hemorrhaging once out of one of the rooms like a prank or a special-effect. The kind Ferris Bueller rigged up in his bedroom to scam his parents into loving him more than his sister. Sometimes it felt like the house was all Joanie's and she lived there all by herself with all her male movie star posters tacked to the walls. She had a big room facing the bay all to herself. There were four bare windows in it, curving like a smile. Joanie liked to undress in front of them while the sun wrapped up for the day, never bothered. She'd ask me if I wanted to fool around or touch her or kiss her, or have her do any of those things to me. I'd say no, feeling the sexual tension go from me to her, while an entire panorama of movie-eyes ogled me like a guy. I'd done things with girls before, but Joanie wasn't exactly my type, physically or emotionally. Cinematically or for real. I didn't really have much in common with her. She didn't really get me. She did what she did with everyone. She was a starfucker and I'd just listen to it. But really, I needed some company, since I was always alone and didn't know anyone. Being alone was my thing. It might've been Joanie who talked openly with me about masturbation, who might've even done it in front of me once or twice, or threatened to. I remember being amazed that another girl my age rubbed herself against things with a target in mind. During the winters, Joanie lived in the South somewhere with her parents and her little brother. When I'd come by, Joanie would drag me up into the two-storey tool shed and we'd talk and hang out by the lawn mower and old furniture. She usually had something to show me. Or she'd tell me about some plan she had to try something new on one of the boys. She liked having an audience. She liked putting her mouth on things.

In the empty kitchen she'd eat or offer me cereal. I think she rarely left the house, and if she did, it was only to go swimming in the bay. Everyone came to visit her, never the other way around, but I have no idea how I first did. Joanie was always horny and ready for a petting session with someone, a girl, a movie poster. There were no *real* boys. Joanie said she liked older men, so she gravitated towards movie men because no one would disapprove of it that way. At seven, you can be in love with Rob Lowe or Michael Douglas and nobody cares. Everyone thinks desire is make believe when it comes to famous people and movies. In that case, you can go all the way. Nobody worries. Go for it. But Joanie was serious about her crushes and about making a move on them. Even on paper. Whereas I'd go to the movies in town, imagining I was all alone in the world. Joanie would watch movies on her VCR by herself. In bed, so that she could be alone with her lust. Our strategies were totally different.

One evening I came over, maybe even slept over, and Joanie offered to perform what she called a "French kiss séance." I didn't know what that meant. So she showed me. In the séance, Joanie set up a chair in the middle of her room like a stripper or a school-teacher in a classroom. Then she pinned a poster of Tom Cruise from *Top Gun* to the wall—the one where he's floating up in the clouds, body-less, while Kelly McGillis is perched on his right shoulder, acting as his "good" conscience. In the poster, Tom looks moody and tight like a fist. He's squinty eyed. After Joanie unraveled Tom's poster, she spread him out and pinned him up. Then draped a blanket or a towel over him, I can't remember, making a tent. Then she sat underneath it on the chair with her back towards me and made out with Tom's glossy paper face to "*Take My Breath Away*," which she had on tape. Halfway under the blanket, Joanie's head would move around in a lot of semi-circles, her body hooked to the chair.

Sometimes she sang the lyrics. To Tom, or to me, or to the general imaginary situation. Sometimes, pretending to be Maverick herself, Joanie would quote Tom's lines from the movie. Like when Maverick, the hot-blooded, impotent cowboy says, "The only thing I ever cared about scares the shit out of me now." Or when Viper, his flight instructor tells him, "That's the best flying I've seen since Nam." Joanie knew the movie inside out, but had no idea that without the required approval of the Navy and the cooperation of the Navy's *Top Gun* school in San Diego, *Top Gun* would have never been made.

Desire is so communal and Joanie knew that. She was into symbolic orgies. The third person was always the image. The ideal. Both *"Take My Breath Away"* and Gun's big kissing scene blasted in the dark as Joanie copied it and I sat on her bed watching. Take after take, her wet mouth took in some more of the picture. Sometimes she'd offer me a turn as if she was passing a joint. But I'd say, No thanks. I wouldn't have minded doing something like that in private, and sometimes I did do it, but not with Joanie plastered all over me. Like a madam, she said I could have my "pick of anyone, not just Tom." She said, "Pretend I'm him." She said, "You're not paying attention." She said she had a whole collection of men but was in a "Tom Cruise phase." Mostly, she didn't discriminate. Joanie took turns making out with different movie-boys in front me. There was Harrison Ford in an *Indiana Jones* poster, there was Emilio Estevez from *St. Elmo's Fire* and *The Breakfast Club*, there was Matthew Broderick from *Ferris Bueller's Day Off* with his arms folded behind his head like he was in the middle of getting a routine blowjob. Once, she even made out with a *Miami Vice* poster of Don Johnson, while Tubbs stood on the side watching with his gun hard in the air. But the vibe was very different that day.

It was Joanie who taught me you could kiss anything if you needed something to kiss, or if you "needed the practice"—the wall, your hand, a pillow, a picture. I'd watch Joanie the way I'd watch older girls make out with their boyfriends. I was worried that someone would walk in in the middle of it. Maybe Becky. Did Becky know about these kissing games? Did she play them with Joanie? I didn't know how to handle it. Joanie was so in love with images, she didn't feel at all real to me. It was like she was just another poster. Next to a poster. Don Simpson, the "concept" producer behind *Top Gun*, and also known as the "Beverly Hills Cock," described the movie as, "two guys in leather jackets and sunglasses standing in front of the biggest, fastest, fucking airplane you ever saw in your life." But that was just an image too.

It's clear, I think, that no one's beauty means anything unless it's depicted. But when I remember him, I think he mattered to me because of the secrecy encompassed in my look and the idea that I didn't have to share it. There was no consensus, and maybe, no one else even saw it. Most of the time, I didn't say a word about it. To him or anyone else. In *Celebrity*, Chris Rojek says fame and star-fucking are the result of the rise of public society. A society that cultivates personal style as the antidote to formal democratic equality. The only Me that exists is the self that's seen by others.

Maybe it's easier to be sexy when you're not being yourself. Johnny and Baby do a whole song and dance using "Love is Strange" as their key script. Their lip-synching is synchronous with possession. They are Sylvia and Mickey—another singing "couple"—like Judy Garland and Mickey Rooney in all their sexless MGM productions. The whole thing is a puppet show and the voices and the lyrics do all the talking and explaining. They use Johnny's sunny dance studio. They're on their knees. They're sliding towards each other across the white wooden floorboards in jeans. Cowboy boots on Johnny and white Keds on Baby. All in black, Johnny is a working class threat/hero, and I can't remember if the sun is shining or if it's raining outside his woodsy shack. They're auditioning each other for the role of summer-love and freedom.

In *Badlands*, Martin Sheen and Sissy Spacek also dance to the song "Love is Strange," except it's no big deal. They don't even look at each other. The whole scene takes two seconds, part of a transitional montage on the inevitability of boredom. Kit is half-leaning against his dusty car while the song's playing and Holly's kicking dirt, with an open book swinging from her arm. The song is private for them, diegetic, a fly in the background. They just barely move. They're beyond what it has to say. I wouldn't call it dancing in the "expressive" sense. Mostly they kick dirt around with their feet, bored out of their minds. Ambivalently plotting. The American road odyssey is squashed in a big way. Movies always make it seem like everyone in the 1950s wanted to slow dance with their sweetheart. Movies like *Grease*, *Back To The Future*, *American Graffiti*, and *Peggy Sue Got Married*—as if nostalgia can solve everyone's problems. In *Back to the Future*, Michael J. Fox's love object just happens to be his Mom. But really all the dancing happens as a way to circumvent sexual repression and conformity. Movies pretend that there is something about the 1950s we should miss. Since most movies are repression vehicles themselves, instead of being honest about history, they make people dance through it. Or on top of it as if it were a stage. *Dirty Dancing* takes all of *Badlands'* violence and schizophrenia and ambivalence out of "Love is Strange" and pretends there's a cure to America.

Whenever I remember our childhood date, I want to toss it around nostalgically and pretend there was nothing wrong. But it's the biggest key there is. I think of Brecht's poem, "I Never Loved You More," as if I'd recited it to him that day:

Everything was grand that one night, ma soeur
Never thereafter and never before—
I admit it: I was left with nothing but the big birds
And their hungry cries in the dark evening sky.

Kit and Holly do the same romantic things that Johnny and Baby do, but they don't believe in them and that's the difference. America is about *believing* and they don't feel a thing. They dance but they also kill. They make out but they also steal. Kit and Holly do their dancing in symbolically different spaces. Spaces where people and ideas don't exist. Only big gaps spread thin across the country. The idea is that there's a *nowhere*, a nowhere which no longer exists, and doesn't exist in the movie either. While driving, Holly and Kit gossip about movie stars. It's the 1950s and bombs are considered the perfect blonde. In the 1960s, *Dirty Dancing* wants to try to change all that. Towards the end of the *Badlands* trip, Kit pulls Holly out of the freedom/boredom symbol of the American convertible, and forces her to slow dance with him to Nat King Cole in the desert at night when there's nothing left to be but ontological. But stars. "Do you like people?" a sheriff asks Kit after he's arrested him. "I don't know," says Kit. I wonder if Holly knows that about him. I wonder if Holly's on Kit's misanthropic shit list.

When Kit sees Holly for the first time, she's twirling her baton on her front lawn in Fort Dupree in South Dakota. Since she's the only thing out in the open, Kit walks up to her and says, "I'll try anything once." "I got some stuff to say. Guess I'm kinda lucky that way." Holly (maybe short for Holly-wood), a red-headed vehicle for Kit's fame and escapism, doesn't react. Holly's a shy fifteen year old, but not so shy that she won't kill people or fuck a garbage man who does. It's Holly who does all the talking, all the "writing," throughout the film, tells us *what Kit has to say*. We're told about what Kit thinks, or what she thinks he thinks, but we never hear him think himself. As a life, Kit gets all the credit. But it's Holly's voice and Holly's script that makes him exist. I don't want to be another female narrator of masculinity.

Holly is a writer, a posthumous one if you think about how *Badlands* is the death of their previous egos. Their ego-trip.

While driving through the Great Plains, Holly reads "Celebrity Rumors and Facts" magazine out loud to Kit, then tests him on it. Most of the time Kit answers correctly, scoring high on the quiz. Although he may be a marginalized outlaw who hates his country, like everyone else, he's faithful to his pop idols. *Badlands* reveals that no matter how much you destroy and how much you try to outrun (escape), you're still a star fucker cleaning the ruins of mass media like a kitty cat. Idolatry, thinks Kit, is the only place to go.

Absconded, Kit and Holly don't want to be Sylvia or Mickey. I don't know what Holly wants to be, she never says. She only says what Kit wants their life to look like. But Kit wants to be James Dean and won't rest until that's what he is. The philosopher Leszek Kolakowski said "the intellect cannot conquer vanity. Nor is it an accident that the word 'vanity' is close to 'void.'" Handcuffed, awaiting execution, Kit hands out his comb and lighter to an adoring crowd.

Rumor or fact? A few years ago I learned that Sissy Spacek had one of the first Hollywood nose jobs and it really depressed me. I'd always thought she was a "serious" actress, proud of her oddities, which included her nose. And while I never liked her nose for its skeletal severity, I did like it for the fact that it was *real*. Hers. In the movie *Carrie*, Spacek's face looks like a terrible skull under a film of blood & fury. But then I found out that she brought her own horror to the horror. I wonder if Spacek ever thinks the plastic surgeon fucked up her old face? Whether she hates her new nose, that's now old. I rented *Badlands* again because it felt lost in my head. The song, "Love is Strange" detached from the rest of the film. I wanted something to make up for Spacek's vain (void) mistake. I wanted to make up for it for her. So I focused on her eerie ability to play dead in every movie.

I want to get all the movies over and done with. Out of the way. I don't want to remember everything unless it's for an argument or an idea or a way out. But the movies keep coming in. Keep stringing me along. And no dam is big enough. You have to do something with everything you've seen.

The biggest smile on Kit's face comes not when Kit earns his status as an outlaw serial killer, but when a police sheriff tells him he looks exactly like James Dean. A wave of relief and peace finally wash over a handcuffed Kit in the back seat. The desert cooling down, the running and murder worth every penny. The perfect flattery, boys loving boys. The ultimate compliment makes Kit feel like the entire killing spree has been a beautiful celluloid dream and someone's finally asking him for his autograph. Now he can go to his grave in peace, without Holly, without anyone, without even James Dean—having become him. Kit knows that men travel in packs, but stars don't need to. Stars can die alone and people will go on living with them. For them. Every enemy Kit has—the police, society, the fathers of the law—suddenly become his fans. And as a celebrity, part of Kit's new found fame is to treat his fans well. He wants to look like the prettiest man to come out of the 1950s. A man who, above all, *died pretty.* James Dean convinced a generation of American males that if they can look like someone else, they can *be* someone else. At the military airbase, totally star struck, the police let Holly go while they question Kit about his murderous life. He works the crowd. Handing out his personal possessions as Hollywood tokens. Kit provides stories for his "old lighter," his "favorite comb." It turns out everyone's an immoral American phony. Not just Kit, but the *entire* country. And the phoniness is only going to get worse with time. By the time I see the movie, the phoniness is *in its last days*. On top of itself. If Kit reminds everyone who looks at him of a Hollywood legend, an icon of rebellion & death, but isn't really either of those things, he thinks it was all worth it. Maybe the crimes can be swept under the rug. The James Dean coif. He does get to die famous, after all. "You're quite an individual Kit," a policemen gushes. "Think they'll take that under consideration?" Kit asks.

Love, love is strange
Lot of people take it for a game
Once you get it people take it for a game
Once you get it
You'll never wanna quit (no, no)
After you've had it (yeah, yeah)
You're in an awful fix
Many people
Don't understand (no, no)
They think loving (yeah, yeah)
Is money in the hand
Your sweet loving
Is better than a kiss
When you leave me
Sweet kisses I miss

Since it's not clear what Kit's feelings are, music is used to tell us, to tell him. "*You're in an awful fix.*" Music loads him emotionally, the way music always does. Loads a scenario. Gives it a tune that can be hummed. The way it's dangerous in movies and in life. "*They think loving (yeah, yeah)/Is money in the hand.*" Dancing with Holly to Nat King Cole's "The Dream Has Ended," Kit looks up at the stars in the Dakota Badlands and says, "If anybody sang a song about how I feel right now, this'd be it."

Holly writes the way I do. About Kit, the way I would have written about him if we'd had all that adventure. Men can fuck up women's lives in so many ways. He could've fucked up mine. He could have made me homeless. But I thought about him too much for that to happen. I reworked the story. Maybe it's Holly's journal, maybe it's Holly's novel: "*One day while taking a look at some vistas on Dad's stereopticon, it hit me that I was just this little girl, born in Texas, whose father was a sign painter, who had only just so many years to live. It sent a chill down my spine.*" Everybody loses everybody for one reason or another.

On Love: I think his body and its consciousness must be my home. At least, it's a huge reference point. I lived in the perfect village, next to the perfect sea. The village was a repository for everything I would need. I know this is all part of the romantic myth of Western culture, but I also know that that myth is built more on the allure and romanticization of Obstacle & Death. An obstacle Hollywood is stuck with. The love-story is always presented as inevitable tragedy, as deferment of pleasure, as Oedipal consequence. But what happens to *actual* love? Unless there's a death tag attached to it, we don't see or hear anything about it. Only how sad it is. Only that it's worth being in a movie. Catherine dies in *Wuthering Heights*, both *Romeo & Juliet* die, *Tristan and Iseult* perish, all the Greek Myths. The name Tristan itself means sorrow. In his reading of the Tristan and Iseult story, Denis de Rougement argues that passion requires obstacles, where desire for passion's obstacles supersedes an interest in passion, and the "inclination for a *deliberate obstruction* turns out to be a desire for death. The basis for developing a passionate relationship becomes tragedy itself, and the enactment of death (death of love, death of the artist, death of the gift, death of passion) must follow as a scapegoat to rationalize self-imposed obstructions or sabotages. The desire for love in Western civilization is really a desire for death. And movies about love are often centered around death because in Western culture, love has a better shot at being dead than alive. Every Western love story comes in a body bag. Either we never get near it, or we get near it through glimpses, memories, flashbacks, wars, and fragments in order to focus on the psychopathology of its breakdown. Even *The Lover's of The Arctic Circle* is more of a metaphorical goose-chase, a wraparound, then any actual portrayal of love.

In *The Lover's Discourse: Fragments*—a book I spent years reading as a teenager—Roland Barthes writes about love as a form of semiotics. I thought that if I understood love this way it would help me improve (decode) my relationships with men. Barthes writes that the greatest attacks on love are those mounted by the theoretical languages, which, he believed, either "ignore love completely, as do political or Marxist languages, or they speak about it with subtlety but in a deprecatory fashion, in the manner of psychoanalysis, which even then, mainly deals with 'love' in terms of sexuality and not in terms of passion or desire."

In *The Lovers of The Arctic Circle*, Ana & Otto are supposed to be the same thing. The same circle. Ours is: all of this happens before anything between us even happens. What happens between us happens five years later. Happened fifteen years ago. The real stuff. Before and after the movies. At the movies. Through the movies. Like a movie.

At Chloé's place, the water was high and flooding in. The staircase that went down to the bay from her house was vanishing under the water. It was a full moon, but since I wasn't on a menstrual cycle yet, I didn't feel it. It was around 5pm. Somehow he was there, standing with us on the deck. The three of us were spread thin. We were all in jackets because it didn't feel like summer anymore. It was almost over. I wanted to keep him there. I felt him wanting to leave, or he kept threatening to, or worse, he didn't care either way. He had on some purple. I wanted to stall him. Give him a reason to stay, since I wasn't enough. Children have no concept of time, being so outta-sight, outta-mind. But I was always full of nerves about it. Uncomfortable. What was being lost was a constant pressure cooker. He kept moving to go. He wouldn't stand still. I couldn't stand it. I made jokes, asked him to postpone going home for dinner. Amazingly his house was just across the street from Chloé's. He said his father was making fresh clam chowder for him. The one with the milk in it. They'd been at the beach all day collecting. I can't remember where I'd been. The water was silver and bending over backwards to pull up to me the way I wish he would. I said, I'll jump in the water with all my clothes on. I'll swim in the rough tide. I'll dive right off the deck. I'll do it now. Watch me. I didn't say, I'll do it for *you*. He said he didn't believe me. He said he would watch me try. It felt like he didn't even care if he did. A dog doing tricks for him. He was already turning away. I fell in with my jean jacket and sweater on. Floated on my back as my clothes bubbled up, so I could watch him and talk back at the same time. He shouted, You're crazy and walked away. He smiled, but I couldn't read it. He said David Bowie was playing in the city. Maybe he'd see me there? I felt like a little bottle cast off with a message inside. I thought he might come in when he saw me do it. I thought I'd broken his will. After all, it was for him that I'd thrown myself in.

2

Kleptomania

For me stealing's always been a lot like sex.

— *Bound* (1996)

Judy

Marnie, Judy, and Diane all walked out of the building together. Not arm in arm, but close and somewhere along those historical lines. They were in the same boat, a ferry, more or less. I felt seasick just looking at them. I don't know if they were all employed at the time they walked out, or just having separate meetings at the same time and place, but actors stay in the picture even when they're not in the picture. Like memories. It was a Tuesday morning, a November, everything was transparent. Wind was blowing, parted a curtain, and I saw in. I saw them. Architects were starting to use glass lingerie frivolously all around the city and I could shamelessly see through everything, those women, the way that Superman can see through women's clothes. The doors, the lobbies, the elevators, the ceilings, were all lacy bras. The windows were spreading out into full clarity, full likeness, and no one could look at each other with so much sun in their eyes.

I felt paranoid and hypersensitive, open, the way that only paranoia can open things. Everything felt politically tied and doomed like in the movie *The Parallax View*. I wore sunglasses so that I could have some privacy with my vista. Or some relief from it. I didn't want anyone to recognize my mood, which was all an act anyway. I could see the three women riding down the escalator together as if I'd planned it. Except they weren't looking at each other, or me, the way I'd be looking at each of them if it were a movie and not just something I happened to see on my way home from the park. In New York City, you can watch movies being made all the time. They shut down traffic the way I can never shut anything down. When I saw that Marnie, Judy, and Diane weren't looking at each other, I wasn't the least bit surprised, since women usually only look at other women if they think one of those women has something they might want. Envy has always been in the picture. Even before the picture. Descriptions of other people and word of mouth spread it around like water levels that rise up from too much rain and move onto the street. They were all sort of in the same frame.

Diane was probably there that day having coffee and self-consciously laughing her way through *The Godfather* script with some producers in a glass room on the 17th floor. She was being panoramic in her outlook. Thinking about the future. Thinking ahead. They talked about when the film crew planned to go to Italy to shoot Michael's wedding while he left Diane behind to marry someone else. Someone easier to deal with. They talked about Diane's shooting schedule, and what she would need to wear to get in character for the period—the whole nine yards. It was like Diane was really married and not just acting it. This bought her some time in her personal life. You're good, they told Diane, but you could stand to lose some weight and look a little sadder. Thin people are always more permeable, you know. Their motor never goes off. But then you'll need to cheer up, they said. You'll need to look happy again. In the first *Godfather*, you'll be trapped inside, in doors all day, and in the sequel/prequel, no one will let you come anywhere near the property. Diane was an actor after all. She could look like and say a lot of things she didn't mean.

Eight years before Marnie had been *Marnie*, Judy was already dead. More than 21,000 people lined the streets to view the open casket. Judy wore the silver lamé gown that she wore at her most recent wedding. The casket was white metal, and lined with blue velvet, with a sneeze guard for her protection. James Mason delivered her eulogy. They wanted someone with a unique voice to match Judy's, plus he'd been her right-hand man in *A Star is Born* and, rumor goes, committed suicide too. Judy's mourners included: her daughters Liza Minnelli and Lorna Luft (who was probably already contemplating digging Judy up to sing a duet), her son Joey Luft, her ex-husband Sid Luft, June Allyson, Lauren Bacall, Jack Benny, Sammy Davis Jr., Cary Grant, Katharine Hepburn, Burt Lancaster, Dean Martin, Mickey Rooney, Frank Sinatra, and Lana Turner. I wonder if any of these people actually gave a shit. Or if it was just another Hollywood party. They'd had the funeral, televised and everything, overseas. It was the swinging '60s and Judy finally died in a way everyone could relate to. Sleep. It was hip to pass out. Cats did it, jazz musicians, rock stars, drug addicts, Marilyn Monroe, and kids who liked to stay up all night. Everyone who was young wasn't home or awake to watch Judy's coffin get carried in and out of buildings on TV so early in the morning. At night, all the teenagers were out, leaning lazily on buildings like graffiti, with one leg up. A bunch of John Voights in *Midnight Cowboy*, trying not to seem too naïve or rural. And maybe they heard someone say, "word on the street is Judy's dead." Everyone pretended to be clean and blank, chalkboards with only the faintest haze of script.

Judy must have been alive that day, or she was up the way songs stay alive and float around in people's heads and mouths. Or are just in the air sometimes, like a ghost or a soundtrack. Maybe it just *sounded* like Judy was there. That was her thing—being a sound. A song & dance. Or maybe Diane felt so angry after her meeting, she was humming one of Judy's tunes to herself: *is that all there is?* And, like the saying goes, "seeing red" all over the place, the way Marnie did before she was cured. Judy sang through the space between the two women, erratic, like a bluebird hitting the windshield of a car.

What if Diane and Marnie decided to go out and get a drink together? I wonder if it would have helped ease the tension of acting all the time. The generational fibers hooking up and linking. A dream where anyone can be with anyone, in any form, regardless of the date and time. In a dream I once opened up a chapter that needed it, and made love to every detail rolled into one like a checklist. Everything I'd ever wanted or thought about was there. I was an envelope of mixed-up love letters, opened and sloshing around in a bag of *past*. I was on some amorous planet, maybe Venus, but more varied, in the blanket of a barn, where the hay was silk and pillows, and this everything plugged into me as though I was an ancient electric socket, a giant movie screen at a 1950s drive-in, which I am anyway. And then I lit up, like a sentimental atomic bomb, the one in *Dr. Strangelove*, and the whole world tuned in and got scared. I wasn't poison. I didn't have an orgasm. The whole thing was one, not just *The End*.

It was still early and maybe no one would see Marnie, Diane, and Judy or bother them, and the bar would be empty and warm, only a few blocks away. They could take their coats off. Except Diane, she likes to keep everything cinched, even if it's unseasonal. Maybe the bartender would see the three women, get excited, but not excited enough to scare them away, and slide open the bar just for them. It would be like a movie scene in a bar. Where's Hitch? He'd ask Marnie as a joke. Slapping his knee hard with a bar rag. I wonder if Marnie would tell him, the way most people do when they get around bars and bartenders, that her and Hitch had stopped talking because Hitch couldn't tell the difference between what he wanted to see on screen and what she was in real life. Marnie got caught up in the curtain. But maybe Marnie, like

Marnie in the movie, kept stuff like that stuffed to herself. Like Norman Bates' taxidermied animals in *Psycho*. Seeing colors, instead of feeling emotions. I like that Ingrid Bergman doesn't do that in *Notorious*, said Marnie on the way there. She's so in touch with her feelings. Diane wasn't like Marnie either. She was more upfront about things that bothered her, or at least she was in training to be that way. Diane had a psychoanalyst who told her not to star as Joanna Eberhart in *The Stepford Wives* because the movie gave him "bad vibes." I guess he got good ones off of Woody Allen. Plus Diane was independent. She said she didn't plan on having any children. At least biologically. She was different in a jokey, androgynous kind of way. She wore pants and ties and masculine hats just like a man, but she was all over the place and neurotic and self-deprecating, pulled by a thread, just like a woman. She was what Woody Allen wanted, just like Marnie was what Hitchcock wanted. Except Diane accepted Woody's come-ons and Marnie rejected Hitch-*cocks*. Diane didn't attract too much attention walking to the bar with Marnie because Diane's days on the screen were all in the future and Marnie's were all in the past. Combined, it was like neither of them existed. They cancelled each other out. This is before *Annie Hall* and *Looking for Mr. Goodbar*, so really, no one was expecting Diane to show up anywhere in her boyish Ralph Lauren—tweed jacket, tie, vest, hat, suspenders, tennis racket. No one thinks that kind of gender-bending is cool until it shows up on the cool-*screen* or on a cool-someone-else. Maybe the confusing clothes come after the movies and not before. Once people know you,

you can get away with more and less. It's amazing that Diane was able to get her own style into the picture. When it comes to famous people, that kind of shit doesn't fly anymore. Everyone's got a stylist now, a clothing publicist. In interviews these days, Diane talks about that a lot. Looking back on the "good old days." Now, she says in so many words, no one will let anyone get anywhere near anything that spells *personal* or *independent*. I'm unique she says, but doesn't say. That day, in the bar, Diane was close to her film *Interiors*, which she would make seven years down the line. A prophetic number. A number that gets shit done.

In *Interiors*, she's stuck with a bearded rapist for a husband who writes poetry, only not as well as she does (a subject of dispute throughout the film, the way it wouldn't be if the more talented one was the husband). The husband tries to get back at Diane by trying to rape her talent-*less* sister in a garage. In the movie, Diane is pensive, curly haired (the result of a bad perm), dressed in sepia tones the color of dried menstrual blood. Or amenorrhea—no blood at all. Her genius supposedly makes her unfeminine, unfeeling, depleted in *other* ways. Though, since she does have actual children, the barrenness is more associative and metaphoric. It's how she makes other people *around* her feel. I don't know how she's able to write brilliant poetry if she can't *feel* anything, but that's how Woody Allen is, full of secret assaults. For example, it's no fun to fuck a woman who won't let you be all Woody, all the time. Through the looking glass door in the Hamptons, Diane peers at the cobalt ocean waiting for her crazy mother to drown. No sun to blind her.

At the bar Marnie and Diane drank what Judy drank and drank a lot of it. And when she was old enough, Melanie followed in their footsteps, and later went on to mix it with bigger and more immediate things on the set of *Working Girl*, or whenever she was with Don Johnson. There are things that go on forever, like an inherited technique for swallowing problems. At the table, where they sat in the back by a real fire, Judy picked up on Diane's weariness and told her and Marnie that whenever she was asked to starve for a new movie, which was all the time, for weeks at a time, MGM would only let her eat chicken bouillon and downers. And then they'd give her uppers so that she could work through the night and through the depletion. There's even a picture of me at an awards ceremony, she said, eating soup. Just soup and water. Over the years, people will become familiar with that picture and they'll talk about it. They'll make sad documentaries about it. She asked Marnie and Diane if they'd seen it? Marnie said, of course. I'm in black and white, at a banquet table sitting all by myself. I'm in a white gown that barely fits, and boy do I look terrible with all those pounds on, girls, but I'm inches away from shedding all of them like a bloated snake. I struggled to keep it off until the day I died. I was a rake the last years of my life. While everyone else is having fun and drinking, walking back and forth collecting their awards, Judy is starving and eating soup all by herself like she's got the flu. Only instead of looking healthy and refreshed, the way people who eat strawberries and drink celery juice all day at health spas do, Judy looks tired and worn out and white like a

Kabuki performer, only without the bright streaks of color on the eyes and lips. Her face is a trick mask for someone who wants to look old, but isn't, like Marnie's mother in *Marnie*. Or just an archaic Mother. And I think it's impossible for someone to look old, so young. Looking at the three of them, I think problems get passed down like houses and photographs. Jesus, Judy, said Diane—a very different kind of woman from Judy I guess—it really sounds like they were trying to kill you! They were, said Judy. They did.

Staircases

MOVIE STAIRCASES ARE so Victorian. Something familiar to get us on board. We know them first thing. Houses need people and reap the rewards of having people in them. They're like sex crazed animals, always wanting more and more of you. Hitchcock did it in *Psycho*, lured people into his house because the hardest thing to say to a house is No. It's a sexual invitation, a total cunt. People get sucked in all the time and can't help wanting to go in. When I was little I remember seeing a photograph of the *Psycho* house getting dragged down the Bates hill and across the Paramount lot on a leash like a dog. It looked so masochistic, I thought. In photographs and film stills, the *Psycho* house is always by itself. Alienated and guilty, an outcast. It sticks out like a sore and lonely thumb, hitch-hiking its way through the country of terror. The house is long and thin like Anthony Perkins, who in pictures, is standing beside it, leaning to the dark side. He's the Tower of Pisa falling apart in endless sequels. I thought Norman's house was a gothic mystery, but it was just a loading dock for all these women, in *Psycho* I through IV, to keep fucking up by going *inside*. Or back to themselves? I guess all horror starts off, like a sperm looking for an egg to bring it to life, in the gendered body. In the late 80s, I saw Anthony sitting on a street curb outside of Benetton in Provincetown just before he died of AIDS. Like he just couldn't *help* being attached to some famous house. Since he was in the closet, living a heterosexual sub-plot for half a century, seeing him sitting there seemed a lot scarier and a lot more schizophrenic than anything Hitchcock ever made.

Road/Me

MY CAR IS a washed black, like the licorice road, and while driving, I felt the sides of it melt off like chocolate, until I was just thought and space and identity broken down, split. Like the Fred/Pete character on his drives down the *Lost Highway*. Split like corn from its husk. Yellow down the middle. Corn is as American as the American freeway, and the Beats had likened it to *splitting* way before David Lynch had. For Lynch it was more like: *there's nothing else, there's no getting off, there's no truck stop.* Everything is asphalt and asphalt looks like a permanent black out. It's true, though, that it's always been easier for a man to hustle two lives. A woman gets situated.

Everything I know feels so perishable.
I feel my body rebel against retaining anything.

Nobody knows what I'm talking about. I don't know why everything isn't really the same thing.

Split

2003: IT'S NOT EASY TO just take off, split like the Beats, or evaporate into thin air on the freeway blackout 50 years later. There's too much at stake. So much work goes into everything I do, I can't just drop it. *To hell with it.* But I can't say that, can even barely think it. I certainly don't feel that way. I'll fall off the face of the earth and people will let me. I'll be the red afterlife ball that rolls around in *Don't Look Now.* Something that's dead, but keeps showing up in people's dreams and old cities. These days it costs too much to disappear. I'm no horror movie. I can't vanish and show up whenever I feel like it, demanding attention like those furious midget babies in *The Brood.* It would take earthly things to get me around: a bottomless savings account, tank after tank of rising gas prices, outrageous rent everywhere you go; it takes a lot of paying, it takes being a man.

I can't just drop off all over the place like a teenager with the same old crusty bag. If you want to drop off, you can't keep your stuff. For men it's a trip, for women it's a new life. Most people won't remember the one I had. I've done it on so many occasions. Dropped out 3 years in a row, for 6 months at a time, in different parts of the globe, and came back a different person without anyone noticing or remembering what was different and what was the same. Without anyone giving a shit either way. No one gives a shit about what

I'm trying to become. No one gave Marnie's Getaway Plan any thought.

Holiday Blockbuster

OVER CHRISTMAS I tried to celebrate. No one I knew was around, so I went to the movies. I chose a theater that played things really late. Sometimes even later than I could stomach. You can count on NYC to not call it quits even when you want to call it quits. Inside I watched a film in which Jack Nicholson describes a passionate woman and a successful playwright as flinty, obdurate, and austere. "You're like a painting," he tells her mockingly. Meaning paintings don't budge, no matter how much you try to seduce them. In the *Scooby Doo* cartoon, paintings always do something behind your back: they transfigure, they wink. They try to murder you. They make fun of you or step out of frame. I scanned the theater, sizing up people's facial expressions and reactions because a movie theater is still the best place to figure out what people are like, or not like, and wondered if half the people in the theater even knew what obdurate, flinty, and austere meant, or if they cared, and why it came as absolutely no surprise that Jack would use those words so freely when talking about a woman. He's always doing antagonistic shit like that and being loved for it. For his mean honesty and phallic bravado. He's always *free*-basing. You know, taking artistic *chances*. Like the time, early on, when he smacked Faye Dunaway across a room, or when he terrorized Shelly Duval, with Kubrick's help, kicking and screaming in the snow like some baby in a sandbox.

Or, the time in 1996, when Jack faced assault and battery charges for not paying two prostitutes after he hired them to fuck him. Then when one of them protested and demanded her $1,000 fee, he tried to knock her off the face of the earth.

In 1989, while filming *Batman* at the age of 52, you, your famous Hollywood drug buddy/drug dealer, Newman, and your scatologically obsessed best-friend/producer Robert Evans, would hire hookers together like blood brothers or boy scouts and stay up all night doing coke. Or just "drugs." Newman said you would come straight from the Gothic fairytale set to Evans' house, stay high all night and then go straight back to Warner Bros. the following morning. Not referring to watching Jack rehearse his part, Newman found it charming and even said, "Nothing is as funny as seeing Jack do lines." In *Easy Riders, Raging Bulls*, Peter Biskind has a section on how you used to put coke on the tip of your dick just to really nail it home. But according to the dead producer Julia Phillips, a lot of guys do that. You are Jack the Joker, you are Jack Torrance, you are fun-house Jack, and house-of-mirrors Jack. How come you get to be Jack so many times? Jack times infinity. Avatar Jack.

Julia, who knew you, talks about you a lot in her book *You'll Never Eat Lunch in This Town Again*. She hated *Easy Rider*, a *Male*-rebellion film, but loved you in *Carnal Knowledge* so much she even wanted to do a female version of it in the 80s with Madonna playing your character. One dick replaced by a wanna-be dick. Guess what? It never got made. Or, maybe *Thelma & Louise* is what happened instead. Like the same man who made *Top Gun, Days of Thunder, Beverly Hills Cop, Crimson Tide*, blah, blah, blah could really offer women anything other than a double-suicide pact off of a geologically ancient precipice. The geological erosion of the Grand Canyon is on par with the feminist backlash of the late 1980s and early 90s. *Thelma & Louise* says: Take that! You greedy fucking feminist convicts, and then dumps it all back into hardened Nature. Julia was behind you for a long time. Everyone was/is. A period of about twenty years go by. Then she ends her observations on page 555 with a conversation with her daughter about *Batman*. Kate, who's sixteen, has just seen you play the Joker:

> KATE: "I loved Jack Nicholson,"
> JULIA (despondent): "Oh, Kate, he's been over the top for fifteen years."
> KATE: "He's over the top, but he has such a good time doing it, I had a good time with him!"
> JULIA: "Oh, I don't think it was really *with* him. More like at your expense…you don't know any better…"
> KATE: "Don't blame me for my taste. It's not my fault. I was born into Sequel Hell."

BUT JULIA, who helped make it as much as she laments what she did and didn't do, was and wasn't, was inside it for so many years, the least she could have done was help her only daughter write off the shit that she knew about first hand. I wonder if Kate stopped putting up with your on-screen/off-screen dissoluteness after that mother/daughter dénouement?

"I don't like movies anymore." Julia gives up. "…Certainly not this gilded turd *Batman*, which everyone told me I'd like because it was so dark. Not dark, I wanted to tell them. More...*corrupt* than dark. More *shiny*, more...*big* than...visionary. Call it the Trump of movies."

What casts the shadow is not the wing of a man/bat, but the 1980s. *The End* of them, no less. How the movies just imbibed the decade and got so drunk.

Jameson says the ghost in *The Shining* is history itself. Or the history of capitalism at its historical peak—the 1920s. The movie makes this point at the beginning of another economic revival, the 1980s. Retro-peak. Jameson finishes up by saying that a nostalgia for hierarchy and domination allegorize Jack's "possession." What else is new? Jack's not the only one longing for the "Veblenesque social system of the 1920s," buying coke and spreading it all over his dick like cake frosting. And in her essay, "Bringing It All Back Home," the film scholar Vivian Sobchack calls the reconfigured father, Jack Torrance, "the mad face of patriarchy." But we don't need the 1920s for that. I think your self-parodies (or patriarchs in general) are the real fucking specters in *The Shining*. They bounce off the Overlook's walls like gaudy coins. And as the Devil, you've bullied and plotted against the trilogy of Cher, Susan Sarandon, and Michelle Pfeiffer, and despite all that, all 3 of them *still* decided to spawn your children. You're always out of your mind or losing your mind or explaining why you are the way you are, and why you can never be anything else, and everybody thinks you're this rebel, this genius, this rogue. This pure charm. And all these young women keep fucking you like it's so fabulous to fuck you—a used band-aid. Even though your hair's fallen out, you're fat, you're repetitive, you're *Jack*! But Jack wouldn't fuck an old(er) woman if his life depended on it. Jack's always in the newspapers trying to fuck, or already fucking, some new, young girl. Or some old, young girl. I think Jack is like a broken record. His talent

has been on a

sound loop

for decades.

AFTER YOUR MOVIE was over I asked myself a question that lasted like a recurring nightmare: Do audiences know what you mean when you said what you said to that Pulitzer-winning female playwright? And if they don't know, or don't care, and the real meaning is lost because they don't know, without knowing the meaning what does the movie really mean? I get the horrible feeling that movies are so fucking sneaky. That they get through no matter what. Either you know or you don't know, but either way, you still get worked over by a tractor-trailer. Like the reconditioning finale in *A Clockwork Orange*, where Alex's eyes are pried open with metal spiders so that the movies can slip in like burglars.

How *do* you get away with it?

The Witching Hour

I'M CHER, and I'm afraid of snakes. And like Susan Sarandon, I used to play the cello, only not as well. But I'm really nothing, nothing, like Michelle Pfeiffer, who's off swimming in some deep primeval miasma of pro-creation. Or as Elizabeth Taylor likes to say to Richard Burton in *Who's Afraid of Virginia Woolf*, a "swampy." Michelle Pfeiffer keeps trying to multiply her void (vanity) and is up to her knees in a river of little penises and vaginas—all the same intense reproduced color blonde. With Pfeiffer, the whole Devil ordeal is supposed to make sense: it's in *character* that she keeps all of Jack's babies at the end of the movie because she already has a predilection towards that kind of thing. It's congenital. So why stop with the Devil? But the Cher and Sarandon characters should have known better. I mean, they were artists! They had gifts of their own. They didn't need his libidinal charisma. If I were any of those women, or just myself, I'd never get near Jack. I'm more like that religious older woman in the movie, Felicia Alden, who wears pearls, dresses head to toe in Laura Ashley, and has some kind of allergic reaction to Jack right from the start. She even vomits in church (or is it at home?) all over everyone (or is it herself?) who likes him, or could've, if it wasn't for her river of puke cascading them all away. Like a bulimic, she's trying to get him out of her system—all those empty male calories—or out of the Female System. Jack infects women like salmonella bacteria. Believe me, I would have vomited too. I would have kept vomiting like a waterfall of contagion. I share the ability to abstain with that staunch church-abiding woman, even though my reasons are totally different and I don't wear pearls or Laura Ashley. I don't need God to tell me what's creepy, I just know, or figure it out. I hate creeps and Jack is the King.

Felicia Alden's vomit is hot and silky. Violently flapping around like an aviator's scarf in Jack's Hadean wind. I think it's full of cherries. She's just had them for breakfast or a snack. Her projectile vomit is refrigerated, cold inside of her, but has steam rising off of it, like a hot, fiery spring. For Felicia, it feels like heaven to get Jack out, to somehow transcend him. She feels better right away. But for the 3 women, the 3 "versions" of beauty—red, gold, and black, like the fable of a fairytale —it's a death wish they gobble right up.

He fills his head with culture
He gives himself an ulcer.

Wonder-full

I THINK CULTURE is also the way men think about women and the way women think about themselves. And who is it that really gets stuck with the ulcers? The bleeding? Who was he kidding? I've had stomach problems my whole life, but I've never heard of Jack having any pain. I'm clogged with culture. Bursting with it, and I can't help it. It's a done deal. It's a Bavarian forest I can't walk out of. I'll always be its regurgitated fairytale. This isn't Richard Pryor you know, this is a middle-class white boy, who, okay, doesn't know his father, and was, God forbid, raised by his mother and grandmother, but who's been pretty much hailed from the beginning. Though people have and will deny that. More than anything else, I eat culture. In particular, I watched this program on TV before I got into my car:

No mention of race is made when the survey on White (Wonder) Bread is taking place. The white market researcher has a laptop computer open on a desk like an alligator's mouth, but blue. The room looks like school. The white man looks like a bad teacher, the kind who is missing a sensitivity chip and could ruin your life. Instead he rummages through it. For twelve grades your anger has nowhere to go. He holds the answers, and his notes, to himself in the plastic square. There are a series of questions, but they're all on white bread. Ultimately, its merits. Though some of the questions allude to the possibility of White Bread being a boogey-man for some. The man answering the questions on the white bread, or, White Bread, is black and in his early forties. He looks fed up. Tired. He's solid in body, with intelligent eyes, and he knows better than to be doing this, but he's caught in some kind of trap. There's no one else in this classroom. It's not clear if the man is there because he's professed himself to be a fan, a life-long eater and lover of White Bread, or if they caught him in a parking lot with a clipboard of questions on cotton-ball dough. None of that is explained. Just questions. From this White Man who is *completely serious* about his questions. There's no tongue-in-cheek here. No way.

WHITE RESEARCHER: Does White Bread make you feel accepting?
BLACK MAN: Accepting or accepted?
WHITE RESEARCHER: Accepting.
BLACK MAN: Accepting? I guess so.

WHITE RESEARCHER: Does White Bread make you feel angry?

BLACK MAN: Angry? No. Not angry (looks puzzled).

WHITE RESEARCHER: Does it make you feel tense?

BLACK MAN: No, not tense. (His face gets tense).

WHITE RESEARCHER: Does it make you feel happy? White Bread?

BLACK MAN: Happy? Not really. What do you mean?

WHITE RESEARCHER: (Next question) Does it make you feel lonely?

BLACK MAN: Lonely? That's a strange question. Lonely? What do you mean by that?

WHITE RESEARCHER: Lonely, you know. Just yes or no. Does it?

BLACK MAN: No. It doesn't (looks visibly confused and annoyed now).

WHITE RESEARCHER: Does it make—?

BLACK MAN: Can I ask *you* a question?

WHITE RESEARCHER: Okay.

BLACK MAN: When you ask people if White Bread makes people feel lonely, has anyone ever said yes? (does not say a lonely white person versus a lonely black person?)

*White Researcher's answer is not provided or shown.

Re-(A)hab

IN *One Flew Over The Cuckoos Nest*, you played Captain Ahab, wore a fisherman's hat, and made institutional misogyny your mandate in order to climb over your insanity like a fence. The cold-hearted nurse-bitch,

Wrachet or Hatchet, was the mighty whale who kept you locked up in the sea and gave you shots in the ass, but also shielded you from the abyss 'cause that fight is right on the threshold. Like men are the only ones living incarcerated lives.

California Wildlife

ON THE ROAD to the pond I felt him change his mind about things. Otherwise it was always the other way around with men. People said the crystal meth shacks were the wildest things up there. Aside from the frogs and the snakes. We stayed below by the water. The rain ponds and the ocean over the sandbars. He said he spent Christmas there last year and felt a beige cougar tracking his every move as he worked in the field beneath the starless eucalyptus trees that he thought was an invasive species, but I thought smelled great. I had no idea they were a problem.

Whenever I felt close to you, which meant I could feel closer to everything else, or further, I wrote you letters. Back then I was stuck to you like such a honey on a stick. I couldn't get off of you, and you, not the world, were my oyster. I wrote:

Dear:

After I strip search and throw out the Christmas tree, which you know I hate doing, I'm going sit to down and watch one of the movies from the pile we've got. Probably *Notorious*, or the other N movie, *North by Northwest*, where Cary Grant spends all his time running around and ducking under the crop-sprayer airplane in his silver mod suit, and Eva Marie Saint climbs Mount Rushmore in a pair of heels, poking the presidents' eyes out. I don't think Cary Grant washed his mood suit the entire time he was running around/ away. And if he did wash it, it was only once. And somebody else did it for him. It made me wonder if his suit got smelly, and if it did, did anyone notice? Did Eva Saint Marie? I can imagine that all that trepidation and sweating over stolen identity must have really stained Cary's shirt collar, armpits, and crotch. Big time. Was he even showering?

After I'm done, I have to send the movies back to the warehouse. Back to Netflix. All those movies are like orphans waiting to come home with someone. On a couple of occasions, when I couldn't bear to part with a film after I'd watched it, I'd sneak out in my pajamas at 4 in the morning and click onto the "Report a Problem" section on my Netflix account. I'd pretend the movie went missing in the mail and would describe the abduction in detail in the space they'd provided. Most of the time, I would get an email back saying I'd used too many characters, and I'd have to go back and edit, delete some surplus phrases like "Where could *Shivers* have gone? Do you think it got delivered to another warehouse? Do you think the mailman stole it and is watching it as we speak? And "A lot of people want to see Cronenberg die." The letters I get back from Netflix never address my questions directly, and they always send a generic auto-reply like "We'll be glad to replace *Shivers* for you, free of charge, because we value our customers." They never say, "Angelica, you're *such* a good customer. No one watches as many movies, as many good movies in one week, as you do. We make absolutely no profit off of you. You're a waste of our time."

I'm smoking a cigarette, and after a shower just now, and a pimple that evidently won't make its retreat back underground into the abyss of my epidermis, I've taken note that the heat has arrived for today. I was stupid enough, baby, after weeks of it, to think that since it was still cool at noon, it might stay that way. The dream of lakes and rivers flood into my own water supply. My tits get bigger every month like carnival balloons that wanna be popped. Like the tide coming back in. I'm fantasizing about being strong enough to shed it. Interpol is back on, and I can't help myself but think of you, us, in all those car rides back to retrieved kisses—a me and you resurgence. The boy on the dock is mine now. I caught him on my fishing line, clogged with all my fishy history. In "Narc," Interpol likes to imagine me: *She keeps on waiting for time out there...* And because you do too, they're also your favorite Interpol words.

How are you my sweet yellow feathers? You're like a nest I took down from a tree. And you didn't mind being separated at birth because the elevation is still high between us. I love you and wish there was all day to inspect it. The love we've managed to catch up with like a good conversation. Did we know? I can't believe we didn't.

I would love to come back to 18 and 20 just for a day with you from all those months of 24 hours we didn't even try to spend together. I pursued those other disappointments without knowing you'd save me from all those falls in the end. "*The anatomy of kisses.*" Yours... please don't ever go anywhere. I love your holds.

Yours, very resurgently.

Diane

ON TV, Diane said she would never have been able to do what she did without Jack. Win her award.

Marnie

HOTELS AND MOTELS always guarantee you a movie. They're so nice about running movies for their guests. They have an appreciation for nostalgia, for why someone like me might be in a TV situation in the first place. Or in a hotel situation. In other words, not home. Not anywhere. They know all about the *good old days*, when TV was like a blood transfusion and kept you alive. They'll do anything to make you stay longer. Maybe a bed is a movie theater. A primal scene and therefore perfect for the typical fantasies that movies explore. These days I can never find even a trace of something I want to watch at home. Where've all the movies gone? The *Godfathers* and the *Omens*, The *Don't Look Nows* and the Hitchcocks, the *Draculas*, the *Godzillas*, the *Casabalancas*? Once, I even saw *Peeping Tom*. All the movies have been hoarded by cable and PBS. Have gone to a realm you either have to pay extra or stay up until 3 in the morning for. But I'm not gonna lose any more sleep over popular culture. Now TV gives people movies like some kind of cheap I.V. drip for good behavior. Everyone gets the occasional Halloween, Christmas, and Easter treat for all the shitty and dirty sitcoms they've ingested all year long. The culture of movies, like the culture of food, is embedded in the lower intestinal tract where it really hurts and turns to shit. Ingested in hotels and motels through room service and PayPerView. But even then all the movies are new. Are gone. They never show anything old anymore because they don't want you to know how bad its gotten or how relatively good it used to be. They don't want you to hold up some standard they've long gotten rid of. Maybe if no one sees anything from another era, if no one has an overview, they won't make comparisons that could get America into trouble. Like how it's changed or hasn't. When I was little, I watched TV just so I could see all the movies I'd missed at the theater or had no idea existed. I don't know what I had heard of.

Overlook

IT'S GOTTEN SO BAD that I miss horror. The real kind. I need it. Horror scares it all away. All the shit that's not supposed to be scary, but is.

Every weekend, mostly on Sunday afternoons, I 'd run into the movies. My sweaty little hand, a puppy's paw, was everywhere. Dripping all over the remote control, drowning the numbers and the red on/off button in my own dead-sea of fear. The transgression of watching what I wasn't allowed to watch: someone losing their mind, someone growing claws and hair at night, someone naked, someone reacting strongly to the moon (are werewolves and vampires just women having their periods?), someone panting, someone fucking a woman's neck with their fangs and turned-up collar. Mostly I remember *The Shining*'s flirty elevator gushing blood as the doors came open like a woman's legs. The way the blood tossed and turned like a secret ocean in a closet of skeletons. A cranberry horizon, some sailor's dream-image of seasickness. Drunk on horror, now it makes me think of champagne sloshing around in a glass. Jack celebrates his rage and makes a toast to it. Getting shit-faced on a world of murder. The film throws it like a ball and this is why people in costumes keep popping up in the subconscious that gets named a hotel, though that's more in the book than in the movie. While teaching a class on *The Shining*, William Burroughs defends Jack and explains, "Guy goes crazy, guy shoots his wife, it could happen to anyone." Women being the proverbial anyones. I always have my finger on the power button when *The Shining* is on. When the cuntish maze finally bites down on Jack.

Tried to escape by figuring out where I was, by finding out who I was, but I couldn't because I was in a maze (Amazed)(Kathy Acker). Let's just say this means amazed with terror, or amazed at the terror Shelley Duvall feels. Shit, she doesn't fit through the space between the cracked bathroom window and the ledge of snow. But a little man does! A little son who can sled down the hill of his father's mess and into the maze where Jack will open his mouth and freeze to death, turning into a patriarchal icicle. Danny is Shelley's surrogate escape, her message in the snow. Danny is his mother's surrogate freedom—it takes a boy—like putting on a disguise that has a new dick and knows its crazy father well. On Christmas people lose their minds. The outside is totally in.

A palm reader, Danny knows the maze like the back of his hand and Jack doesn't stand a chance in Her universe.

Once in a hotel, I watched a documentary on Egyptian mummies and thought that movies are like a kind of mummification, and if it were still okay to do it, to pull someone's brain out through their nose to make something last longer, to seal it in, people would. But I guess there are other ways to make something last forever now.

Things wind up at the Overlook Hotel that no one plans to see. A dust cloud of repression. The corridor versus the foliage maze versus the snow. Things no one wants to see end up being reddened all the time in movies. Little psychic Danny rides around on his bicycle. A movie star, he keeps getting clogged in the fibers of the hotel's red carpet. The red-ride isn't as smooth as he thought it would be. It's a ribbon of blood that clots and leads him astray. Then the twin girls show up together in the middle of the hall like the uncanny: ubiquitous, old, and sliced down the middle like a juicy red apple. As if Jack/Jack could chop a vagina in half like a log or a spiky pineapple.

I saw *Marnie*, a "sex mystery," when I was 13, the year I got my period. And then again the other day at the *Home Grown Inn*, at 11 o'clock at night. After a shower, I got into the hotel's huge bed, my face and teeth clean and slippery like bathroom tiles, and slid over to the right side like a sardine in a can, hanging on the edge. I pretended I still shared a bed with you, instead of sticking my ass out and my leg up as if I were getting ready to run away. When someone sleeps like that, it usually looks like the shape of a dead body outlined in chalk. If that person were frozen in place or dead. After that I turned on the huge TV, and there was Marnie's face stained red, her memories burning up like mine. I looked at Marnie carefully the entire two hours and eight minutes she was on. Her high fore-head, her seagull shaped eyebrows, her implacable face. Her lips are pink like only a sliver of what a sunset has to offer. I saw the young, flat-chested, Melanie Griffith show up a few times in certain angles of her mother's nose and mouth, in the thin lines. Like the image of half of David Banner's face turning into *The Incredible Hulk* at the cemetery. His old self buried to death. I thought about how the name Tippi Hedren always showed up in quotes as "Tippi." I thought: *Your mother's a quote, like some "tippi-cal" fad that flew out of fashion.*

When Marnie shows up at her mother's house and swipes the red flowers her mother already has in a vase for white ones, a new little girl is there, a surrogate Marnie, waiting to get her hair straightened out like a problem. The Marnie that pretends she didn't kill anyone when she was that age. The non-homicidal Marnie. The red flowers that Marnie asks the little girl to take home to her own mother, stir up the murder Marnie committed in the name of her mother. In the name of lust, sex, rage, and passion. All the stuff that Marnie can't stand to look at or feel. All that desire gets shoved into the stealing. Marnie gets off on being a kleptomaniac. It's her sex. Breaking into the safes, stuffing the money into her tight little purses, splitting and taking off, dying her hair and then stripping it back to candle-light blonde as she lifts her head out of the sink like a post-coital rise off a body. She looks fully satiated in the hotel mirror. But the men spoil the fun by not letting Marnie get away with it. Oh, and then Sean shows up.

Blondes

MARNIE'S MOM says: "Too blonde hair always looks like a woman's trying to attract a man."

She won't let her get off. She doesn't want a man. She wants to skip town, ride horses, and keep doing it. Keep doing it.

Hitchcock always employs the proverbial blonde to entrap. He switches her on like a porch light over and over again. He loves the clicking sound. In the process, he screens all the brunettes like a phone call he doesn't want to get.

Sometimes I can see the old Melanie so clearly in "Tippi." It's there, in the fear.

In *Body Double*, where Melanie is still fox-nosed and barely herself, her hair bleached a baby-chick yellow, she looks like what "Tippi" would have looked like in bondage gear, if Hitchcock had kept going another thirty years. I mean *Frenzy* is pretty harsh, pretty sleazy. Melanie was best-friends with Jamie Lee Curtis at the time. Another daughter of a famous mother, paid and shot to look scared in Hitchcock's frame. Both were Hitchcock's frosted little buttercups, melting with fear. Just dreading the idea of hanging around. Both Marion Crane and Marnie were little light-haired thieves. One took the train, and the other one drove around in the rain, while Norman shoved his eye into the wall like he was trying to fuck it.

Red and white. White instead of red. That's Marnie's big dilemma. Sometimes she switches the red with white. Sometimes she sees just red, and sometimes red on white. The only thing Marnie wants or aims for is white all the time. Either way, it sends Marnie over the edge. Jane Eyre had the same problem. She went ballistic locked up in that attic. Behind the velvet curtains, she bit down, gagging on her rage. Bertha would have been Jane's doppelganger, if Jane hadn't been so English. Being English saves Jane—saves the day. Marnie knows how to fuck, you can tell by the way she rides her horse. A lot of girls learn to do it that way, or don't like to do it any other way. Who would want to relinquish that kind of control? Sean Connery was so jealous when he saw Marnie ride.

Roadrunner

ON THE ROAD, I didn't eat for three days. I wanted to be light as a feather. Like the roadrunner, who's made almost entirely of smile, I want to outrun. To get that dick-faced coyote off my back.

[Lyrics in the text. from "At Home He's A Tourist" from Gang of Four's *Entertainment!* words and music © 1979 Gang of Four. "Narc" and "Take You on a Cruise" from Interpol's *Antics* © 2004 Interpol.]

3

CINEMATIC SYNCHRONICITY

THERE ARE A LOT of ways to be close to someone. To Peter. I am looking for those ways. Just the other day I was looking. I do all kinds of things. Some of them work and some of them don't. I don't know how much Peter feels, but I feel a lot. In fact, the less Peter feels, the more I am driven to feel. Or the more I try to feel. Like a sneeze, most of what we feel happens when no one's looking. People don't see half of what I feel. But I don't have to be near Peter to feel or to feel close to him.

From what I remember, it was easy for Peter to feel things too. He would often tell me, *I'm sad, I'm angry, I love you.* And when I said that *I loved him*, that *I was hurt by him*, that *I was relieved by him*, Peter looked visibly happy. Peter and I could make each other cry just by saying any of those things, *You've upset me, You're wonderful, No one has ever said the things you say to me.* If he didn't want to say how he was feeling, Peter beckoned me with his eyes. It was easy. Peter wanted me to know he felt, he thought it was the best thing about me. He thought I was like a snake charmer gently pulling him out of his basket. It was dark in the basket and Peter had been sitting in a knot of partial light, down at the very bottom. He liked my taste in music. I could make him unwind.

In July I went to the movies in another country. It was the season of outdoor screens. It was warm every night and I had stars above me that reminded me that the roof is always the same no matter where you are. I was far away from things, but determined to feel close. I chose Hitchcock's movie *Frenzy* because it took place in London and Peter was in London. True, the movie took place before Peter was born, and was not the mood I was looking for, but I felt like the city already contained him. Since I knew what year Peter was born (1973), watching *Frenzy*, which took place in 1972, was like looking at a photo-album of Peter's parents before they had him. Maybe, if I looked hard enough through the album, at the film, at the cinematic city, I could see his mother's small belly poking through time. There are some things you can find any-where, everywhere, no matter where you are, like movies and books and coffee and pregnant women. And I don't just mean those things in form, a Coffee or a Book. I mean the same movie and the same book anywhere.

I once watched *Saving Private Ryan* in a medieval stone court-yard on an island in Croatia called Korcula. I entered a castle through a chained drawbridge and sat on a plastic chair. The place was ancient, but the chair was new. I was alone and the stars were on me again. The water was around me on all sides. It was like I was in a small boat watching a movie tip on the horizon. I was rocking, gently swaying, in my boat seat. Children hung out of the windows like laundry, trying to sneak a peak at the screen without paying for it. From above, the screen was just a floating image, shipwrecked, and didn't belong to anyone. The children were like extras on the set of a *West Side Story*. Immigrant communities hung out like boughs, dipping into a common courtyard. The buildings, looked like they were cut out of colored construction paper, standing under a saffron watercolor sky. Maria felt like she could be with Tony anywhere.

While looking at postcards of donkeys on a dusty pharma-ceutical rack, I learned that Nabakov also spent his summers in Croatia, on the island of Ráb, but due to a lack of technology, did not see the things he saw in Croatia in America. Maybe he said, *Thank God. I don't want to feel close.* In Rome, I watched the same movies I would have watched if I was in New York. In Rome, I could have had the same coffee if I'd gone to Starbucks. No matter where I am, I can be somewhere else. No matter where I am, I feel close to Peter. Sometimes I wear a coconut suntan lotion, just so I can feel close to the beach. To coconuts. A lot of people travel to bring everything with them.

Watching the aerial footage in the opening sequence of *Frenzy* made me feel like I was in a helicopter looking for Peter, charging after Peter, a missing person in my life. Like a war pilot going crazy in the air, only gently without any desire to exterminate, in a London I wish was still around. In my fantasies, in my thoughts of fantasy, the bushes would swing open like doors from the helicopter's wind and Peter would be revealed, hiding like a bunny rabbit in the grass. Peter rabbit, caught and afraid. Something I could softly scoop up.

I was sitting outdoors again, on a hill it took me twenty minutes to climb. The good news was I could smoke on my way down. The stone tiles looked like teeth. The entire city looked like a smile. I had run out of cigarettes as soon as I found a table at the theater. I asked the three people I was sharing the table with if the bar sold cigarettes, since it sold books, coffee, alcohol, and movies, and the man on my left, said, *no, but you can smoke mine.* He slid the pack next to me like a love letter or a high school note. He slipped it like I was his friend or girlfriend, and whatever he had was mine to have too. He said, *Don't ask me. Just smoke as many as you want.* He gave me the lighter too. He spoke English as if I had taught it to him. If the offer didn't inevitably lead to my death, I would have felt even better. He made me feel close to him, and as a result, I felt close to Peter. It's easy. I thought, *intimacy is transmission, transfusion, a game of telephone.* And even though there are all these other operators on the line, I know Peter is always on the other end. Some people don't need to be lovers to be close. Some people are lovers but aren't anywhere near each other.

In the movies, nothing is ever random. Nothing shows up unless it's meant to be there. Everything is there, in the shot, because it's planned that way. If you see something you don't expect, or insert something that wasn't there initially, it's called art direction or cinematography or projection. Editing. The beauty comes out of the camera. It's no coincidence that I was watching a movie outdoors about London in Spain. Peter had lived in Spain, spent a lot of time outdoors growing up, and was from London. I had all the elements of him. I had lived in London with Peter and was now in Spain. In *Frenzy*, the color of hard egg-yolk, I watched Covent Garden unfold on camera and remembered the Covent Garden I'd been to with Peter, the asparagus I'd bought with Peter for our lungs (we're both smokers) at a vegetable market that was no longer there, but somewhere else. Besides seeing it in person, I had also seen Covent Garden in *Oliver, Darling*, and *The Red Shoes*. I took a picture of the aerial screen and it looked like a postcard I could write on and sign and send to Peter. It looked like a photograph of Peter's city, and somewhere, Peter was in it. Back home, I showed my pictures to friends and when they asked me, *What's that?* I'd say, It's Peter. *It's a grid of Peter.*

It was like one of those aerial cameras on Google Earth that can zoom in on any street or house in the world. The way your memory can zoom in on you or be pulled out of obscurity. Before the close-up, everything looks like the ocean. Like one amorphous pool. It isn't until you go down and come in that you can see parts. Minutiae.

When I first met Peter, I didn't know any of his details. I didn't have anything localized to go on. He was just generic, unknown. But I said, *Oh, I could get something crisp out of this blanket, him.* I wanted a tunnel in my shape, but at first Peter was just a layout like everyone else. I wanted him to pop through me like dough filling some symbolic, cookie shape—Christmas tree, snowman, Gingerbread Man, heart, dog. I was on the edge of my seat waiting for Hitchcock's camera to plunge into some alley, to show Peter standing with a coffee, smoking a cigarette. Sitting on a couch, eating bread. Sleeping in a bed, fucking himself. To find Peter like a carrier pigeon with one of my messages. Peter had never been random to me, just too far below for me to see him. I saw a spot of Peter and I enlarged it and enlarged it in my brain and heart and then I let it burst like a broken blood vessel. I remembered the red stain that takes over everything in *Don't Look Now*.

I never think I look older until I see someone else looking older. I never think Peter looks older until I see someone like Sean Penn or Al Pacino. Most people watch women age and get hysterical about it. But I pay more attention to what happens to men's faces. Whatever time they've put on, I realize, Peter's put it on too. I have a photo-album, and an actor has a movie. I have pictures I wish no one ever saw, and an actor has movies they wish no one would ever see. Once an actor has made a film, they can't choose oblivion or hide any more. It's out there to be looked at, as many times as people want. People get embarrassed by films all the time. "Caught on tape," actors get humiliated by their roles, trying to forget them like old girlfriends. And audiences get embarrassed by what they see on the screen—bad acting, or bad sex, or just sex period. I go to the movies to be closer to things, or to see how close things can get. Whatever my mother and father taught me about being a woman, a movie can take it and run with it. Can run away with it. A movie spoils you rotten. A movie rots your teeth like your favorite grandmother.

I can't stop looking. A movie can accomplish a lot. Can do anything for you. Can be a love letter. Once, in a newspaper article, I read that in the movie *28 Days Later*, London's Westminster Bridge, The Embankment, and the whole of Manchester, the whole city, was put to sleep like a beloved dog for the crew. They needed the city to look wiped out, to be one single companion for the male lead, Jim. A survivor. I wished a movie could do those things for me. Make a city stop. Make room for my life. Make desertion happen. Remake the world. A city that waits for me without disappearing. A city that says, "*Remember all the things you said Peter? Remember how I took them to heart, how it took me and made me stand still? Cleared everything out. How you blew through like the plague?*" Love flies like an aviator over parched land. In a city that clear, Peter and I could become clear to each other.

It's true, I wouldn't want to be strangled the way the women in *Frenzy* are. But it's not like I don't know how it feels. It's all in the head and throat. To be choked up. None of those obstructed women could swear off men. The necktie murderer beats them all to the punch. It upset me, but it didn't surprise me, that in the movie Brenda Blaney is a modern cupid, trying to match people up, while tragically mismatching herself. Didn't she know that her and Bob were a bad fit? Why did she even let him into her office? I think they knew each other. Had gone on one bad date she never forgot. He gave her the creeps. More than the creeps. She was smart enough not to go on a second date, but not smart enough to lock her door. That pissed Bob off. When Brenda dies, it's like a power failure, her bow and arrow shut off. Blowout like a neon "Open for Business" sign. Once Peter and I watched *The Birds* together in bed. There was all this hidden anxiety flying around, mixing and looping. Collecting like a million elephants in a room. A tower of sexual tension. I kept thinking the black birds were like fingerprints at a crime scene. Does DNA have karma? Do movies?

Like me, Brenda Blaney is too open. She was too open and in England that's a crime. A crime that Hitchcock, an icicle, believed deserved to be met with a crime. I don't blame her for it. I under-stand her, but still wish she'd used a different approach. Wish she had seen the red before it cut her off completely. Bob Rusk, the killer tomato, who works at Covent Garden, and oversees all the vegetables, has rusty hair. Bloody, red hair.

I keep Peter close by editing. Storing. I watch the movies I remember he liked or the movies I taught him to like. Peter still has a box of my movies up in his attic. Like spit or germs, like buried desire, my handwriting is on the tapes. The title, the year, some notes on the labels. Whatever I could fit in: *A Clockwork Orange, 120 Days of Sodom, Wittgenstein* and *The Last of England* by Derek Jarman, *Jaws, Ghost Dog: The Way of the Samurai, The Red Shoes, Frankenstein, Metropolis, Who's Afraid of Virginia Woolf? The Shining.*

It was winter, 2001, and for weeks I stayed up to record Film Four's movie retrospectives while Peter lay sleeping beside me. I was in London. Sometimes we slept while the movies droned on like a radio or a dream, and films I didn't plan on recording would end up on the tapes too. Our beds were so low it was like we were the floor itself and the movies were walking all over us. Fucking us over. Like in *Videodrome*, the movies affected me, went into me, sometimes warped my sleep. I woke up with a new feeling. The videos were surprises. I gave them to Peter as if he didn't know about them. Did Peter ever watch those videos? Did he ever look at my labels? My inscriptions. Those labels that are like some kind of puny love letter. "*The videos became the only form of discourse.*" Peter's attic's not easy to get into. You literally have to go vertically through his mother's room first. There's no ladder. You either have to use a chair or jump. I buried the movies up in a mind-hole like a squirrel that buries its nuts for later.

I've seen the way a movie can drain a room like a bathtub. Turn it into another movie, turn it all into movies. Movies that scare you away or bring you closer to the thing that's scary. When I was eight I rented a movie for my birthday party that sent five girls/guests running out of my house like a burning building. Out of the burning gymnasium in *Carrie*. And like *Carrie*, everyone thought what they saw was my fault. That I'd made the mess. No one works together in a scenario of fear. It splits things like a walnut or an atom. The deal was: I thought I'd rented *Alligator*, which I'd once seen part of on TV, the part where the prehistoric alligator is hiding in a Suburban pool on Halloween waiting for the little boy in the skeleton costume to fall in. But instead I'd rented something called *Eaten Alive*. *Eaten Alive*, it turned out, was some kind of sexual-slasher. The first scene shows a prostitute getting anally raped by a deep-South hillbilly wearing bi-focal glasses. I don't know why the video clerk didn't say anything when I asked for it. Maybe it turned him on to rent horror-porn to a little girl on her birthday. Or maybe he didn't have a clue. I was by myself when I rented it, since the video store was just across the street. No one else was in the store on 87 Chambers Street. Also, I liked being independent every chance I got.

From what I could tell, *Eaten Alive* took place in the bayou. Everything was wet and sloppy, green and red. The red part was blood. The green part was Spanish moss, nature. In it, the women are fed to alligators—also green—like minnows to seals, and disappear screaming in red lipstick, into a lime-colored swamp. In another scene, the hillbilly rapist raked one woman up (he used an actual rake) like dirt and then knocked her into the alligator abyss. After this happened everyone at the party looked at me in horror—an appropriate reaction I guess given that was the genre—and I felt really ashamed. What the hell was I showing them? *What the hell was this shit?* What kind of mother let's her daughter and other daughters watch something like *that?* All the parents, the ones who were still there, went totally berserk in a time of Reagan's family values campaign. Was I using the movie to be overtly hostile to my classmates, or society as a whole, to say something like, "Leave, I fucking hate all of you"? I was a bad girl and a bad friend, and maybe, even a bad American. It was true, I didn't like any of them very much, but they didn't like me *at all*, so they would've used any excuse to get the hell out of there. Rape, alligators, etc.

The movie cleared the room in a nanosecond like a scene in a horror movie when something horrible clears the room. And the party that no one wanted to come to in the first place was over in a camera flash. It was still light outside. We'd seen all that horror with the sun shining. Afterwards, my mother asked me a bunch of questions, but was generally very understanding. We returned the tape unwound. It was the mid-80s, so no one was really asking anybody to rewind yet. I can't remember who returned the video. I might've been too embarrassed after what happened. But I do remember that none of the girls at my party said, *Shut it off, but let's stay with her anyway. Let's not let the movie ruin things, run things. Let's keep going.* But that's how movies are. They take over. They bridge or they divide. And that's how people are too. The movie decided, that at age eight, or almost eight, I should be left the fuck alone. I see Peter in every movie. I look for him.

4

Metablondes

M HAS ALWAYS BEEN LONELY but loneliness isn't M's problem. If it was, like it is for a lot of people, M would have been L from the start, but from the get-go M wasn't L. M didn't want to say too much, but M didn't want to say too little either. She felt both could lead to flatness. It's the first of day of sixth grade and the first thing M doesn't like is L. It's no secret. It's not their secret. L gets more attracted and holds onto M as though she were a kite moving away. L sat next to M in every class and wore a post-Labor Day ensemble of all white, but skimpy. More like a bride than a junior high student. White tank top, white pumps, white mini skirt. M couldn't stand it. She had on her Adidas sneakers with the green book-marks in the back, which she liked because they made her feel androgynous and multilingual. More was better. More was complex. At that age M, eleven or twelve, wanted to confuse boys and teachers, not tip them off. The first few months of school, L's shoulders were bare. Among other artifices, L had blonde hair that she regularly snorted through her scalp the same way that drug addicts snort cocaine through their nasal passages. Maybe they feel colors, or colored, when they get high. There are different ways of feeling better. L encountered something like, instead of the sun shining, I do. Even at eleven, she worked on getting blonde. Her hair had never been light. This felt antagonistic to M's dark locks.

L lived in the East Village, in an apartment she shared with her mother and stepfather. L's place was dark and dingy, tangled like fallopian tubes, and facing a dead-end of brick walls, so maybe the hair was a way of lightning the mood. A way that only cost five dollars a pop at Food Town, where M often went along with L to do her weekly food shopping for L's family. It was the mid-80s. M was little, but tall, and into adopting surrogate families as a way of having siblings, which biologically she didn't, and as a way of moving around geographically. For weeks, M was a nomad and spent time in different parts of the city. M got to know these areas really well. L and M walked around everywhere. No one drove them around, like they do in California. They walked up and down the spray painted avenues. Where they ended up, really wasn't very kid-like. M got rid of boundaries that kept most people going. This meant M was one of them, whoever "them" happened to be, but distanced within the actual nucleus of the things she was in. L's world.

All the vegetables at Food Town looked dismal. M knew L was poor just by looking at the vegetables she bought. They were on a list for her to go and get and looked like they'd been put through the ringer and blasted against a bad stage-act. Old lettuce leaves and popped tomato skins. The kind you see laying in the gutter at the big London market in *My Fair Lady*. The only thing that looked vaguely middle-class about L's life and purchases, was her family's vegetarianism. Instead of hot dogs, they ate tofu and tempeh franks from a can. M watched them bread everything and fry it. M thought broiled fish would have been a healthier option. At least she thinks so now.

After dinner, L and M watched *The Simpsons* with L's stepfather, back when it was still part of *The Tracey Ullman Show*. Mostly he liked the show and would invite L & M to watch it with him. Besides being a vegetarian, L's mother transcended her poverty by spending all her free time at a trendy East Village café on the corner of Avenue A called 7A. M, sarcastic and already fed-up at a young age, always called it 7Up, even though she never drank it. Even as a kid she didn't. When M's parents took her to art openings, she asked for club soda with lemon. She didn't want to get poisoned, she said. When she was very little, M's father told her that Dr. Pepper, which she once loved, was made at one of the freeway factories that smelled bad and that they passed on the way. After that M always correlated Coca Cola and Pepsi with shit. The wine & cheese people thought she was delightful for abstaining from all forms of mass sweetness.

L's mother went to 7A with her students, her older son, or with M & L all the time. She was local, she was the neighborhood ambassador. She was fat and often depressed. She would lock herself in her room. She was a singer and gave singing lessons 4 times a week. Her red hair matched her red lipstick and the restaurant's dark, red chairs. M loved the used bookstore across the street that's not there anymore, not by a long shot, and that looked like a living room up to its knees in pages—M could sit anywhere, on a pile of magazines or dictionaries, or she could sit on some history book and warm it up with her ass. Sometimes L & M hung out at the Polish coffee shop Odessa's. They sat in the brown booths eating fried peroshkees with sour cream, self-reliant and independent like boys. Everything was intimate, was marriage. They went to the newsstand next door, where M tripped on the ledge all the time, and bought cream sodas like it was the 1950s. L taught M to like them, but M never finished one on her own. She liked the first three sips. The rest made her sick. They were boys, or M was a boy and L was a girl. Both of them pretended. L always needed some male energy to bounce off of. L & M walked through Tompson Square Park all the time by themselves, arm in arm. It was a chance to see the leaves change and the fire coming out of the garbage cans that had been in the news for weeks. L's sister was beat up by the police in the riot. They also broke her camera and threatened to rape her and her friend. Men on the street called L & M dykes. Little dykes? They didn't specify.

L carved "I love Matt" into a park bench, across the street from her house. She did it with Matt one morning, maybe their last morning, while M was at school and L wasn't. Matt was a man. L's parents made her get rid of him, after she'd been fucking him at his apartment "in all kinds of positions" across the street for months and writing about it in her journal or telling M about it everyday at school. L said Matt was twenty-six, almost twenty-seven, a Scorpio, which, she said, was why "he was so good in bed," but after looking back on it, and doing some easy calculations, M thinks Matt was only nineteen. The park bench stayed—like a hand shape in cement. All the lines were there.

After their breakup, L wrote: "I love Matt" across her bedroom wall in red lipstick, her favorite color, as a form of protest and then cried in her bed for two weeks. Matt's bio was: he sold used books on Saint Mark's place on the weekends, across from what was once the big Drug Rehab. Two weeks into it, L arranged for M to meet her and Matt at the Café Regio by Washington Square Park. Matt kept starring at M seductively, in front of L, like M was a peep show, only stern. He was grinning, not smiling, waiting for M to crack. To leak. M would have been fine, maybe, if Matt had been smiling, but he was oozing adult bullshit all the way. M thought he was really boring and manipulative and disapproved like a cranky mother. Over coffee Matt said, Nothing bothers you, does it? If you saw a car accident, you'd probably keep a straight face the whole time. Matt didn't know a thing about M. M was always upset and seeing something like a car accident, or anything unfair, would've destroyed her. Then and now. M thought, but did not say, *some older & wiser man you are.* What Matt said to M was his way of saying, *I know you know. I know you know better than L does and I'm just going to cover my tracks with you.* It was a silent pact. M didn't keep it. Years later, M looked for L and Matt's bench carving, but found it had been painted over in green. Years later, when it was M's turn to be nineteen, she went to visit her bestfriend Lee in Oaxaca, Mexico for a month. M & Lee were sitting at a café drinking coffee and orange juice after being sick for days, and Matt was sitting over M's shoulder talking to a friend, who looked his age, at the next table. In the sunlight, Matt looked the same. Much younger than L had pretended he was. By six years at least. M checked three times. She always checked everything more than once. M told Lee the story.

Most of the time M wore her hair in clips and avoided it down at all costs. It was the sixth or seventh grade. L called M Edgar Allen Poe and said she was too serious. She didn't mean it literally, since M was always being funny and making L laugh. L meant, your sexual style is too harsh, scary, or non-existent. Even though M was a chronic masturbator. L didn't know that, even though M knew that about L. That's something guys say they are all the time, to each other, about each other, "Johnny's a chronic masturbator," relayed like it's a skill, or a character trait when boys do it. Like a lot of men, L couldn't read between the lines, only on them. Within a year, M's two front canines were in trouble, protruding. Eight months later, M was covered in braces. There was a chance she'd be hideous if M didn't do something about it, since teeth have a way of making or breaking a face. M hid her mouth for two years and didn't know how to smile very far. She didn't get a kiss in edge-wise. She didn't want to, the choices were so dire. Then she did, and contrary to all the 80s movies that showed people with braces getting stuck in an orifice, S, her first real boyfriend, said he never felt a thing.

Two years later, L had worn M down and they were together all the time, at school, after school. L read a lot of new books and saw the movie *Wild At Heart*, so she started asking people, mostly boys and M, to call her Lolita, and later Lula, after Laura Dern's character. Anything rebellious and hyper-sexual that started with the letter L. A name that was short, compact, and loaded, like L. For a while L toyed with the name Lola—Lola from the Kinks song, not Lola from Barry Manilow's *Copacabana*. On Friday's, L and M went to *Twin Peaks* through L's TV set, or rented horror movies like *Suspiria* from Kim's Video on Avenue A. M walked the aisles and scanned video boxes in the horror section, observing the covers of things, while L ignored her, and stood leaning against the counter, flirting with Rob and Steve, the twenty-five year old video clerks, who, when they weren't working at Kim's, L was convinced, were doing incredibly interesting things like painting and singing in bands. The usual cliché male artist schtick that most of the time doesn't amount to anything except for clichés, but gets taken seriously anyway. When M was little, she thought everything was original. Or maybe that was L. Or maybe everything was original except for boys & girls.

Mostly, it was the fucking Rob and Steve did, while L was supposed to be doing her homework that L thought was really original. Would they fuck her, a twelve year old, after work? Yes, sometimes they would. L thought about that question up in her loft bed, which was too close to the ceiling. She rarely changed her sheets. M could smell them a mile away. The sex question made her sick and made L lucky. Unlucky.

L knew a lot about movies, or pretended to. She watched them, but that's not the same thing as knowing what's going on with them. She wasn't watching *Pretty in Pink* or *Girls Just Wanna Have Fun*, she was renting early Robert Altman movies, *MASH, 3 Women, McCabe & Mrs. Miller,* and reading *The Tropic of Cancer* and Freud. It was so Freudian, it made sense. Everything was so male-identified. Women were identified with men, and with each other as a way to know men, and men identified with men, and with women, but only as a way to better understand each other. Can you imagine a bunch of boys reading Kate Chopin's *The Awakening* in order to feel awakened and rebellious?

L and the two video guys talked about that, their interests, but left their main interest covered under a sheet. In the background, M thought the whole sex thing was haunted, cursed. At least the kind L was always getting wrapped up in. The boys thought the L movie was far more entertaining then anything at the store. Unless they had a section for kiddie-porn. They sneered and elbowed each other. They were cute M thought, both dark and in glasses, one of them even looked like M, an elaboration on dark colors, but also sleazy and dangerous, like L, so M didn't get near them. At least not the way L did. What separated M, what M had going for her, was a knack for proximity, periphery, a panoramic view. She could see into the future of each little moment. The Rob & Steve moment. M liked Rob's shoulders, he was thin and wore musky tight plaid shirts, and his collar-bone was beautiful and nuanced in a way that he wasn't. It made her think about mind/body lapses and how tiny slivers of things, like a bone in the body, is sexier than the whole deal. Especially since the whole deal disintegrated small landmarks like bones and windows of skin. His skin was brown, garden dirt brown, fertility rich, but like a lot of brown people, boys and men, Rob had a preference for things—girls—that were lighter than him, which M wasn't. But L was. And girls had a preference for lightness too, for their own thing to lighten up. It already started to drive M crazy at thirteen. M thought, that winged collar-bone is the best thing Rob has going for him and the most underused. Figures. It was underactive, low key, while the most boring qualities were always milked and blown way out of proportion. Totally unpacked from the suitcase. She scowled at L. Don't you think you should see if you want to stay first? She wondered. The place looks like a dump.

M already knew that people, men, are not what they seem and L knew that too, that's how she even got them to broach the subject. Rob and Steve seemed public, but what they did required a lot of privacy. M was the tougher obstacle course, the brunette. M had dark roots R & S weren't interested in exploring, only tugging at. She flared up like a horror movie and retaliated. Since M didn't run away or flinch, maybe *she* was the monster, the chaser. That's how they made her feel anyway, which is another horror technique— repression. Rob & Steve liked to joke around with M, about M. School stuff. They said M was the prettier one, and marveled, as in a dog that's amusing when it's agitated, at her sarcasm and suspicion. She seemed so free of them, like a drug habit she'd kicked. They said, you're gonna be gorgeous, you're our first choice, you know. L quivered, and compensated, took her blonde hair out to sparkle like a diamond in the shop, ostentatious. Blinding M. Her eyes tightened without protection. M was the dark mining cave housing L's canary yellow. What is it with female politics?

L stepped on M's brain and the way M thought about things like a foot-stool. M always pulled the stool out from under L. It was their routine, a circus-act, until they were fifteen and M split off like the Siamese twins in *Sisters*, killing L. Except L still calls and M still hangs up.

Rob & Steve, a package, told M to: take it easy.
They said: What do *you* have to be so pissed off about?

Rob said: You should see *Stranger Than Paradise*. You'd really like it.

They said: You'd be gorgeous if you weren't so bent out of shape and so personal in your responses.

Most girls won't pay attention when they're called to. But M wasn't about to miss her chance to be equal. She wanted to know why Rob had made that particular suggestion about seeing *Stranger Than Paradise* to her in particular. Not who he'd rather fuck, but who he'd rather listen to and think about. Not picture, *think about*. Since M is so young, she wanted to know, without already knowing, about that question as much as she wanted to know about the actual film. Was the film a clue that would lead M to M? Or him to her, or her to him, or M to the world? What got M into trouble was thinking about ideas and analyzing them. For example, she asked: Why? Why do you think I should see *Stranger Than Paradise*? Why do you think I would like it? What about me makes you think of *Stranger Than Paradise*? She wanted someone to score the jack-pot with the perfect answer. M knew that everyday interaction, before you started writing it, was the only poetry.

Rob could say something like:

Well M, I've thought a lot about this, thought of you. And this is why you'd make a good pair. You and the movie. A beautiful combo. I think about you. I think. You make me think. I want to think. I think you, as young girl, want to watch movies and think. I think the fact that you watch movies seriously instead of just wanting to be in one, or some version of one, is sexy.
M would say: Oh, the drama of the brain is better than any movie Robbie.

M BECAME a writer so that she could write the things no one ever says.

M wondered if Rob & Steve ever really looked at her "bent" shape the way that she knew Rob & Steve looked at L's. She felt she'd been x-rayed instead of being safe like Oz behind the curtain. M's breasts were slightly asymmetrical. They were just starting out. Had only been around for maybe a year and a half. Her legs and torso were very long. L on the other hand, asked people to look at her, scope her out, so she had answers and details and clues to work with. A paraphernalia of junk answers. All kinds of external elaborations that M didn't enter into and didn't enter into M. Scopophlilia, like a file on "Sexy." Movies aren't the only things that people watch, but they're the main thing people think of when they do.

M remembers.

Back then, no one said:
Anything about models and actors on a daily basis. Only movie people, but the profession became everyone's.
No one brought it up when you walked into a room.
No one made them the center of a subject or the theme of existence.
No one made you feel like the poster or the screen was always better.
No one brought the look of the entire world into the picture.
M didn't hear about it all day long.
Why should everyone's bad taste affect my life?
Back then the image was just a puppy.

L DID: A lot of bad things to M. And she did it on purpose.

Whenever M felt like Rob & Steve were describing a physical deformity in her, she went ahead and slouched more. Made fuck-you faces. She didn't correct what they saw as mistakes the way L did, if she made any mistakes at all. Funny, M thought the fact that Rob and Steve knew all about her aesthetic preferences via the movies she'd rented over the years *was* pretty personal. If they'd looked hard enough, they could've figured out everything about her: Her sexual taste, the boys she liked, her cataclysmic side, her hang-ups, her sensitivities, her obsessions, her heart, her soft side, her sick side, her intelligence, her moods. But being that they were so fucking lazy, they never did that. M thought most guys weren't interested in that kind of range. Even twenty-five year old guys. And she was all range. M was, if you find a way to get to me, I am all of these different things and I won't just be one, or one or the other for You. L said it was only a matter of time before guys realized that, and left her behind for a woman like M. Blew out of L like an old ghost town. L was the legend that movies and books and guys construct about what would set them free, what they'd like to have, or at least get them going on their horse. L was the facade of desire. But really what would set them free is a woman who sets herself free. M's mother, a feminist, said men really want that, but aren't prepared to deal with it yet and don't know how. They're not enlightened enough yet. In this case, "Yet" was really a historical and political term. M flinched; it was a bitter pill to swallow.

Whenever she was around in the video store, M turned Rob & Steve's act upside down and put their whole show out of business. L was pissed off for days. She said, You always fucking ruin anything that's fun. M said, Why are you always so fucking obvious and traditional when it comes to having fun? L didn't have any demands, or commands. The ones she had, she hid. M taught sexy boys to like something they didn't think they did, like girls who read books and talk back. She thought this was progress. M's mission: to work with what could be, instead of what was.

In the store, Rob said: What?

M said: What?

Rob said: What *you*?

M said: You're the one who's looking at me. *What?*

Rob said: I'm just looking. I like looking. *Jeez.*

M said: Go turn on a movie. You've been working in a video store
for too long.

Rob reacted: You're so mysterious.

M said: Why?

Rob melts, not in M's arms, but with videos in his hands. He
wants to be younger for M, or for M to be older for him. Or
maybe he just wants to stay young for himself, period. Rob's
putting back the returns and airing out all the rental titles like
dirty laundry—everybody's sick or sappy or clean or bad selections.
He looks vulnerable and sorry, so M gets excited. M gets sorry.
Where was L's awareness when all this was happening? When M
had L's entire audience in her lap for no reason? L moved over and
talked to Steve.

Rob & Steve looked like the gynecological twin brothers in
Dead Ringers, which came out around the same time. Who knows,
they might still be looking that way. They weren't twins by blood,
but by common desire and practice. They were guys into some
similar thing. M was asking for effort and a level of detective work
that L never made anyone go through. It automatically made M the
boy, or the sadist. The "off" one. L was a Hollywood plot, which
while everyone likes to watch, they also always know the ending.
On the other hand, M was some difficult experimental film. Some
other language. Something unisex that made Rob & Steve drool on
the inside. It was a good sign. It was also a bad sign.

These were the early years, so M was just starting out. It was just starting to get clear. M saw *Suspiria* on a pull-out couch in L's living room. They felt like adults with adult preferences and routines, lounging around in all the horror. They laid around in bed like lovers. Sometimes M did love her, when all the boys were out of sight, seduced and adored, and that's why M stuck around. L's parents weren't home. Her mother was out at the café. They watched all the dancers at the ballet academy in *Suspiria*, except Suzy Banyon, die. L & M loved Goblin's synth-rock score. Goblins making music about witches.

There was:

    a rain of maggots
    a bat attack
    a woman who flees a pursuing maniac only to fall into
    a labyrinth of razor-wire.

When M was thirteen, her mother's friend, Veronica, told her, *you're going to have a very hard time with men*. She didn't tell M why, or what she meant by "hard," but it obviously meant suffering. Veronica assumed that men were going to be in the picture, the way everyone assumes that, and the way men always are, but M never forgot Veronica's curse, which wasn't a curse, but a social observation. Later M understood that Veronica thought about other women the same way some men do. As *difficult*, and was against it. Maybe M had said something to piss Veronica off. She knew that things, words, come from all kinds of places. Then again, Veronica didn't explain what she meant by *difficult*. She just thought hard was bad, or worse than it normally is.

That's where M comes in. Men go really crazy for M, but, just as her mother explained, were not prepared. This is why M can't fuck lightheartedly. It isn't that she doesn't like to, or has some religion stopping her, it's that there's nothing lighthearted about M. Or how she does things. M thought lightheartedness was a myth, and probably a Buddhist one. In the beginning stages, M is always told she fucks like new, or that she makes men feel that way after she's fucked them, or after they've fucked. A light goes on. She wants it to stay on. That means M teaches them something and they relearn. Everyone has a regime of their own, M's is very pared down and clear-cut because she's eliminated a lot of the shit by being so specific about what she is/isn't. While L was willing to go through a mile of trash, M wanted a boy-preacher to preach with. Someone really electric and beautiful. A William Blake who liked to have sex. M didn't know anything about the way Blake actually made love. Maybe he didn't. But M liked that too. It depends. She could like it, given that passion was really just executed and performed by the body. It's the insides that are so riddled with sex. M'd never seen Blake's shoulders, or his collarbone, but the idea of a man like that wanting to do it all the time was her ultimate fantasy. Passion and ideas were her goal. But making it took a lot of energy and Rob & Steve were definitely not up for that. M knew that at thirteen. They'd never be up for that. If seeing that, and abiding by it, made M difficult, then Veronica was right, she was going to have a shitty time.

In bed, next to L, M thought: There are a million ways to touch someone.
She thought: There a million places to put your hand.
She thought: There are a million variations on pressure and force.
She thought: There are a million combinations of hands and body.
She thought: There are a lot ways to break through.
She thought: I've been doing it to myself for years, so someone better match it or be even greater.

L said: Nothing.

Then L said: You're so neurotic.

When they were fifteen L stopped M in the hall of their high school and said: I always knew you were going to be beautiful, I just didn't know it would happen so fast. L had a pleading look, like she wanted M to pour gasoline on her face and set it on fire. Like M owed her that. Female envy being so destructive, M told L to fuck herself, or something to that effect, which M knew L did every night anyway, and went to third period. In math class they'd pass notes around, until L would tell M to, Sshh, shut-up, I want to pay attention now. That said a lot about L. She was always deciding when she'd had enough of M and wanted to trump her with something else. There was a lot of dominance & subordinance going on between them. It had been years of that, and M was fed up. The math disappeared for M and she couldn't catch up. She still has nightmares. M read her own books under the table. Namely Kafka. When L wanted to write about sex, having it, she wrote in French. M wrote back in English since she didn't speak French very well or have sex, and L accused M of being naïve and repressed. Unsophisticated. But it was M who left the country and didn't come back for years.

Back when their shitty sixth grade class swam in the pool down in the school basement on Thursday afternoons, L's hair looked green underwater and followed her around like algae, or bad lighting, while she did her laps. M thought her own hair looked even darker wet and pretended she was a mermaid and her tits needed shielding. At eleven and twelve, one of M's breasts was bigger than the other, and still is. M thought the jaundiced look that clung to L's hair until it dried, which was fast since her hair was thin like blades of grass, was punishment, a side-effect, M had read about on a box of hair dye. Or maybe it was L's anger leaking out due to an invasion of chemicals. Like the Incredible Hulk and the chemical-syndrome that got his rage out of the bag.

M would go home after whole weekends with L. She can't remember what she did, but she did it forever, for years, all through high school. To get home M had to walk out L's door, cross the street, take the bus, then another bus or the subway further downtown from Christopher St., the Western point, then she'd walk again. Or she'd just walk the whole way, the whole time. Down Broadway, down West Broadway. Taking different directions each time and almost always on Sunday mornings or afternoons. One time, M peeked through the glass wall of a clothing shop without realizing it was glass, and banged the hell out of her face. M felt like she'd been royally fooled. Like someone, other than herself, had pushed her face into that wall of glass that M hadn't seen and that M thought was just more air and space to walk through. She stood on Broadway and Houston for five minutes just throbbing. Just wanting to cry.

5

PETER & PICTURES

I just died. Remember how we used to just die?

— *Eyewitness* (1996)

WHEN I WAS ALIVE I was full of death. Full of *this happened* and *this reminds me* and *this will end up killing me* and *if this doesn't do it this will*. A garlic clove, the summer I was nineteen. Buying aspirin, the headache I spent with Peter. Peter was crying, Peter was crying in the garden after dancing at the club. He thought I wouldn't find him lying there, behind the bushes, with his bicycle lying there with him too. Peter was lying flat on his back, in a garden at night, as though he was dead in his grave. As though he was grass. I stopped dancing. I came looking for him. I came to find him, then kneeled down when I found him crying. It was summer and we were both crying because we were both in love. We were making each other miserable. We were killing each other. We were dying with love.

When Peter left me I wanted to die. Over the telephone, Peter slipped out and never said another word to me as though he was dead. Then he carried me around all winter like death. Eight months later I came back, an extra hour of light, and hung around, and it was summer all over again. Peter and I rose up from our separate coffins and came back to life. It was bright outside. It was warm. We had the sea on our backs like a parole officer. The memorabilia of shared salt tossed at us. Leaving people is one way to kill them. When people refuse to be left, it's one way to stay.

While Peter was gone, I pictured him everyday as a ghost, as something I could see and could not see. Some of the things I pictured Peter doing, Peter did. But Peter also did things I did not picture, did not predict. Peter did not always act like a ghost. Peter tried to be a body and tried to have one too. Men can do things like that, be two things at once. I thought ghosts couldn't fuck, could only fuck around, but learned that I was fucked for thinking that.

As a ghost myself, I didn't do much of anything. I thought separation would lead to return. I collected dust, cracked like paint, peeled back from an old color. I licked what Peter gave me clean like a dirty dog then distributed my very own grime over it. I watched the image take shape over and over like a photograph in a tray of developing fluid. I was in my own darkness making pictures of it. I was the tragic movie waiting for my end to perk up. I wanted to start from scratch every time.

Peter dreamt in purple and photographed an owl sitting on a roof across from his window. The owl made sounds that reminded him of what he had left behind, of what he had had, of what he had done. The owl was stranded and alone and bad luck, like Peter. By photographing it, Peter was identifying with the owl. A bird, that by definition, no one sees and no one tries to. The color of ash, the color of the roof and the rain in the sky, the color of Peter's entire roll of film. The sea was there too and snow and a photograph of me on the wall that no one, including Peter, talked about as though I were dead. Peter acted like the photograph of me was a ghost, or like it was a ghost that put the photograph of me there.

The photograph was double-exposed, blurry and red. Indefinite. It looked like a ghost and so Peter never looked at it. Peter never looked at ghosts, but couldn't help creating them. Peter did not want to have a ghost in his room, on his wall, but the ghost was there anyway. Not wanting it, gave the ghost a reason to be there. Peter never looked at things he didn't want to see. Even if they were there looking at him. When Peter left me I had no choice but to become a haunted house. I was never revisited. I talked about Peter. I talked about what Peter was like and what he had done. I talked about how Peter was missing and how it was me that missed him. I talked to the house.

There were days when Peter remembered me, or thought of me, or didn't, and in those moments, I was on the periphery of existing. I was a ghost. Something Peter could keep in his room, like the photograph of me on Peter's winter wall. Something of mine, something of me, something I'd given to him, something he'd taken of me. That Peter kept but didn't keep. Ended up with, even though he didn't end up with me. The way people end up with each other. Or don't. Or the way they struggle to stay. I have a photograph of Peter standing in a room full of people, next to a small, low wall covered in pictures of me and Peter, or just me. All these things in one picture. All these lives in one frame. The picture space, the wall space, the space between me and Peter. The space that was there when Peter and I were together and the space that was there after Peter and I weren't. Peter in a picture, next to my pictures, next to pictures of himself, next to pictures of us, next to people who weren't in any of the pictures. I was in a different city. I was no longer with Peter, except for when he stood and slept beside that wall of photographs, which he did every night. A composition that said everything there was to say and everything that Peter didn't. I was desperate to hear from Peter and the desperation left me saying things about Peter for years. I was alone looking at all these things. I was in the background. I've never gotten over the duality. I've never had anything of anyone's except duality. I've never been anything except a reminder of some man's duality. I'm duality now. Want and unwant. I'm wanted and unwanted. I just want. I'm Peter's passion and Peter's ambivalence. It's not what I want, it's not what I wanted, but it's what happened to me. And more than once. I am dead after all.

Once, Peter told me that he loved the photograph of me on his wall because of the expression on my face which revealed how fucked up I thought the world was and how upset thinking everything was fucked up made me. Peter felt moved that I could express two important things at once. I felt red like the photograph of me, and was dying over the love that had died between us. When Peter first fell in love with me, he declared it in two stages. Both times it was night. The first time, he was preparing both me and himself for it. He said, "I *think* I'm falling in love with you," and he was both in love and upset when he said it. We were walking on an empty highway. Peter was crying and I was crying. The sky was black and the road was black and we were walking further into the blackness. The second time Peter said he loved me, his emotions were in front of a sea of emotions, which was the sea itself. It was night and the sky was black and I was coming out of the blackness of the water into Peter's arms and into Peter's black teeshirt. Peter was standing in the sand, on the line between the sand and the water, treading it, and I felt so alive. Peter refused to go into the water and waited for me to come out instead. And like the water taking in more and more of the line of the sand, there was an indiscernible difference between Peter and losing him, between Peter and remembering Peter, between having Peter and not having Peter. So you see, this isn't the first time I've been dead.

6

MOVIE MEN

JACOB. THE SHARK under the water. Why didn't Jacob ever come to get his things? Why wouldn't Jacob give me back mine? I asked, Jacob didn't. I mean, I said what I wanted. Jacob didn't say anything. Because if things are kept, it's like no one ever left anyone. In the history of leaving. In a world of leaving.

I wish it were true. I wish Jacob's shirts and glasses (you need them to see) and watches meant this whole thing never happened. *And some days, I forgive you completely. No one fails on daily basis like you do.* I wonder why, with all the time in the world, I loved sad men? And despite my death, still do. Men who could only offer me their sadness on some platter I handed them. Who was the first sad man I ever loved? Yes, there was the scarecrow from the Wizard of Oz, but I was onto something by then. More like, who was the first sad man I ever knew? Takes knowing it to want it back. It wasn't my father, so who? I was a sucker for a secret and a heart that can drag. My lips to a rubber raft, blowing it up, making it bigger. All the color on the water is a boy I help float across.

I am a thing that never let's go. I was. I was convinced I'd be rewarded for this. Being an unflinching trooper, a devotee. *How far will you go? Everyone is testing me.*

When I met Jacob I was convinced my solitude was over, in the all-encompassing sense. That it was wrapped up, over and done with, and thank god for that, if you want to be honest. I was wrong. It happens. But it was a huge surprise party of slaps on both cheeks, and punch, and kick, and crash. A cinematic reference would be *A Clockwork Orange*. When there's a brotherhood, it's easy to demonstrate what women go through. *Viddy well, my brother.* If I had wanted to, I could have really laid down the law in breakdown. But I knew that every second, so I watched the tide closely because I was part of it and could storm and make myself seasick at any time. Sharks are stories of the past, unconscious, and when I was alive I watched *Jaws* many times.

IS THE SHARK a woman who won't let go? One way to say it is the vagina dentata. But that's only because men think strong women are breaking balls in a game of culture they're trying to catch. In the business of sea. *Jaws* would go right into my bones like shark teeth. It would go right into the deep place it comes from and I would get such pleasure knowing this pain was old, knowing it could swim so well, that it had existed for so long, that there was even a photograph of three men, scientists, standing in the mouth of a prehistoric shark. The picture to prove the wound is inevitable and where we end up. That the wound is a trophy you can stand in. Scientific. Photographic. Cinematic. A frame around men. I think there were three.

Let me tell you about all the fraternity, the trinity everywhere: There were three mechanical sharks, three men, three R's: Roy, Richard, Robert. *"I was intuitively floating in a sea of male images."*

Jaws gave me such deep pleasure I almost couldn't believe how shallow its reasons were. The ripple effect was so strong, coming from so far away. I could feel it everywhere. A movie about a shark, but really so much more. Really it's about wounded men, which is where I began, and where I ended. Three wounded men in the water, sinking. It's where the holy trinity picks up and floats and gets eaten and spit out, and then swims back to shore with missing pieces.

Whenever I watched *Jaws* I thought it was a love story about the relationship between the wound and the rage. Male, but part of me because it took up so much space. The story ends up in us, women, by association. Like a plunge, we learn to live with at the bottom of the ocean, find resilience in spite of, or don't. Mostly don't.

The plot goes: meeting in the middle of the ocean like a bet, the wound gets blown to pieces because it's already everything. Already in everything. Has already consumed and eaten everything. That's why it swims so well. It's been around the block. Knows what it's doing. And one man goes home. No, two. A love story, I told you. They way they peddle back with their legs together (with their arms around each other?) on something fragile they made (how?), held up by the air barrels that were meant for the shark, but failed to keep track of the wound they tried to keep track of. No push. And the soft talk between Richard and Roy, when it's all said and done. About ordinary life, the days of the week. How to get back home. The movie is over, but the story isn't. The credits are for eternity, and roll. Over two male dots in the bulk of earth's water. And we've got words again to make us feel safe. They credits tell us who did what so that we can read all about the men who helped build this with cameras over the course of two long years.

Back to the subject of surface again, the surface we've already lost, the surface already in view. Land. The blue lines of their loss, onshore, in the sand dunes, slung deep, where other things have happened. On top with the sky, below with the water. Time so exposed on a handle of grain. And all that water. That was what I loved. How much just that water alone had to say. *Jaws* was one of the few movies ever to film water in real water and that made such a difference. It took time, and in the end it paid off. The exploitation, the ode. Fake water: you're not fooling anyone with your fooling, so let's just agree that it's just an agreement to be fooled. That's how it goes in Hollywood.

At the end of *Jaws*, the two men go back. Swim out of the gash. And I'd think, okay, but what is there for women in all this? For a woman? Is that what *Jaws*, a microcosm of men in America, is trying to tell us? What room? In the end, the land, like the tide, is already moving out of summer, out of the camera's view. Like these men have been there for ages, away in their boats, in the death that got blown up and sank with hallelujah. With its meat and blood to the bottom of the ocean. A giant bloody valentine sinking in the water.

When Roy Schieder screams with joy, with catharsis, with surprise, with relief, at the end, my heart got broken. It did. I told you sad men make me happy. Make me soft. It's what finished me off. I wish I was what I was. I wish I wasn't. I'm not. Thin and in Jacob's arms everyday. What I liked most was that it was everyday. Duration was always so crucial for me.

It got better only after they'd been on the boat together a few days.

After it was over (I hope you question that word), I kept wondering when Jacob would write again, would call, would come to see me. I waited for it without waiting. With others, I waited like you wait. With Jacob, I didn't wait in any visible way so that other people would think I was experiencing my loss correctly. The contemporary American way. Forgotten and slipping away on a ship—like the rest of its formulas. Jacob topped it. Topped me. Surpassed everyone else, which I could say ruined everything, but was what I asked for. With Peter, I let myself cry, sink. The wood rotting. The shark getting in. With Jacob, I didn't dare. I knew better. Knew because I was. Jacob was in me like an anchor. Of loss. Of what I wanted and lost, and then an anchor. My life in slimy chains like seaweed. Seaweed on anchors that scratch the surface of the bottom, but don't move. I'll call this love. This metal object, ruined. Wrapped in wet, mineral softness. Love. Which part was I? An anchor, because it is ancient history, of the pirate variation or the Iliad. Rusty and permanent. Because it holds ships. Because I did. Because people rely on anchors to do this. It's their job. A sea of men. It was mine.

7

THROUGH THE LOOKING GLASS: OR THE GRASS IS ALWAYS

GREENER IN THE OTHER SHOE

A FEW MONTHS AGO I started working for a tall woman named Aileen. When Aileen was barefoot, she was shorter than me. But Aileen insisted on wearing four-inch heels the entire time I worked, and that convinced me that I was smaller, more than it gave her the illusion that she was bigger. I don't think she gave that part—how it made me feel—much consideration. But what I knew wasn't enough. The fact that I am tall didn't save me. From anything. I kept walking around all day, reminding myself it was the *shoes* making Aileen seem huge. Nevertheless, I found myself buying into the illusion, instead of logic. How could I let myself be so manipulated by a pair of shoes? By two disposable platforms? A platform I, too, could have stepped onto and claimed as my own at any time, but for some reason didn't. Aileen did it first, and if I showed up one day the same height, Aileen would know something was wrong. Would see the compensation and the mimicry on my part. She was always so precise, so accurate. Not a trendsetter, just a good businesswoman. In any case, I hate being second best and unoriginal. I shrink over anxiety, I don't compete.

I kept wishing my employer would resume being barefoot so that everything could go back to normal. So I could rise again. Strut around, clicking on the floor. I wanted to look over Aileen's head and see the view—5,000 square feet of hardwood flooring—

undistorted and untampered with. Mine. I knew that if people were to look at us, which they would and did, they'd see Aileen as the taller one. Plain and simple. They wouldn't bother to lower their eyes to look at the heels she was wearing. They wouldn't think to look at my feet to see that I was barefoot (Aileen liked her floors clean). The only thing people would see was the end result: the undeniable difference in our height, forged or unforged.

For the sake of etiquette, I was forced to look inadequate. Aileen was paying me to be humiliated. People would no doubt conclude that my height was lost beneath Aileen's—the false and unjust outcome of a pair of four-inch heels. In the end they wouldn't see the great lengths that this woman had gone to in order to be taller than me. They'd treat the hoax as exactness. Because connotational procedures are not strictly part of the photographic structure. I see it everywhere. When it comes to the final signified of the image, notes Roland Barthes, fabrication is always read as natural, not cultural. The cultural becomes *naturalized* through denotation. Once you see it, you can't help but feel floored.

When Aileen was away on business, I wore heels while I worked. Not hers, my own. I'm tactile, but I'm not a pervert. I brought them with me, taking off my sneakers to put the heels on indoors, not the other way around. I don't need other people's things to have a good time. I snuck my heels into Aileen's apartment like a secret lover while she was gone. Then I snuck into the secret. *Is it enough*, I wondered, *to put on an extra three inches while I clean this house all by myself?* Or is being seen by the other the whole point? And is symbolic actualization more powerful than the reality of the actual? I tried to determine whether "invisibility can be a way of achieving freedom "from the trap of visibility." As Peggy Phelan notes, visibility provokes voyeurism and fetishism. Maybe shrinking away from "visibility" is a blessing in disguise, since the people doing the looking are so dangerous and so lame. After all, it's the audience that converts you, not the other way around. The media says you don't even exist if you aren't being seen, that you should want to be, but maybe the opposite is true. If beauty is everywhere, if it's so easy to get, then beauty is no longer beautiful.

I developed a foot fetish, which only became a foot fetish because I was desperate to reclaim my enormity. My excess. In my heart, I paid more attention to my height, my feet, than to Aileen's dirt. But I didn't have the stamina Aileen had. Unlike me, she didn't *have* to go anywhere. Inevitably, my feet would get sore. I twisted my right (bad) ankle over and over again while vacuuming. Mopping 5,000 square feet took hours and there was a chance I could slip and fall. In the end, the shoes just weren't practical. And in the end I hated that. Not while I worked, mopped floors, changed sheets. And not really at any other time either, since I was always working, mopping floors, scrubbing toilets, changing sheets. Altering and laundering the sheets always made me feel like I was going to have a nervous breakdown. It was the chore that always made me panic and just want to give up. Not just on the cleaning, but the whole thing. On top of that, I had to change my own sheets every week. Aileen and Chazz's bed was such an abstract symbol of intimacy and repose, and yet so much of my hard work went into it. Was responsible for turning it into that for them.

Unless there was something there to bounce off of, who the fuck actually cared about the extraordinary height I was trying to reanimate? To bring back from the dead. The spectacle was wasted on an empty house. On all the empty houses I worked in. And on me, an empty house.

Aileen and her husband, Chazz, only had one full length mirror in their house, on their bedroom door. In it, I could watch myself going crazy. Being English, their huge bedroom mirror could have meant something extreme on both ends of the spectrum. The long mirror made my legs look short. Again, I was reflected inaccurately—

fuck—improperly, and who would correct the mistake? Who, but me, would even spot it? If people looked into the mirror with me, would they think it was the mirror that'd failed to look right, or me? The mirror widened me instead of pulling me up. It confused me. It was confused about me. The heels did nothing to disprove it. By having someone else like Aileen around, I would be forced to stop focusing on myself. Or it could also work the other way, the way it usually worked. I could go home feeling worse than when I left home. If I didn't have the right weapons, I could easily get wounded again. Knocked down. *And then*, I thought, *there's the whole outside world to contend with once I leave the building, that's even worse. There's Soho turning into fascist forgery. I'm just another thing out of season.* Never underestimate the violence of props in this world.

When I was dusting inside the closets, I often investigated Aileen's shoe collection, which was by no means excessive. No, she made up for that in the inches department. All of Aileen's shoes looked barely worn and were some version of a stiletto. As if she were trying to spite me, every heel was the same. Designed for an acrobat, a woman of privilege and slutty aspirations. Only women who worked at a burlesque circus could pull off such a risky walk. It's a learned thing, involving invisible tightropes, and normally they get paid to do it. Stilettos were the only kind of shoe Aileen had. Or was willing to wear. Maybe back in her other house in London she had a more diverse collection. But in New York, where I cleaned her loft twice a week, for nine hours at a time, Aileen was taunting me by showing me that she could walk on that stage forever and ever.

On my knees on the floor, close to the dirt, I massaged a Pledge-sprayed cloth around the tips of each heel, and by doing so, made a perfect trace around each shoe. Underneath each shoe, the shelves were still gray, but everything else was clean and white. Smelled like lemon. Even glistened. Better than Aileen's shoes, which were a crime scene. I really should have used Fantastic instead of a wood-based cleaning product. But I wanted to be rebellious and make the paint on the shelves peel. Eventually. Once, to see if I could ruin a pair, I sprayed Pledge on some brown suede. But only on the bottom of the heel, where she'd never notice.

Aileen was committing a crime against me by wearing those shoes, and the spotless outline I left each time I cleaned them was proof that she was doing damage not just on my back and knees, but on my heart. On my height, which was rightfully mine. Something I'd always had, even when I didn't want it. The dirt underneath each shoe, which would always be there, week after week if it weren't for me, was me.

After a few weeks, Spring came along, which meant with the snow gone and the pavement dried up, Aileen would be wearing her stiletto shoes and sandals non-stop. On the broken and cracked fatal slices of New York City streets that *Sex and the City* always neglected to show because Sarah Jessica Parker was only ever required to walk from short take to short take between scenes. One Friday morning in the beginning of April, I crouched down in Aileen's closet and started to feel nauseous. There was no point in crying. This was existential. I just lost my appetite. I got up and stormed into Aileen's huge industrial kitchen and pulled out a knife I was responsible for keeping clean every week with stainless steel polish. I brought the knife down into the closet with me. I wanted to slice the heels off of all of Aileen's shoes, which was arrogantly, most of each shoe. Who could stand on pins & needles all day, anyway? Didn't she need any support?

I thought: this is Aileen's way of getting high, injecting herself with stature and superiority. You could never pick up the pace with those kinds of shoes. Never get serious or determined. Never out-walk anyone, never out-run anyone, or anything, never get pissed off. Which meant Aileen had nothing to run away from and nothing to be pissed off about. Besides, New York was no longer the kind of place that signaled Danger. There was nothing to fear, except loss and boredom, and being stuck all day with a nostalgia that no one else bothers to feel. Everyone with money is safe and New York is finally the kind of Big City everyone had always dreamed of. *No one will accost you while you shop*, some young yuppie pregnant wives promise. They reminded me of Rosemary from *Rosemary's Baby*—the way she's totally oblivious of any demon progeny, pitching tent while she shops for baby clothes. Aileen was in sync. But Aileen had money, so Aileen did most of her synching and speeding in taxis. Like in the movies, they quickly took her where she wanted to go. By chopping off the heels from her shoes, like logs for a fire, I would be doing her feet a favor and burning all my dread away. In honor of how ridiculous her shoe standards were, I would leave only the heels and confiscate the shoe carriages for myself. At the very least, I could enlighten Aileen and lose my job in the same hit.

Alice in Wonderland suffers from some kind of breakdown, some longing for a retouching. Down the memory hole, she has anxiety and drugs herself with various substances, and then retches whatever she can't swallow. I don't filter anything. More stays in than comes out. I am exactly what everybody says I am, or am not. I was tall when everybody said I was tall. I am short because everybody says I am short. It's a lose-lose situation. Bodies have to roll with the times. Bodies have to roll with the punches. Unconsciously, all the girls and women I've chosen as friends throughout my life have been mega-short. Mostly 5' 3" to 5' 5". Did I somehow do this on purpose, surround myself this way? Were they ever jealous of being smaller? Did it ever affect them? It never seemed like it. They never said. Or I never noticed. They were always happy to acknowledge what *I* was, and what *they* weren't, in way that I've never been able to do. I never held anything against them and they never held anything against me. We all felt fine the way we were. But in the funhouse, the mirror gets turned into a horror movie and you never look good.

Most of the time I'm pretty relieved to find out that fashion models are actually much shorter than I'd expected. Other times it turns out I'm exactly the same height as they are. There are rare occasions when it turns out that some of these women are vastly bigger than I could've ever imagined. Most magazine articles are full of myths about beauty and stature and always misrepresent the facts about a model or an actress. They almost always say she's thinner than she really is, that she's taller than she really is. Sometimes some of the women, depending on their increasing status and allure, fame and the illusions surrounding it, increase in size over time. Their size increases in relation to their rising status. The more famous they become, the more "beautiful" and "thin" everyone thinks they are. For example, once I read Uma Thurman was five ten inches. A year later, as her fame increased after *Pulp Fiction*, someone on the news announced that she was a mind-bending six feet. Now that made me mildly anxious and suspicious. At five feet ten inches I was even, equal—surpassed only by money, fame, and depending on who's looking, beauty. But at six feet, I didn't stand a chance. I was buried underneath all that, *plus* an extra two inches.

I feared that people would only believe what they saw in that room with me and Aileen. They'd see one woman who was taller, regardless of how she got there. Are people only concerned with the things they are nearest to or furthest from? I could lose it any day. I'm losing it all the time. Cultural zeitgeist proves that abundance and lack is always subject to change, to reversal and retraction, and so are you. You might have to wait a hundred years to be in style again, or out of it again. I started off one thing and became another. I went from extra-ordinary to ordinary. I'm jealous of being tall because I am, and because sometimes, depending on who's standing next to me, I'm not. I want to have what I'm close to having, close to losing. I want to be what I'm close to being. I want to be known for what I was once known for. Being tall.

8

Mean Streets (Or Jacob Part II)

If jacob had his way, *what* would happen to Jacob? Or, what did Jacob do when he *did* have his way? Pure and simple, before me. He fucked girls he didn't know or like. That seems pretty standard, exhausted. By the time I met Jacob, I was halfway over the tragedy of what boys do when they don't care. When they don't want to. Assign themselves to it. It's more act than real ability. I wasn't a whore, it wouldn't happen to me, or I could take boys that wanted to be *Rambo* in a house with a party (*I fucked her with a vengeance*) and turn them into soap bubbles. I lifted them and then it would all burst. We talked about this a lot. Jacob knew what he was dealing with, and had a vocabulary for it, which I loved. Men with vocabularies for their past.

Jacob had plenty to say on the subject of where he went when his way was a field trip. A grave. It was the first thing I recognized and believed about him: *I was such an asshole, I really regret it, really an asshole, you don't understand.* I took it as a sign of enlighten-ment—a breakdown always is—or possible flash of light. All those words he gave me about himself when we crossed the street in London. I thought the statement, and what it unlocked, was more important than the harm it revealed. Jacob was on my right, it was winter, more wet in London than cold. Jacob was buried under an inflation of red. His red parka was sealed with silver duct-tape over his arms and chest, like he'd been injured. At some point, his stuffing had come out. He put it back in, like the scarecrow in *The Wizard of Oz*. He wore it to work. To me. I watched his lower lip while he cried. *What men do for me, if I ask.* Like an awning, it gave me high emotional shelter. But I wasn't shorter than Jacob, he was shorter than me by a hair. But now I think Jacob was warning me as much as the light was warning us not to cross or turn. Jacob was under a spell. He didn't see anything but me, what I was, no one else had it, he assured me. But maybe that also made it easier to leave. No one else would. *It's a gift, the way you left. I'm full of things to say.*

Even though I'd seen *Mean Streets* many times, I'd never noticed, that it's Scorsese, without his beard, who's ordered (as an assassin) to kill Johnny Boy. From car to car, he shoots Johnny Boy in the neck and it's Johnny Boy's blood that goes off like a gun. The blood has a purpose, it pours out like some kind script or reward. For two hours it's had no place to go. This blood that all these men have been trying to keep inside by making less of it, turns into a joke. The blood streams out shockingly from Johnny Boy's neck and Johnny Boy holds his neck with his hand, holds his sinking head, and never lets go, like it's noise he's blocking out, not his death. Johnny Boy walks out of the car when it hits its wall, away with his holes. His neck is a watering can making everything grow. He immediately covers up the holes, runs into the alley, falls. Or lays down. Slides, but it's more graceful than that. It's more of a collapse. Masculinity, boyhood and manhood, unwinding from its tight screw. Screwed. You know how a rope lands when you drop it? It undulates.

The police are there, another alley. Johnny Boy is down, but still walking his newborn wound like a baby. Both him and the wound are babies. We're back to that again. Scorsese films the entire movie in red, Shakespearian red, meaning the red comes back full circle; it's there to do something: to get you. You don't just dance through it, in it, underneath it, like Harvey Keital does. You end up being its message, its vertebrae. It delivers you. Johnny Boy is Charlie Boy's baby. They flirt the whole way through and play like puppies, but only one of them can do the looking after. Charlie holds Johnny Boy's face and looks at it when Johnny cries against the wall. It seems like they might even kiss. They need a hard surface to undo things. They could almost kiss but they don't. It wouldn't end well.

How many times have we seen Robert De Niro cry? When he cries in *New York, New York* it's better than when he cries in *Mean Streets* because he does it on Liza Minelli's turf: on her stomach in the hospital, just after she's given birth. He's got more to regret this time. He's older now. He has nowhere to go but back. Liza's just had a baby and De Niro won't look at their son, won't name it with her. I think that's the last time De Niro was willing to say goodbye in tears, because a few years later, meanness took up almost all the space he was aiming for.

The men of *Mean Streets* are absorbed in red. Scarlet with their lust, their fear, their attack; their bodies dare-deviling. We drown in it too when Johnny spills out like an ink stain. Holding his holes, his faucet, this time he doesn't ask for help. Just runs with it and dies with it. Johnny Boy's a colorful piñata with all this intestinal candy showering from the rooftops he crawls around on in the dark. Shoots a gun from.

Are they really such animals? We drown in Johnny's bowels and it's a surprise he was asking for. Is the movie trying to say that male violence is a sacrifice? A wind-up toy? A religious odyssey? That men are giveaway lambs in a wolf's collar? In the name of. To the system of. Or in *Mean Streets* to the dance, because it's still playful and tender too, like small animals with their sandpaper grip. And is that what Harvey Keital's obligatory religious meditations, abstinences, guilts, self-burns are? The finger in the fire is what Jacob was telling me about himself that night, and I was falling in love with a lineage of burns, with a civilization of self-hatred. Self-infliction, infliction on others, more on yourself. Isn't it the same? That it's a shuffle and a script so absurd and mean, it jumps, and then later in *Goodfellas* it death-hunts and crashes. In *Goodfellas* it's all there is and all that's done. No longer mixed up like a nice salt in the dance, in the brotherhood cake. What's the difference between the threat of the baby tiger in the basement of the bar where they all hang out in *Mean Streets*, and the sweet fangs of Johnny, who could also turn? Who watches his tiger self get stroked and loved from the top of the couch in the basement (Johnny is always on top of something, he's afraid to come down: billiard table, couch, roof). Both are sour milk and warm in their harm.

Jacob looks like De Niro once did. Exquisite and hurt, a shadow. Both had moles making them eggshell, crisp. Italian. Fluorescent yellow light screwed into their skin like bulbs. No one gave into paranoia the way De Niro did in *Mean Streets*. Flick, like a raging on and off switch. Can't decide what to do. Goes back and forth to punch someone's lights out. Kicks existentially with his shaky leg, itching with ants. Another boy into the pavement. We don't see him. He danced it. He did a lot of dancing back then, wouldn't get into the car when Charlie was getting ready to drive and save him. The odyssey coming to an end, going to hell. It made Charlie laugh. It made Charlie nervous. The dancing: repetition, compulsion, butterfly, how they're stranded in the air, ever notice? But it turned into rigid cement. I'm telling the story of boyhood and manhood. I told Jacob what he was doing. He was so soft. I told him every time. You think I'm not self-destructive? Well I am.

What is it about me that freezes not like ice, like a deer, whenever I love a man? Looks straight into the eye of a light that runs you over. I don't move. It wasn't something you could see, me freezing. I'm talking about inside. The way I used all my being to frame the feeling. The man I love. So much of me paid attention. Got in. Few people really do it that way. Underneath the sleet, underneath the mattress. I did. Swam below, held onto. The legs of a boy, Jacob, so that he wouldn't fall. And in the end he did. Johnny Boy did. I pulled back too far and Jacob's legs fell out from under him. Like a platform when you hang. Charlie was always leaving Teresa to find Johnny. The hallway, the car crash.

I woke up with all this water. I went to sleep an empty tank. I used to come home crying when someone would hurt me. The wrong word and all the trust would go out the window. I'd ask Jacob if I was a good person and he would say, "The best." Then he would do more than say it, he'd get down on the floor with me. We'd take up all the room. Acting out all the words we meant like charades. Holding the leaves as if we were branches. He'd stay there for a long time, reinforcing it. Maybe someone would walk by. Then tell us what they noticed. We weren't always home. We were that kind of summary. Witnesses are important. People would see me and Jacob and make a note to themselves: *They love each other.* Jacob gave me his effort and I'd say it's what I was looking for. Someone's effort without budging. I wonder, now that Jacob's left me, now that I'm dead, does he ask himself, "How could I leave a good person? A person whose goodness I gave space?"

9

A Note on Why Gentlemen Prefer Blondes

I thought you would be blonde. I don't know why.

— *A Star is Born* (1954)

THERE'D BE NO BLONDES if it weren't for the others. All blondes are reoccurring, are metablondes. Same thing about metawhores, or metawhoring. And in general same thing about Beauty. I've never believed that the "face that launched a thousand ships" was actually the same face, more a prototype—the face that launched more of the same face. I'm more interested in blonde as symbol or cultural strategy, than blonde as some arbitrary color. Becoming a blonde or being one never happens by mistake. It's harder when you're working with a break in tradition, with antithesis. When it comes to commodity, the whole point is to break away, shun prior texts. Taste is tribalistic. Taste is inheritance. A hand-me down.

In "Thanks for the Memory," Ann Rower let me know that the whole blonde thing did a massive u-turn in the 1920s with movies like *Gentlemen Prefer Blonds*, and has kept going that way ever since. Brunettes became the plain and sensible, a symbol of endurance and domestic longevity, but that that wasn't always the case, and being such an avid reader, I really should have picked up on the switch, the where and when of it. She says 19th century romantic literature is full of dark-haired raven mystique, and not just female. Edgar Allen Poe, Heathcliff, Rochester, and Maxim de Winter from *Rebecca*. Was Anna Karenina blonde? I can't remember, or I don't know. I know that I am dark-haired and I read those books. I know that the books made me feel better than movies or TV.

Witches have always been dark haired, or bad witches have, or bad guys, or people who're in conflict with themselves or everything else. Even Tom Cruise, the hot-blooded cowboy pin-up in *Top Gun*. Good witches are blonde and all-white. Goodness is sheer and transparent, like 19th century novels. In *The Wizard of Oz*, Glenda is daylight and weightless, while the bad witch, the wicked witch of the East, is chalky, green, and weighed down by history. Her skin is the color of Regan MacNeil's demonic projectile vomit in *The Exorcist*— as though being female is really the deepest illness that needs to come out. Is the Wicked Witch of the *East* a Communist thing? The Eastern one's so heavy with spite, retaliation, and ideology, she needs a broom to lift herself up and get herself around. Glenda only needs a wand. And her heart. Snow White's narcissistic Stepmother had black hair, wore black clothes. You can find more recent examples in films like *Betty Blue*. Dark and crazy and depressed, Betty fucks herself into a spell and goes blind doing it. She's a light that goes out. Some lost meaning. These inky women are the pitch-black, rat-infested—really the avatar of evil—attic in *The Exorcist*. Later, the same French actress shows up blind again in Jim Jarmusch's *Night on Earth*. Maybe a ghost of Betty's. Maybe Betty's twin.

Ann spells blonde differently, spells it without an "e" at the end—blond. In one passage, she describes how the binary always takes turns: "The blond is the plain Jane, blond=bland, pale, home-hugging Anglo you marry while the dark raving and ravenous beauty the hero is allowed to have a fling with in the *forest*, a wild ride, is brunette. Is Eastern, exotic, Semitic, foreign, possibly with a name like Miriam as in Hawthorne or Rachel as in Scott. And, if he can't tear himself away from her to get back to the blond he left behind, the dark one dies." Whatever was once fiery in the brunette is now bad, bad-girl, and leaves people cold. And the blonde, who was once the cool ideal, the local, the opaque movie screen; the repository of aesthetic clichés, and who made Jimmy Stewart impotent in *Vertigo* and *Rear Window*, is now hot and trashy. She's only ever been watchable. The instant igniter. The one who's there to remind you that nothing's changed, and that she doesn't want you to either. You can give her *any* script, and she'll memorize it for you.

What started off as a blonde mystery became the end of the world.

Being blonde and cool works wonders for Catherine Deneuve's monster in *The Hunger*. But I'm more interested in figuring out what it means to be blonde, what it meant, so early on, that my friend L was. Cool can coexist with a lot of things, but blondeness, being so specific, so hyperbolic and signifying, can't anymore. A lot of things set this inquiry into motion for me. Miriam, the name of Deneuve's vampire, is a name that could almost be spelled backwards, a palindrome. Here's a brief summary: Originating in the Far East, Miriam Blaylock has lived for 2000 years, ancient like the pyramids, and even before the culture industry, everyone agrees that she's sexy—her sexiness being the main reason for her longevity—and either everyone's been bitten by her, or wishes they'd been. This goes on forever, without any kinks. In *The Monstrous Feminine*, Barbara Creed argues there are all kinds of explanations for what things mean when it comes to women & movies & abjection, but there isn't much that challenges what makes beauty *beauty*. How something goes from beauty to monster, or vice versa. How even critics can't figure that out. Mainly Creed just gets into the monster territory, and mainly she sticks with texts, but everyday women and situations are texts too. So why do so many critics and theorists cop out and stop at movies & books and *politics* politics? Privileging some realms of the political over others. Like when brilliant male theorists who criticize *everything* go out with 20 year-old blonde girls who have nothing to say or are expected to say nothing. Is that just a way to make sure there's more space for men to say more? Or is it because since they know the world is fucked and don't believe in anything anyway, they might as well take advantage of the cultural cynicism they hate by sleeping with powerful clichés? Does a powerful cliché make you more powerful? "Beauty" pulls the wool over everyone's eyes.

The social theorist and philosopher Leszek Kolakowski wrote, "the intellect cannot conquer vanity. Nor is it an accident that the word 'vanity' is close to 'void.'" In other words, it's not women who are vain, but men because they want women to be vain so they can enjoy them and sidestep their own vanity. It's a depressing hypocrisy. There are a lot more. The only thing Creed never examines is her own use of words like beautiful, sexy, and glamorous, as if when it comes to what something looks like, we automatically stop being accomplices in systems of value. As though everything but a face is a social construction.

There's always a gap and it's the common gap(s) that makes me write about things that no one else would even touch with a ten-foot pole. Like, how come when it comes to what's pretty, who's pretty, no one has a thing to say, except "That's Pretty"? Even the brightest are stupid and gullible about beauty. Even critics aren't critical. But Barbara Creed does explain things that *The Hunger* never gets into. Most notably, where Miriam comes from.

Miriam's the Sphinx, she's the archaic mother, she's forever. She's archival. A mummy, she lives in a coffin endlessly repackaged. She's a sure thing. She's what science dreams about every night. The vampire phenomenon is really similar to the celebrity phenomenon. Same seduction, same split between private and public self, mortal self and iconic legend. Same being-hooked-kind-of-feeling, same principal narcissism, exclusivity, elitism. Miriam started off as an Egyptian Princess, a fusion of Carmilla and the Countess Bathory—one lived for centuries vampirizing women, and the other is a historical 16th century Hungarian woman, who'd supposedly tortured 600 young virgins and as a beauty regime soaked herself in their blood. The whole race & looks must be interchangeable, part of a zeitgest.

By the time we see Deneuve-as-Miriam in the film (the dark-haired/dark-skinned raven gets swapped for a blonde), it's the 1980s, and she's with David Bowie who's also in a blonde phase. They're WASPs pretending to be new-wave punks living in an old-money mansion on the Upper East Side across from Central Park. They've been together for 200 years: the perfect couple who've managed to make the elusive "it" work. They also look alike, which plays heavily into the whole synthesis/double/narcissism aspect of vampirism, the way that beauty & eternity are generally about that, and blondeness is splattered across America in every movie, magazine, & TV show. The pair of them set out into the New York club scene and succeed in seducing just about everyone—though I'm sure there are a few exceptions to that rule and I'm not sure that their luck has as much to do with their vampiric status as it does with the general sexual climate—everyone fucking everyone, vampire or not.

They look like WASPs, they've chosen to, but the vampire-as-Dracula myth has always been upper class, a horrific elitism. Whether it's Victorian society or the 1980s, the similarities are palpable: it's the same kind of hypocrisy, the same yuppie two-faced (two-fanged) shit. The vampires are not immune and yuppies aren't afraid to dabble while keeping their dabbling a secret. Like corporate businessman who snort coke and fuck prostitutes before and after every big deal. Maybe there is no vampire, just the eternal reincarnation of class & privilege. Maybe elitism is an infection. There are a lot of interpretive directions I could take, but I'll stay along these lines.

It is the 1980s and Reagan's been around for a few years. Miriam knows things will go more smoothly if she lightens the mood. Lightens her eyes, lightens her hair. Lives like a tax-paying queen who gives music lessons in her philanthropic spare time. The rich have always been patrons of art. Though both Deneuve and Bowie would consider eating their cello student, it's not their first choice.

On Fashion: Miriam keeps her clothes dark and her shoulder pads big to remind us that darkness & night are her primary conditions. So are hard lines and primary colors. Her style is historical, ahistorical. It's retro, an homage to the 1940s, but with a 1980s high-tech sleekness. She wears the equivalent of a man's business suit and evokes the premise that surface is a reliable, tangible reality, a theory so prominent in 80s culture, even a vampire can come across as law-abiding with the right politics. Miriam wears skirt-suits. Everything's buttoned up, or rather, buttoned down: controlled and cool on the outside. Everything is in the shape of the 1940s, politically and aesthetically, and is perfect and square, masculine and bleak, since it's wartime. AIDS is starting, so it's wartime. I think Deneuve's clothes look great because I'm a fan of androgyny, or anything between the lines, and to some extent, masks, which is what the vampire myth is all about.

To emphasize this, Miriam is bisexual. Temporally and sexually. She's fucked everyone, she's fucked all-history. She's lived with, not just fucked, both men & women. She's probably been both too. As a blonde, Miriam won't be as lonely, her vampire tooth—now a blade disguised as a gold hieroglyphic cross—is the only thing left of the black Egyptian she used to be.

As the film's title points out, Miriam will not go *hungry*, but she'll always feel that way. If Miriam had stayed an Egyptian in a 1980s right-wing America, she knows she would have had racism to contend with. She's already had centuries of dealing with it. In a flashback sequence, Miriam looks like she might have even been

Nefertiti in 14th century B.C. She is the Queen of Egypt, the wife of Akhenaton covered in blood. Maybe she's even just killed him and gone from there. The film doesn't specify, but he's black and she looks white, so who knows what she's killing? Maybe it's race, the mutation of race; the selection of whiteness. Miriam doesn't need that much exoticism. She's got enough by being the exotic blood-sucker circa 1983.

Are brunettes the modern Dracula? Our relatively new aesthetic Other? Is being with them just a biblical mess or a bore if everyone says so? And is it a dream to be with blondes if everyone says so? Things are what everyone says they are. I wish I'd been around to see the switch from one ideal to another. Like seeing bombs being dropped. W.K. and I have this joke, an exercise we like to do while watching TV or a movie where a famous "blonde" actress becomes serious and important and wins an Oscar by portraying a serious and important and *less attractive dark haired woman*. Usually weight gain also figures prominently into the change from beauty into "real," flawed woman. We call this exercise, "Put A Blonde Wig On It." The best examples of putting a blonde wig on a woman (this really just means a dye-job or a bad wig) to signify "true," "ideal" beauty are Cameron Diaz in *Being John Malkovich*—who becomes ugly, maternal, and sexually deviant just by adding dark, uncombed hair to her head—and Charlize Theron in *Monster*. What's monstrous, the fact that Aileen Wuornos killed the men who raped her and wasn't sorry, or that fact that she was in a physical/economic dump? Even though she is the kind of blonde that is bleached right out of a trailer-trash box, and it's why men want to fuck her to begin with, the more important kind of blonde-ness, is blonde as intention, politic, state of mind.

People couldn't get enough of how ugly they thought Cameron Diaz—was or *became*—in John Malkovich. How beautifully she performed brunette ugliness. People said what was ugly about her was her "hair," the rest was the same. But her features didn't change, I told W.K. "They're the same!" But no one talked about that. I thought she looked ugly because she is ugly. Ultimately, shouldn't a beautiful face transcend a bad hairdo? As if color can really trump everything else. Being that Cameron Diaz normally walks around in a blonde "wig," I guess no one thought it would hurt her feelings when they said she looked ugly in a brown one. *With brown hair.* As if the main thing were to save Cameron Diaz from insult, and not all the women who aren't blonde, by birth or by choice. Cameron Diaz certainly didn't contest it. She gladly slipped back into old form when she was done filming. She was eager to restate her own cultural signification of blondeness, to give everybody what they were dying to get back.

Since Cameron Diaz didn't gain any weight in *Being John Malkovich*, we'd have to assume that her "beauty," or "anti-beauty," hinges solely upon wearing, or not wearing, a blonde wig. Pamela Anderson is also a prime example of a woman who's become what she is because of all her Blonde redundancy. Would Pamela mean everything she means with *just* the fake tits? Without the blonde hair to top it all off? It's something at least Dolly Parton is totally honest about.

The face inspires so much: What would happen if we actually thought about faces, or broke them down and intervened in how they're delivered and described? What if we unconventionlized them? What if beauty wasn't word of mouth, verbal and visual pro-paganda? How come we rarely acknowledge the politics of beauty when it comes to something as loaded as how people *look*? How we want them to. It seems like the only time we let ourselves be ana-lytical about a face is when we want to break it down for conversion (cosmetic surgery). Or for some reality-TV show like *America's Next Top Model* or *The Swan*. Which preoccupies itself with: "This needs fixing on her," or "I need to be fixed." Read any online blog on Hollywood faces and you'll find pages of petty deconstruction about what should be done cosmetically to particular people and why. The merits of one face versus another, while both faces are equally lauded. It's in those spaces that we have the most to say about what's working and not working, and why. When a face gets broken down, it's because it's seen as slum housing that needs rehabilitation. Houses that need to be knocked down so that new condominiums can be built in their place. Whole acres of look-a-like formula.

Getting back to Ann Rower's point, are we back, or did we never leave the era of safety, plainness, and copy? Beauty is like slipping into a set of institutions—the presidency.

When Judy Garland walks into the publicity office of her Hollywood set as Vicki Lester in *A Star is Born* for the first time, she's greeted with instant disappointment that's plagued her all her life. It's a throw-away moment in the movie, but to the real Judy, and to her character Vicki Lester (AKA Esther Blodgett), and to me, the comment means everything. It let her down for good. It meant she wasn't Lana Turner or Marilyn Monroe. It meant movie stars come with strict conventions, or at least a willingness to take them on board. You can find a list of famous blonde phrases everywhere if you just look. Listen. Phrases like, "*I thought you were going to be some blonde beach beauty*" or "*Pale, like angels*" or "*She's got a sort of Aryan quality. I think she would go down extremely well in Germany*" or "*With platinum and peroxide, there's no lack of blondes these days.*" In *Annie Hall* or *Manhattan*, the movie where Mariel Hemingway is like seventeen and being felt up by Woody, Woody Allen says something stupid about how twelve year-old blonde girls are the secret to the universe. I guess that's bad news for all us post-puberty smart, brunette girls. "I thought you were going to be blonde. I don't know why," Miss Markham, the woman who runs the publicity department, tells Vicky/Judy when she walks into her office. "I don't know why."

10

THE TRUTH ABOUT NOSES

"How do you like your hero? Over easy or sunny side up?"

— *Last Tango in Paris*

I can't understand what makes a man. It takes another man to make me understand.
                                        — *Depeche Mode*

TOM WAS HIS BEST SELF with a dog. Anybody's dog. If he saw one, he walked over to it. It's not that animals bring out the best in people, or that they unthreateningly enable you to disclose what you're really made of, it's that animals are in fact all there is to most people. To Tom. Why go beyond a dog, thought Tom? Why strain yourself, why push your luck, why complicate, or maybe, Tom didn't even think any of those things. Dogs were as good as Tom was going to get. People could see how attentive Tom was, after all, he didn't have his own dog, so all of his care was always on open display, in front of other people. Riding horses is an act of extreme kindness. How can anyone doubt someone who spends all day in the company of so much shit and ignitable dried grass? They're not doing it for fun. Tom believed that everyone thinks highly of you if you have a pet, space full of cats. A cat for every cat. In the movie *Lovely and Amazing* that Tom had just seen, it's the character that can't say no to rescuing stray dogs who is told that she is "lovely and amazing."

Tom was stroking something horizontal with fur—all animals are indirect, interstitial. A gutter you can install yourself into like a pipe. Tom could feel connected like plumbing, his heart flushing with water. Tom's hand merely had to reach under something, and something like a dog would sneak out from somewhere unrelated. Tom acknowledged that, like Hollywood, dogs are intent on illustrating how total their interaction with you is, it's like never wanting to have an affair again. Dogs, confirmed Tom, are the perfect breast.

Tom was drawing a breath, maybe through his nostrils, comparing noses in his mind and the unforgiving contexts of noses. Hollywood is a map of the face. There are borders everywhere, nothing is free, and either you can't get in or can't go back. It's all anyone wants to see or pays attention to. It's the conspicuousness of the face in relation to all other inconspicuous things. No one really gives a damn about the physiognomy of a dog. Tom paid attention to his own nose, and to the noses of the men who get away with everything. Being blonde and a WASP, Robert Redford got away with his less than perfect proboscis, his facial bumps. Tom studied the surprise crack as Robert cocked his head in *Legal Eagles* to watch Daryl Hannah enact performance art. But there was so much blonde and light in the room, no one noticed. People are less prone to noticing sun on a wheat field, than they are to buttercups along dark rivers. This was the difference between Robert and Tom.

Being rich and impervious, Tom Cruise pulls off his steep bridge. At least Tom earned his right, thought Tom. Tom probably didn't always have it easy, lamented Tom. For years, Tom was torn up about his buckteeth that are caught on film forever in *The Outsiders* and in *Legend*. But at least in *Legend*, Tom had mythology and sorcery on his side. And long hair like a curtain over the miserable outdoors. The gothic underbite vaporized by the swing of a sword. Everyone knows fantasy is rampant with imperfections. At least Tom knows what's it's like to suffer, to be just around the corner from ugliness. He was even wearing clear braces until as recently as 2003. Tom had seen Tom proudly flash his wiring on the red carpet, but Penelope Cruz gleamed anyway.

Tom has to work on things. Robert got a free ride just because of his colors. The sun bleaches things out. Alleviates inflexible edges. It goes with the territory, thought Tom. About Tom. What goes with mine? I need to make room on my face for any outside mistakes and disturbances, the face being the most social space there is. There wasn't a day that went by in Tom's life, that someone hadn't seen it.

TOM TRIED TO think of more examples where the system had been beaten. The facial system, which is a microcosm for all other systems. If Tom could straighten this out in his nose, Tom would be free in other ways. At the café, there was bamboo that, like prison bars, separated things like food and cars parked in a lot. A nose was a lot like that, there's no reason things have too be too close or too far away. A face should be like a good community, like a suburban row of house after house. Not hostile, like a recluse in a cabin.

There was a father at a table who gave his 6 year-old daughter two dollars to pay for ice cream at the counter beside him. She ordered Oreo cookie flavor while he ate a BLT. The little daughter, Jasmine, was getting something sweet, and so was the father, as he stared at a 16 year-old model that he didn't know was a model, but wouldn't have been at all surprised if she was, because if she wasn't, he thought she should be. Maybe someone should tell her. Maybe he should, or would. It would be a crime not to, a waste. You don't waste steak, you eat steak. You let steak decay in your intestines, the way all meat eventually gets processed. Most of the time society doesn't frown upon, or even notice, an older man advising a much younger women about things they pick up on. That would explain the staring; he was merely trying to conserve her. After all, the father was the one with the bacon.

At the Metropolitan Museum of Art in New York City, Tom wandered around the Greco-Roman wing. The life-size sculptors, walls; the figures in the paintings, the saints, the gods, the angels, the anguished, the lovers, both the men and the women, all showed off their bighearted Roman profiles. No one gave these subjects a hard time. Instead, they had been invited to take a brush-stroked photograph. To show off what they had in angles. If the lips were red and warm, why shouldn't the nose have as much charity in place? Scope? These oil visages were full of lush extent, even the oneric pre-Raphaelites by William Holman Hunt, John Everett Millais, Dante Gabriel Rossetti, forced Tom to pay attention to the microscopic detail of fullness on display. "Finally, a place, a time, where the nose was free to roam. To be. To just forget about itself and get on with it." Whenever someone told Tom his nose was too big, or just big, which sounds just as bad, in a way that having big lips or eyes is never bad, Tom retaliated with his art education and reminded people of the nose entitlement the Romans had been treated to. "Weren't these people considered beautiful?" insisted Tom. "Weren't they the norm? Weren't they beautiful enough to be immortalized and hung up, pinned to a wall?" People were either silent, or dismissive. "Okay, but this isn't Roman times Tom. This is now. Things have changed, and those Romans were fat and ugly and needed a tan. They had no idea what a camera can put you through." Actors said this, everyone says this.

Tom wondered if the love of the pet above all other things and loves, hadn't translated into the realm of beauty. Like that woman, Jocelyne Wildenstein, who has undergone countless plastic surgeries in her quest to resemble her perfect ideal—a cat. A woman who shaved her nose like it was a peeled carrot dropping into a salad bowl. A block of bitter chocolate she couldn't bear the bitter taste of. Tom was sure that he had heard the cat woman, as she is called, arguing that her facial restructuralizations were as healthy and loaded with emotional potency as any root vegetable. Tom looked at the cat woman's nose-montage on *20/20*, as the cat woman gradually abated and decongested the view. "You see how when I turn my head to the side, I disappear?" Jocelyne asked Barbara Walters. "You can only see me from the front, like a photograph." Barbara could sympathize, she'd changed over the years too, and like any image, you could look at the differences and point them out. Barbara didn't want to be caught looking Jewish for the rest of her life.

Who wants to look at a face and see a face anyway? Nobody actually ever looks at a face. Instead, they hear about what faces should like look and try to keep up. In almost every case, there is room for change. Desire, like a nose, should never be fixed. Tom got annoyed and smirked as he thought about how no one had ever asked Robert Redford to change a thing, probably not even his acting style. It was only when Robert became an old man, did he feel any pressure. He pulled his face up like a pair of pants that were falling.

Tom Cruise fixed his teeth so he could look happier and less impacted. No one wants to look at face that always looks like it's prohibited by food. Either Tom had to find a way to be like Tom, or Tom had to figure out how to be like Tom. Dye his hair, get blue eye contacts to cover up the real brown. How did Barbara Streisand find her way out? Tom thought it had to be a generational thing, as well as her voice, which drowned out the sound of her nose. Dustin Hoffman abandoned any hope of being looked at just before *The Graduate*, so it never came up again. People were there to see Dustin drive circles through his characters, not please the eye. But what about Jewel or Jessica Simpson? It was true, the camera rarely settled on the side, but nevertheless the grooves were there. Some faces do more charity work, more negotiating, for the rest of the face than other faces do. But still, Tom had to show face with his face, and until he could find his way out of it, Tom had to face things.

11

THE GHOST OF BERLIN

TOM WAS HIS BEST SELF. Even now, sixty years later, it makes sense to me to be a spy in Germany, or to seem mournful there. The summer was dark, so I could be too. I was a little bit like Nosferatu, the first one. Very pale, in a black and white world, a foreigner with no reflection. It felt like I came in a box. I was watching everything all the time, but I was totally invisible. On the street people looked at me with sub-titles. They stared at me between the lines and didn't know whether to be sick or in love with me. My hair was dark like a movie screen turned off, or a black bird perched on a windowsill. Do you shoo the night bird away? Do you push it off even though you know it can fly?

Berlin is leftover. Full of punitive damages, both structural and emotional. Everything is missing something, a chip, a tooth, a limb. Part of its memory. Some of the buildings still look hurt like that burnt church in the werewolf movie *Wolfen*, where the church functions as a wolf den and the wolves are Gods, except nobody knows it and nobody cares. The wolf church, a high shadow, is surrounded by twenty-eight acres of abandoned slums in the South Bronx, but the wolves love it there and have no other place to go. They feel oppressed, so they go where the oppression is the heaviest because they respond to sadness. On blog sites, some *Wolfen* fans complain that when the wolves are finally unveiled in the movie, they aren't even scary, they're just wolves. But the wolves aren't supposed to be scary, we are. The same thing happened with Oz in the Wizard of Oz, but I think it's scarier when something isn't scary, but has been made scary through hysteria. Some bloggers also complain about the film's eco-terrorist subplot. Since the movie partially believes that the wolves are the eco-terrorists, anything or anyone that's trying to help them, is also an eco-terrorist—even though wolves were terrorized first. In one scene at the end, hundreds of wolves, in different fur shades, band together like environmental activists on the steps of the New York Stock Exchange, angry as hell but willing to come to some kind of compromise. In Berlin many of the buildings on Museum Island have teeth marks and scratches in them as if beavers and woodpeckers and rats, even wolves, have been clawing at the walls.

I was alone in Berlin the whole time. At first Sam was there because it was his place, but then he left and the place became mine. When Sam was there he acted like I was his wife and owed him something in the house, so I was relieved to see him pack his bags and go back to the States for two months. He called me once a week, during which time he would pause a lot on the telephone, waiting for me to say something romantic about him being gone and him coming back. I don't think he understood that my solitude wasn't a symptom of his absence, but what I wanted to have in my life, and that, like the U2 song, I would have had it with or without him. The night before he left, we made dinner. Some kind of nut loaf from a 1970s cookbook that had no illustrations of any of the things it was enlisting you to cook. Sam said his mother gave it to him on one of his birthdays and then he snarled. I was turned off by his obvious mother-issues. Afterwards we listened to the Smiths attentively with our ears pinned to the speakers, literally, and stayed up until three in the morning talking about Eastern Europe, Budapest, and all the new variations on Klezmer music that we both liked. I told Sam about how much I loved the bathhouses in

Budapest. How many of them were tucked away in parks, behind trees and bushes, like Easter eggs, and how amazing it was to bathe and hear the room echo you back while you did it.

The only romantic thing I did in Sam's honor while he was gone for the summer was rearrange his furniture on a daily basis, then tell him about it when we spoke on the phone. Sam liked to picture his chairs and bed being moved around by me. He was very domestic, so it was dirty talk for him to hear me describe it. "You have some voice," he'd say afterwards. "It's like a beautiful dark wood with no finish." He imagined me as the floor beneath his bed. Maybe I moved Sam's things around as a gift to him. Or maybe I did it to erase him, to make the place feel like it was mine, not his, or at least not his while it was mine. I hated knowing that he had been there and that he was coming back, and that we would be there together when he did. I also talked to Sam's beautiful plants—his jades and iron maidens and red geraniums. I was jealous of all his big windows and wished that I had windows like that at home in America. But mine were tiny and faced other walls, and there were only two in my apartment. Sam had three big rooms, with really high ceilings that I used to look at at night, imagining the flat floor of the North Pole and finding animals in the cracks. Sam's building was pre-war and one of the few things to survive in the neighborhood. All the buildings on the streets in Prenzlauerberg had large balconies that looked like greenhouses and nurseries stuffed with leaves and flowers. I liked that Sam had so many plants. It showed that he wasn't just paying attention to himself.

On Sam's last night in Berlin, I fell asleep first. Instead of leaving, Sam curled up behind me like a horny cat and attached himself to me. To the back of me. He was sneaky and bony—the color of a sweet potato. He had the body of a twelve-year old boy and looked like a French fry. It was gross, especially since he had such high expectations for female proportions. Meanwhile, his own body was such a wash and had never even made its way out of adolescence.

Sam slipped in from nowhere. I had a tiny mattress on the floor in his office that I slept in behind a door for extra privacy. I pretended I was sleeping just so Sam would get bored and roll off. I didn't want any more icing on the cake. Most men don't want to touch you unless they think you're responding to it in some way. That's why they invent stories all the time about consensual sex in nonconsensual situations on programs like *20/20*, *Primetime,* and *Oprah*. They make you think that you're responding even when you're not responding, but usually they at least like to imagine a reaction. Some minor solicitation always helps. They want an audience because everyone does. In Sam's arms, I played dead like a possum on the side of the road, but unfortunately that seems to make most men want to touch me even more. They love to imagine that my feisty side, the wolf side, the side with fangs and claws, is dormant while they pet me like a tranquilized polar beer in a coma of melting ice.

The next morning I woke up feeling pissed off. My sleep felt contaminated and infringed upon. Instead of sleeping, I was on night watch instead, patrolling my own body in my cop skin and cop car. I imagined Sam melting off me, dripping from the bed, and through the wooden floorboards like Mr. Clean liquid. Out of the apartment altogether and without the washed sanitized smell. I wanted a sleep do-over. In the morning, there was a note and a rose on the floor. I don't know where Sam got a designer flower at five in the morning, but I felt like I had fucked him even though I hadn't. Sometimes you can't get away from sex no matter how much you try. Fucking is all in the mind. It was in Sam's and it was in mine as an antithesis. Mind-fucking was what kept me going all those years. Being intimate with things in my head and keeping that intimacy to myself. The note said:

You're a peach. Soft and wonderful. I hated to leave you there. I'll miss you.

The note made me sick because it was full inaccuracies and gross projections.

1. I didn't know what being like a peach meant. Was I a peach because I was fuzzy? Prickly? Juicy? Unripe? Pink? Orange? The pits? Hard? On the phone, my friend David told me that it was a kind of Americana 1950s thing to call a woman, or a girl, a peach, like doll-face or cutey-pie. "It's a good thing," David assured me. "You are." That made me mad at David too. He assumed I wanted to be a peach. That as long I was called a peach, it didn't matter by whom, because I had no peach standards.

2. What was wonderful? That I was soft and a peach, or that I was a whole set of other wonderful things in addition to being peach-like?

3. Why did Sam hate to leave me? Because he felt *I* hated it? I didn't. What made him think I did? I hated the very opposite of him leaving. I *wanted* him to leave. I hated him being there. Plus, he had to think I hated it in order to think it mattered to me that he did.

4. *I'll miss you.* Was that the beginning of me having to say *I miss you too Sam*?

A FEW DAYS LATER, Sam made his first call from the US. I pretended like the note was his dream and not *our* shared movie. I was glad I wasn't in the land of movies anymore.

In bed alone, I thought: *This is why it's better not to mess with being alone. Now I feel like I've imagined the whole thing. All the purity. The new genre. I don't want a cat, but I've ended up with a solitudinous prop anyway in exchange for being female. There's nothing curled up in a ball at the bottom of my bed. Movies are full of so many root vegetable clichés and year after year the Halloween costumes at the supermarket are the same.*

Movies were really the only things I could handle in doses. I took them everyday like small pills—my Valium, my Prozac—waiting for them to make me better. But they just made me pretend-better and drowsy. The outside world of movies pushed me further away from the outside. The more I saw of the movie-everyone, the more phobias I developed about the non-movie me. I wasn't what I saw on the screen, at least it didn't look or sound like it. Plus, seeing movie-everyone naked, or fake naked, or in their bras and panties, really fucked with my head. I never even saw anyone naked or in their underwear in my real-life, and when I did, it was always in context. There's no context for seeing women you don't know naked all the time. After awhile, I stopped being able to look at myself naked and decided that if I wasn't doing it for a movie or a photo-graph, I didn't deserve to do it at all. My being naked had no consequence, no wide-scale effect; it didn't establish me as anything to anyone, the way that being a fashion model makes everyone think about you in the same way. Most of the time I didn't know if I was sleeping, since movies are pretty much the same things as dreams, only your eyes aren't shut. What happens when you fall asleep in a movie theater? Is that like a double-whammy? You can have good dreams or bad dreams, or just average ones, and movies can come across that way too. Sometimes a movie can really turn me on, open me up, align everything into order or chaos, and I can feel that, just like I can come in my sleep.

It was hard even to wake up. I always missed my intended mark, 9, 10, 11 in the morning. I started the day off first thing feeling like a failure, and it was almost always the same thing out-side: the failure to be warm, failure to be light, failure to be early, failure to be fun. The city really disappointed me on daily basis. The city itself wasn't necessarily the problem—it was that particular city in combination with me at that particular time. It didn't understand what I needed from a place or how sensitive I was. It never let me meet anyone. The light resembled slabs of gray concrete. Concrete from the floor above fell into Sam's balcony Geraniums on a daily basis. The building I was in was falling apart and I picked the pieces out of the red flowers every morning. Wolf territory. I went to the park across the street for color. I hurried around by myself in a very sad city.

The impression that a dark movie theater gives you is that you're furtive and safe and tucked away in a cognitive kangaroo pouch. Submerged into something mostly unavailable to anyone but you in that moment, like your own subconscious or a great vintage find. It's why men love to go to porno theaters by themselves and get turned on by themselves. They feel like they're simultaneously in and out of the womb, protected by it and free of it at the same time. Connected to the archaic, while being up against some wholly new thing. It's a no-zone that works. That feeling can be embarrassing to have and embarrassing to watch. It's why in *Taxi Driver*, while looking at a porno, Travis Bickle, a scopophiliac, does it with one eye closed. He makes a hand scissor or a hand-gun—a repression puppet—with his fingers, and keeps switching the movie-sex on and off with it. He takes his excitement in doses and slices. He edits away certain scenes. He can't really handle his own desire. It's too gooey and hot, which is true about most people's desires, so he finds a form he can deal with.

The effect that movies have on the lives of the people who make them is just the opposite. Instead of feeling discrete, things get really sweet and overblown (blatant), really fast. It's like watching cotton candy being spun around in the glass booths that are always at carnivals. When you watch a movie, you feel a false sense of privacy and intimacy. You think it's your baby, your secret, your sexy disclosure, like in the movie *Videodrome*. You're convinced that what you're seeing comes out of a special box—the screen box or the TV box—that you can penetrate and affect, and that it's a personal message for you to decode all by yourself. You think it's magic and that you're taking a risk by looking at what's inside that magic, which of course you are, but no souls pour out screaming and writhing from Pandora's Box, and nothing transpires that quickly or seals your fate for good. Ever. The effect isn't dramatic or mythological. It's slow and systematic. The box isn't even yours and it's not personalized in some special way. And there's no fable attached to it. People forget all the time that movies are ultra-social creatures. The worst kind of extroverts. The kind of person that at a party makes you cringe because they can't help blasting themselves all over the place like images that blink in every single room simultaneously. Even if you're in the kitchen with a beer, you can hear them—they're so wasteful— or in the hallway, you can see them, but there's no sound. Most extroverts work on introverts like an x-ray effect, illuminating the damage inside.

IN BERLIN, I thought about every single thing I watched, in America and abroad, and the network polls that were constantly been accessed about programming and ratings and who liked what. Like a lot of people, I watched the same thing, but I didn't watch it in the same way or for the same reason. Only there's no category for how someone watches something and what they think and feel about it while they're watching it. There's only one poll that says that if everyone watches *A*, then everyone likes *A* the most or thinks the same things about *A*. I want there to be a poll that says that just because everyone watches *A*, doesn't mean that everyone likes *A*. I watched *A*, but ranted and raved and cursed *A* to hell while A was on. I also watched *A* because I wanted to know why *other* people watched *A*. What is it about *A* and why do people watch *A* more than they watch *B*, for example? And why doesn't any one want to watch *C* instead? *A* was one of those spy messages I was trying to decode in Germany. But espionage techniques were notorious for being difficult to get across borders. George Washington had this problem when the British occupied America. Almost all the signs were eliminated as soon as they were invented. Spies ate their secret messages on paper and only dreamed about them in their sleep. Plans went haywire as riddles went unsolved and uncommunicated. The ink infused the spies' bodies with steam like boiling water and the forgotten secrets came out of their pores when no one was looking. *A* was just like the Prom Queen who got fucked the most.

The subways in Berlin were always two things: a world of underground bakeries, meats, and tights & socks shops. I avoided all the brightly lit dough that seemed so dirty and old as it never saw the light of day down there, but bought many socks in an array of clownish colors that had to do with that Kinder-culture quality that Germans love. I thought I might feel better if I wore red or yellow socks. I learned the city by taking the U-Bahn and S-Bahn to different movie theaters. I'd circle listings in the paper. I went to the movies during the day and at night, and sometimes I went to one after the other, either at the same theater or at another one, at a different location, on the other end of town. It was like going to AA meetings. The movies became soothing lairs to sit in. Maps in themselves—calendars, plot devices, clocks—and the tickets in Berlin were a third of the price. I was captain of my solitude. I watched little Godard movies in little movie theaters with a couple of fold out chairs and a piano wedged into a corner below the screen, and I watched huge movies like *The Perfect Storm* in huge theaters, on huge screens on Potsdamer Platz, where an ocean looked so big, it made me feel seasick and utterly alone. I was the only one in the theater when I watched the young Tristan-fisherman drown all by himself in a wave so gigantic it was no longer real, but mythic. He was overwhelmed, but not afraid, by the femaleness of the wave, while he remembered everything he could about the woman he loved on dry land. That way he could convince himself that the giant wave about to take him under, was really his beloved coming towards him. To my surprise, I started to cry when this happened because the way the fisherman faced the death-wave was so un-American, it reminded me of what I was trying to get away from. In *The Perfect Storm*, Tristan had nothing in front of him but that Isolde-wave and what it would do to him.

BBC was the only thing on TV I could understand because it was always in English. They had a twenty-minute program that was all about the latest American blockbusters and it was played on continuous loop. The guy who hosted it looked like a bald eagle and was usually on 42nd Street by himself talking about movies and box-office scores. Since the year was 2000, I was pretty sure the bald eagle wasn't watching pornos. The rest of BBC was more of a news *sound* than actual news. Its presenters and reporters were trying to put together some phonetic meaning that people could receive. It was obsessed with the perfect rendition of a certain British inflection and delivery, as if horror could only be reported using the right vocal technique.

I felt isolated and irritated and tired most of the time, like I'd been bitten on the neck in a vampire movie and my troubles were just beginning. Every day was humid and made me feel weak. There was a part of me that felt sick and distressed. I looked for Victorian white nightgowns to sleep in at my favorite antique stores. East Germany is full of them. But when I finally bought one, I felt more like a medieval man in his undergarment, perusing around the pantry with a candle, than a stung heroine with her locks undone. I had no locks to undo. My hair was short. Everything was so disappointing and off-key. At night, I thought, *October is a beautiful word*, so before I went to sleep, I said it out loud and knocked myself out.

According to various sounds and shapes at night, I wondered if my life was in danger. I was sure all three of Sam's rooms were haunted—especially the big empty one. I slept in it for a few days until a ghost attacked me in my sleep. It was sitting on my chest and trying to get in through my solar plexus. But I'm very particular about what and who I let in through there, so I struggled and wrestled until I woke up. I'm sure something possessed me because for the next three years I didn't feel well and was extremely pale, even though my natural skin tone is olive. When I arrived in England, no one believed me when I told them my face was usually dark. Same old story. For someone who was alone as much as I was, I should have masturbated a lot more. But I couldn't get worked up that easily because my desire was just as incognito as I was. Off on it's own somewhere without me. I wasn't in any kind of sexy shape or mood to do something demanding like raise my sexual blood pressure whenever I felt like it. I didn't feel like it. I couldn't imagine anyone I wanted, and when I tried to, it put me to sleep, instead of waking everything up. Whatever that person was, he was too deep to locate with fingers.

12

WEB LIFE

I KNOW YOU KNOW what I do. I'm always wondering about where you might've seen me. That's the fear. I cover my tracks. You never know. I was on the internet the other day looking at your pictures, studying your face, your hairline, your teeth, your subtle weight gain, worried the whole time that you might discover me there, snooping. My fingers on the keyboard, on your face, coming up to the notes to read them. Sometimes you look horrible. Sometimes you make that face. You've been everywhere it seems. I'm not really invisible, am I? I wondered. I ask around. People who know these things. Yes, some trace does exist. A number or a code. Yes, but does it point to me? Does the code spell my name? Does it say where I've been? No one says anything.

I was shaking like a leaf. It was late. You were probably asleep where you are. It's always three hours later where you are. The clock on my computer sometimes stands still. Sometimes gets stuck. I just wanted to see what you'd been up to these last ten years. It's innocent, just checking in. You know how badly it goes in person. How else can I know? I'm not going to call you. We used to run into each other, but found out nothing through our run-ins except that it was all still there. "Nothing," I'd tell you. "Nothing," you'd say back. Or say first. You already had your projections anyway. About what I was. What I am. And unless I ran into you, I'd having no way of knowing anything about you. I looked at all your pictures—you put them there after all. I guess you want people to see them. But I'd die if you caught me looking at you. Are you looking to catch someone? Do you look to see who's looked? You don't look at your own pictures once you've posted them, do you? This is a great time to be curious.

When it comes to you I've always done things this way. I've always spied and snooped according to the ages. Our ages. I type your name and it shows up a hundred times. In blue. You've done well. Some people only come up once or twice. It's a status thing. I get jealous, it doesn't matter that you're a boy, or that we're in totally different fields, worlds. I've been doing it as long as you have. I shouldn't have given you as much support. It's things like my support that got you there, got into your head. I think I deserve better.

After I've clicked and looked into it, your name goes purple like I've strangled it. Shit, it's a trace. Old blood restricted. Stuck. I am. The purple is a constant, documented reminder that I've been there looking for you. My computer registers it and won't let me forget it. I hate myself and pretend like it never happened. I worry anyone could find out, you, by typing even just the first letter of your name, P. And all the times I'd looked at/for you would show up like a grocery list of you. Not just you. What if at some point I lost my computer? Like a diary, I'm all over the place in it and so are all my obsessions and secrets. And so are you. Some obsessions are public, scripted, but most secrets aren't.

I have these pictures of you. They're not the one's you posted for everyone's pleasure. They're your pleasure. Since they're not *that* kind of picture, only the people who know you, including yourself, get the pleasure. I get the creeps, the one's I've always gotten from looking at something that belongs to you. Even when we were together, it felt like when we weren't, and I'd just steal these glimpses, these looks. I'd just steal from you. Kissing you in your room didn't feel like my fantasy coming to life, it just felt like my fantasy. I felt sick and asked you to stop doing what you were doing. It was shocking how much I'd already imagined. Maybe it ruined everything, actually having you. Hard to stomach that you were really on me. On top, and no longer just in my brain.

I get the photos that maybe you don't even know about. I wonder how many people do. I click onto "images," instead of other kinds of categorical information. Like "News," "Groups," "Maps," or the real biggie, "Advanced Search." I just want to go straight to the face. The Web let's me cut to the chase. Do you know that all these people took pictures of you? Were you posing for them? At different venues and events? Did you want them to be "out there?" At one point or another, I think you did. Anyone can see them. Anyone can have them. So why shouldn't I? I doubt anyone asked if they could take the pictures. If there are lots of people with the same name, who have done things to make themselves knowable, a lot of you pops-up. But I'm only interested in one of you. One version.

I've gotten two things out of being a scopophiliac. I'll make this personal and tell you what I thought of you. Or any man I've wanted for a long time. First I wanted you because I spent years looking at your face. Really looking at it, or what's now popularly called, "zooming in." I was little and took to obsession easily. The thing that made me stop wanting you was the same thing that made me start. I looked until I saw your face emitting. Until what I didn't like about you anymore showed up on your face, attaching all around it like scaffolding. I didn't know that that's what it was, but I loved how Semitic, Sephardic, you looked. How ancient and modern at the same time. A teenager, but thousands of years old. Like you'd been in a lot of places at once.

I thought everything I'd ever wanted was in your face. I spied on you turning your head. I gave up when you started to look so obviously mean. You weren't anything like the boys they made out of corn in the '80s: *Silverspoons*, Luke Skywalker, or some other golden consensus. I wish I knew if that affected you, the way it affects girls. You were definitely something old in my young body.

I went looking for what you'd decided to publish instead. My pride was with me in all the "rooms" you'd made. You're so proud of yourself. That's a nice way of putting it. I read everything in your cyber-drawer like it was a top-secret file. I didn't even have to carefully put it all back afterwards. I listened to the music you'd made, read all your feelings about your latest achievements (your blog), looked at you having fun with all your friends. I felt like such an intruder. A loser. Why are you displaying all this shit that's open for business 24 hrs a day? The best department store in the world, all the different levels of you. What's the purpose? The point? After you'd said No to me, who was I to go searching anyway, but I did it because that's what it's there for, for everyone, the whole world, me, to see, even when everyone tells us we're not allowed to. I wasn't allowed to be inside, but I am anyway because there is more than one way to get there. There is more than just one inside.

I want to make sure I know what I'm *not* missing. Sometimes, in the social sphere of my past, I have to get up close, zoom in, to be confident. It's your face that gets rid of any doubt that maybe I should be with you. Your face out in the world says it all.

I worried that you, being a microchip wizard, would know exactly who and when and how many times I'd checked up on you. You'd love that, I worried. Especially after our last correspondence, also on the computer. I panicked that the hour of my search would look the worst. Say the most. That not only was I persistent and desperate, and an insomniac, but I spent the hours I couldn't sleep perusing around your site. I was looking into you at 4 in the morning. 4 in the morning, that comes as across as so crazy. On paper, it's crazy. You wouldn't know the first thing about why I'd do something like that. There'd be nothing to explain it. My porno is my fear of being upstaged by everyone. My porno is how I scan the past and look into it all the time. My face started to burn, I felt nauseous. It was so late. That's when I quickly shut-it all down, the site, the computer, you, before you got the chance to realize where I was calling from and trace all of it back to me, like Thelma's husband Darryl in *Thelma & Louise*.

There are so many you's. A new you is made everyday. But you all seem the same. You're all the same when it comes to searching. The search engine.

What everyone thinks is on the internet too. About you, a relative nobody, about stars and creeps, about a constant glare of bodies. Pink and in my face if I want them. I get up so close not even your friends are there. I'm a dermatologist in your life pores, I'm that obscene. It's obscene. I feel like a pair of fingers squeezing at the facts, the details in your pimples. You had so many when I knew you, but I never let it get in the way of how good your skin really was. Really could be once you stopped being so adolescently horny. If I put my mouth to the screen, would I be sucking someone, anyone I choose, fellating them, pleasing myself? Would anything drip out of that bone-dry monitor? You can respond all the time if you want to and it just stays there on record. Your whims, your spontaneity, your secrets, your stupidity, your total lack of real navigation and bias. Part of me felt happy when I read what everyone thought of what you wrote in that magazine. A whole nest of reaction, mostly bad, when all of what you'd said, really wasn't. But it grew everyday anyway, warming people up in the circle of feathers. Everything is so light. I shouldn't stare so much and so hard at the screen all day. It weakens my wrist. It weakens a lot of wrists, so how do so many guys beat off all night? I could see I wasn't the only one who doesn't like you. But if it weren't for the future, how would I have ever known that?

I wanted some new bras. But I didn't want to be in some big, fucking store trying things on with a million other women who feel like shit about themselves, but are all over the place, naked, anyway. All stuff that goes right to my head. All those mirrors and all those lights that are supposed to make you want to buy things but don't. The light's always against you. I'll avoid that. I'll shop from far away like everyone else, a desire tourist, a scanner above everything else, and then whatever I want will just show up without anyone knowing about it. I don't even have to tell anyone. The bra site has all these female busts and torsos, these parts clothed in the bra you like. You get to see what you're looking for on someone else first, what else is new? Can't I ever just want something without seeing the Star first? The prototype. So that's what makes you want the bra, someone else's tits, not your own. Not the design of the bra itself. Just someone else, anyone else, period.

Everything is sex. Sometimes there's a face too, sometimes there isn't. Sometimes it's just the breasts. A lot of them. You can display all of them on one single page if you want, instead of going through ten at a time. That's tedious. I just want to scroll through as fast as possible and get out of there. I feel like I'm snooping again. All the displayed breasts are one size, but the bras come in lots of variations. Well, not that many. Sometimes they're all white. The skin, that is. That's usually the case. The bigger the store, the more racial variation they try to come up with. I order the bras, which arrive a week later, and they're huge, they don't fit. They don't fit at all. I bring them back. I don't send them. I'm relieved and pissed off. I didn't want them anyway. I want to get this bra thing over with, but I'm also happy that I have so little on my chest that the world can use against me.

It's a great time to be unreal. How much of me really exists? How much of me gets stuck, like a glitch, in the system? I think I can do everything without having to actually show up. I'm pretty sure that's true. How would you find out if I were there? Before the future, I thought I lost everybody. Wouldn't it be great if no one knew me? The whole world at my fingertips. Before, I had no practice for my fears. Now I have some place to put all of them. This makes it really easy.

13

The Dread of Difference

The other morning I was standing outside in the bitter cold, sharing a coffee and a cigarette with a man named Peter who I met a few weeks ago. Peter's a lot older than me, by at least thirty years, and we talk about all kinds of things people my age will rarely let me talk about. We also talk about things that everybody talks about. It took a while for me to get a word in edge-wise. But once I did, Peter couldn't get enough of what I had to say and how I said it. The very same day we met, Peter started sending me email love letters that I never took the bait on. I knew immediately I shouldn't have proved myself. Men always confuse female brains with female seduction, when really I'm just trying to be smart. Peter likes to dignify worry as much as I do, but his repugnance is mostly vanity. He doesn't really mean anything he says. He doesn't really stay away from the things he says he hates. He fucks the enemy all the time.

The things we complain about don't get under Peter's skin or through it because his skin is thick and full of shit. Like leather, it stretches to make more room for his misery. Unlike Peter, I walk around with my sadness pushing through like too much food in a grocery bag. I don't just report my woes, I am my woes. Peter, like most people, can just as easily let something go, making outrage a temporary persona, whereas I can't. Time and time again, I'm gullible about this crucial difference with everyone.

Peter and I met the usual way. He barged into me while I was reading *The Sorrows Of Young Werther* at a café. Reading on Sundays is really important to me. It's a day for all kinds of mourning and reflection. Though reading on Sundays is almost a religious ritual for me, my reading is diluted by the fact that I do it at noisy cafés. Café's are ambiguous places as they border on being both social and antisocial, full of people who are social and antisocial. People often disregard that I'm reading because I'm seen doing it in a public place with a coffee in my hand, which for most people means I'm *really* waiting for someone to come and talk to me. Plus, I'm a girl. That always leaves the door wide open no matter how many things you use to close it. I'm talked to incessantly. When I lived in Europe for two years, I never got any work or reading done at all because I insisted on doing it in cafés and people insisted on overlooking what I was doing.

People have no respect for books, or they want to invade the space a book excludes. It was Goethe who said, "The decline of literature reflects the decline of a nation." I use books as shields for all kinds of things. I use books as internal and external armor. I use them as can openers to open things that otherwise won't open. In me and outside of me. Movies can sometimes do the same thing. I use movies like an coat hanger to break into the car door to my life. And when things unravel in a theater, I usually like to be alone. I rarely want an audience for what I'm feeling and thinking. I don't want to dilute something that could potentially be important with the presence of someone who doesn't understand its importance. I rarely want to get my ideas across knowing that the across is most likely a shitty destination.

At the café, Peter noticed my hat because I like to wear my hats indoors. I prefer to keep my head to myself. Reserving my energy like an athlete in solitary training. This particular hat is white, furry, and has two long tails on both sides. I like to imagine that I'm a

Siberian princess whenever I wear it. White against the black. It's all about contrast with me. Peter commented about the hat from across the room. Trying to be charming and seductive. When I pretended that I couldn't hear him by putting my hand behind my ear like a wing or a gill, Peter got encouraged by my "hard of hearing" and jumped at the opportunity to get closer and explain. He pulled a chair out for himself and sat down with me. I held onto my *Sorrows* book. I should've kept my hat over my eyes, or my eyes over my book. I should have been cold, like the air outside. Within five minutes of admiring my hat, Peter tried to get it off of me. To see what was underneath.

Outside, freezing, we kept on talking and smoking our cigarettes. The conversation predictably—Peter's turn—landed on the subject of fashion models, and I don't know if Peter knows any, but he definitely had "information." Like a spy or a conspiracy theorist, Peter kept insisting that "these days" women are over six feet tall and walk around like skyscrapers intimidating the hell out of everyone else. I assumed he meant that in a good way. Everyone always means it in a good way. And even when they mean it in a bad way, it still doesn't make *you* feel good because in that moment it's understood that in some cases it's good to be bad if it means you're tall and thin and coveted by everyone else. "Even being a freak has been turned into a convention," I tell Peter. But he doesn't hear me. It's fake damnation. If you're in America, you appreciate big things and treat popular culture as another one of those big things, so I get the drift without asking. Peter said "absolutely" about everything I said. Regardless of what I said, he got closer by the minute.

After he was finished divulging a bunch of urban myths, Peter looked at me, laughed, and concluded (we're roughly the same height, though I'm a bit taller), "We're average compared to *those* women." I knew Peter really only meant that I was average compared to *those* women because as a man he wouldn't feminize or deliberately aestheticize himself that way. At least he's not the kind of man who would do that. First and foremost, being female makes me aesthetic. First and foremost, being a man exempts Peter from broad comparisons. Peter was English and extremely thin, wore tight jeans and pointy mod boots, but he wasn't an outright dandy. There was no cane, no sexual subversion, though there were a lot of exaggerated facial expressions, ticks, and posturing. I wondered if Oscar Wilde was that cruel. He looks so romantic in that famous picture of him reclining on a couch, surrounded by and covered in the most luxurious fabrics. I always think Wilde looks like some kind of Victorian wooly mammoth.

Peter replaced most of his more suspect flamboyance with a compulsively sexist one. Who knows what he wanted. He was above all a narcissist. It's hard to know someone who spends all their time talking about themselves.

Just the other night Peter told me that he got thrown out of a club by two bodyguards for being wrongly accused of ogling a group of young girls. The girls complained about Peter—nearly an old man—making them uncomfortable on the empty dance floor. Peter wasn't dancing, which probably made things worse, and the sparse darkness wasn't enough to make the young women feel safe. From behind a column, Peter's owl-eyes poked through, fixated, not blinking, a drink in his hand. He was in a bad leather jacket. Not bad leather, bad style. He had venom written all over his face like a shiny birthday banner. He turned the story into an example of male injustice and his face looked disgusted the entire time he told it. He skipped right over the shady aspects of pedophilia and sexism. He said he dismissed the allegations to the bodyguard by declaring, "I wouldn't be caught dead looking at a pair of flat tits tramping around in fake Chanel." He was over the moon about his comeback. I could tell all he cared about was the comeback.

Peter said he wasn't angry about the accusation itself, but about the attack on his taste. He said he only harasses the best. Peter is apocalyptic and hedonistic at the same time, which I guess isn't that much of a contradiction, since it takes a great deal of excess to be cataclysmic. Peter's anger made his accent go from Upper Class down to Cockney. He was on his third coffee and marriage. It's probably what keeps him thin and regular. His daughter, Sammy, short for Samantha, is twenty, studies biology at Oxford, and has a black boyfriend whom she sees when she's in New York City on her winter breaks. Peter talked a lot about Sammy's "black boyfriend." For extra pizzazz, his insults and slighted self-image dunked into the gutter. He pulled words out of his bitter drainpipes like sewage. His black leather jacket, that he always wore, shined like tar or his black coffees. Peter's roots were in the theater, so I didn't know if he meant anything by his flip out apart from a love of drama and resentment towards women. Peter had a radio show, so he was used to saying whatever he wanted without fear of immediate comeback. Later that year, Peter started filming a period movie, *The Libertine*, about royal debauchery with Johnny Depp, who could relate due to his own Hollywood debauchery. Everything is acting, even if you love some parts more than others. A director, Peter could have said this, but he didn't. His skin looked mean. He tried to sweeten it with a smile. The light parted and made me want to leave. I'd wasted three hours on this man. But I got them back when I wrote this story. I avoided his kiss goodbye. I wanted to tell him that Chanel can be tacky too.

14

Houses (Or the Uncanny Glows in the Dark)

A house, Ms. Seward, cannot be made habitable in a day. And, after all, how few days go to make up a century.

— *Dracula, 1979*

IN THE END it didn't make any difference how many houses there were. Petra was surrounded by one on each side, and a surge of others down both directions of the road. On the porch, while sitting on it, she watched a desert colored cat that belonged to one of the houses wait to cross the street. Do cats know that cars can kill them? It could have been any handful of the neighbors, and the cat was in fact a house resident as well as a non-house resident. Cats are in between, and so are houses. Between other houses, streets, people. Houses rotate lives. Collapse and inherit. It's not just people who fit into houses, houses fit into people. Do cats know where they're going? That they're moving?

At night, when Petra worried about being in the house, something she never worried about during the day, Petra forgot about all the other houses and worried only about her own, which she believed could be isolated at any time. When people decide to kill you, they choose one house over all the rest and forget about all other houses.

Petra did the same thing when she imagined herself being killed in the house. She was the only one being killed and it was only her house that housed the kill. As the murdered choice, her house was the one that stood out by virtue of being the selected slain, and made all other houses disappear. It's the topic of all horror films, in some way or another, *The Last House on the Left*, *The House on Haunted Hill*, *The Ammity Ville Horror*, *The Texas Chainsaw Massacre*, *The House That Screamed*, *The House That Dripped Blood*, *The House of Dark Shadows*, *House of Evil*, *House of the Damned*, *House of Exorcism*, *House of Freaks*, *House of Fear*. People run from houses, or to them, or hop from house to house, like Jamie Lee Curtis when she bangs on all the doors in *Halloween*. Houses house things. Houses are for housing.

Houses have always been the site of the most familiar horror. The monster, whose windows become lights of dreadful invitation. Should Petra turn them on or off? If someone thinks she's home, will they leave her, and her home alone, or will they decide to enter it? Or if someone sees black, like any abyss, will they steer clear of it? Petra didn't know what attracted people more, darkness or light. Emptied or occupied. The proximity of houses should have made Petra feel better, but it didn't. The topography of houses should ward off people who choose to stray into them, but it doesn't. Fear and death work together. If Petra was afraid, would someone be more likely to kill her? Petra thought whoever was going to kill her, didn't give a damn about what else was around. Focused on her, in her house, they'd forget. The way that being focused on her fear, and her house, made Petra forget about the houses in her vicinity.

The age of the houses, and the trees that slung over them, should also play a part. Who needs an old house that's broken and distracted by trees? Or maybe someone needs it more because it's easy to break into and the trees misdirect the intrusion like a magic act. There's nothing here to want enough to single out, thought Petra. Why not choose the fucked up house on the right, or the fucked house on the left? The fucked up person on the right, or the fucked up person on the left. Why choose the careful, anxious person in the middle? At night Petra forgot about the neighbors too, whereas during the day, Petra felt all they did was lurk around. Watch her walk to her mail, then back. Was it because Petra could see them during the day, but couldn't see them at night? The view darkened, and the lens narrowed.

The houses might as well be any phantasmagoria. It all looked the same. But during the day it was the details that made her confident. Petra felt watched by all the old ladies and completely unwatched at night when all the old ladies were sleeping. They went to sleep before she did and left her all alone in the house. She was the last one to turn off the lights. Sometimes she left them all on. Petra assumed that if the neighbors were facing her, and she could see them, then they were paying attention. But she never felt noticed by people her age or younger. People her age or younger, didn't pay attention. Anyone who decided to kill Petra, was going to have to be an observer, like a bird watcher. And initially, she'd seem inaccessible and colorful too.

People go into attics to hide things and people go into cellars when they want to hide themselves. Secrets and boxes, and people; stored things and things kept away, from top to bottom. Like discussions with their mothers, as in the ones Norman Bates has in *Psycho*. Or where Bertha ends up while Rochester is downstairs with Jane. All kinds of things happen, and rarely in the center. From the perspective of Petra's house, she was off the hook. She had a cellar, but no attic.

Home is where the heart is, or isn't, and the heart can become bigger or smaller according to the home. Sometimes the heart bursts there or gets stuck or unravels and rolls out the door like the ball of dough that fools everyone in the Russian fairytale *Kolobok*. The air of food fills houses; or parties fill them, or sex, or no sex, or fights, or talking, or nothing, but nothing is ever nothing. Houses are bought and sold. Houses are stayed in and then left, or the other way around. You can love them or leave them. Or feel uncomfortable, or too hot, or not warm enough. You barely leave them or barely put in an appearance, or use the stove. Houses can accommodate deaths, accidental or non-accidental. Petra was once in love with a man who, like a bag, left his life behind in a house. Or in a room in a house. The house had a garden, which he stood in the last time he talked to Petra on the phone. Petra had once shared a room with that man. A life. Houses can be huge and irresponsible, or one room you can keep an eye on. Petra knew everyone's house by heart and when the lights were turned off she had no heart.

Allegorically speaking, and houses always speak allegorically, the house is the first thing you know. The first place you're in. Everything takes place in the house at some point. For most of us, houses take up the most amount of space and time. "Since when are you afraid to be in a house?" asked Petra's friend Joyce. "I don't know, " said Petra, "I've never been in one before. Not really. I've been in rooms. But apartments and rooms are a house's amputees. I've been in the limbs, in the fragments, of a house, but that doesn't count. Maybe I started being afraid when I remembered how much I lost. Couldn't I just as easily lose my life and wouldn't a house be the perfect place to lose it in?"

"Norman, is that you?" "Who's there?" "At the door?" "Just a minute." "I'll be right there." Are all things Petra had said in the house, or near the door before opening it. She had also heard many things about houses on television and in the movies. Houses are stars in films. The house made everything familiar and unfamiliar, so Petra double-checked the lock just to be sure. Petra couldn't tell if houses made people safer or made people feel that they had to be more cautious. She had hoped for various knocks at the door, especially when she was younger. But he disappeared like a lake. The ocean remained, and had such a modern way about it. No one even came near it unless there was a plane nearby. Petra thought, at the very least, houses are visited, like museums. It's a ritual. No one remembers very much about them, but everyone knows vaguely where the *Mona Lisa* lives. Because houses are so old fashioned, often, people didn't even call first. Petra got stranded when she moved in. Unlike the movie *Sleeping with the Enemy*, no one arrived with a pie or a basket of apples. She offered the handy man a bag of zucchini from her garden, but he barely looked at her as she handed them to him. He worked on her house, so Petra thought she should give him something that was part of the house—the garden.

Freud thought people were houses. The ego, superego, id, are all rooms joined through the house. Guests and owners take their turns using the rooms, or blend them; open the space by knocking out the wall, push the beds together, take turns fucking in different ones. Siblings get stuck with their rooms, in their rooms, for years, until they leave and pick news ones in new houses. Petra never lived in rooms. She grew up in a modern version of a "house," in an anti-house, an open space called "loft." She could see her parents down at the end of the line. Their bed was on a platform. If she had seen something, the primal scene would have been credited as an official theater. Artists lived in lofts, now yuppies do. But for a while, it was only artists who were willing to leave their houses behind.

15

Travel Notes (Really Trying to Be Happy)

New York City, July, 1999

THE CONSTRUCTION IS FUTILE. Same black day and damp in the same black place, and every now and then I get a whiff from some salt substance I don't have enough of. Some recycled tide, big enough and brought in from Provincetown, comes up to me like a memory. This summer marks the beginning of my sadness and despair and my way out of it. Six hours away and this summer I never get there. I say goodbye, toss the umbilical cord, and send it all away like a child to summer camp. Sunset color and nervous day breaks down like pixels. Neatly falling apart in a designated space of time. Summer. The end of a movie. Everyday there's an evening that strains like an arm-wrestle across the table. I can't go back. And this would *really* mean going back. All the way.

This is how the plot goes: I'm seventeen and live alone. The summer is my reimbursement for winter. I catch up, make up for all the lost time alone, like sleep. I can stay out as late as I want here. I have no dark circles under my eyes. No itinerary, except for the one I'm unaware of. I'm confident, like I never am when I get older. I think: *I can go home at whatever time of night I want.* I love sleeping alone, sleeping late, sleeping in my "boy's" underwear and rarely stay over at my boyfriends' place. I move around like a cat. Never in one spot. He lives in a little plywood, fairy-tale shack on Young's Court that's not there anymore. Or, it is, but it's attached to a big condo now. The shack is surrounded by two hundred year old Elm trees. We make out for the first time underneath them.

No matter how late it is, I usually get up, get dressed, go home. No one's offended. Since I no longer *have* to stay at other people's houses in order to stay out, I like going to sleep in my own bed. It feels more rebellious than sleeping over somewhere. Than sleeping at a guy's place. I like to wrap up a day on my own terms. If I wanted it to be different it could be. At 4 in the morning, Commercial St. is deserted and foggy. Only the gay men who've been dancing at the A-Hole all night, or fucking under the Dick Docks, are out wandering around in their clammy leather suits and butt-less chaps. Used leather is in the air, but so is the sea-humidity, and it makes my hair curl back. And back then I let it.

The tide on the left is always either high or low. I ride up a huge hill on Bradford Street, past Saint Peter the Apostle's Catholic Church on Prince Street, to get to my own bed on the way down. I love not having to peddle for one whole minute. I love all the space I have. *There's space everywhere*, I think. I rarely feel that I have any *space* around me when I get older.

I have a lover. His name is Josh. I spotted him like a gorgeous dress in some store window when I was fourteen, too young, and he too old and occupied. He was riding a plywood skateboard past Town Hall like it was still the 1970s and he was in Santa Monica. His hair was long and curly like mine. He looked like the perfect flower child. His eyes were blue and mine were brown. Are brown. He looked sweet. With me he was his sweetest. It was the second time in my life I'd been undone by a boy's beauty. I befriend the girl he's with and almost forget all about him in the process, instead of the other way around. Josh and Jenny take me, and my best friend Gina, under their wing. They take us to parties. They introduce us to people. Gina and I sit on the benches by Town Hall (also called the Meat Rack) and watch Jenny eat cream cheese sandwiches with alfalfa sprouts. She talks about her diet as "a way of life." She's a vegetarian, she says. Not wearing a bra is also her way of life. I can see the profile of her small breasts through her overalls, which she wears over her bare chest. The two straps hang loosely. One of them is off her shoulder. She's so laid back. My breasts are too big at the time, so being laid back would never work.

Gina wonders where the drugs fit in. She knows they're on them. I don't. How would I? My friendship with Josh and Jenny is how I meet everyone in town and go from being just a daughter on vacation with her cool parents to a cool girl on her own for the summer. Everyone is older and stoned. I try to figure

out if Josh notices me through the haze. His eyes are cloudy and very dark blue. He says a couple of things over a two-week period that I read as a Maybe, possibly, if things were different. If I was older, and he was single. Josh stops riding his skateboard and rides a bike instead. He never rides a skateboard again.

Years later, after they've broken up, Jenny becomes semi-famous and stays that way and Josh keeps in touch with her because he likes how her "glamorous" life-in-the-movies affects him. He thinks, *No matter what, I have great taste, or had it. No matter what, I know people in the Biz.* Josh is an anti-star fucker star fucker. It's what tears us apart. All our arguments a few years later are about movies, their politics, and who's in them, and me "being so critical in general." The second summer we were together, we fought all the time at places like the local video store. Whenever I didn't like something or agree with him about what he liked, particularly some movie, Josh called me jealous. His favorite insult, and perfect for a woman, as it's most likely a female disease. Especially when it came to me not liking some actress. Especially Jenny. But when things were really good, we smoked cigarettes and talked about everything and stayed out all night. We talked a lot about Josh's two-year sobriety, his teenage drug addiction, and his family's drug lineage. He said, "*Being fucked up runs in the family.*" Maybe he meant the world too.

The summer I first met Josh, he told me that I had beautiful hair and that I looked like the women/girls in Modigliani's paintings. Gina said, *because you're so long and your hair is so dark. Because you're un-usual.* I'm not *usual*, I think back to myself, that's true, but that's not quite how people mean the word when they use it. I have a long-standing interest in beautiful and *un*-usual clothes, which comes from my parents. My parents are *un*-usual. In town people comment about how I dress all the time and have no problem letting me know that they appreciate what I'm trying to say about myself with my un-usual sense of style. But people rarely give praise away when they get older the way they do when they're young. When I get older I don't hear a fucking peep from anyone. Sometimes I go years without hearing a fucking peep about any aspect of my life. As time goes by, everyone starts to guard their words and compete with them. Mouths and hearts shut down with age like old factories. But if you want me to be honest, maybe it was someone else, not Josh, who made the Modigliani comment. Maybe a woman. A painter named Deb from the Fine Arts Work Center or The Art Association, who I'd sometimes hang around with and talk to in front of the Meat Rack or at Café Express. She was always appraising me as a painter. As "a visual person." But isn't everyone a visual person? Or forced to be one?

Maybe I wasn't fourteen. Maybe I was 17, and Josh and I were together for a summer doing all the things I'd hoped we'd do and that's why I'm confusing who said what about me as a form of pictorial representation. *The girl in a painting.*

It's 3 years later. I'm 17. I have a brilliant best-friend named Gina back in NY and Josh is my boyfriend now. I sit outside Spiritus Pizza, with a whole new set of town friends, on an arc of low brick that assembles everyone in a bow—any moment we'll snap and shoot ourselves at something. I eat pizza there and smoke cigarettes and ride a handed-down red bike everywhere that I constantly fall off of and laugh and kiss and am fairly relaxed if the conditions are right. I can fight and stick up for myself without any hesitation. It's never as easy when I get older.

I read Dostoevsky and Sartre and write letters, stories, and journal entries. I brood and swim and wait for my older boyfriend Josh to finish working. He's a breakfast & lunch cook. We don't mind rain or getting wet. We ride our bikes in storms. Once, in front of Josh's grandfathers' huge house on the East End, after a swim, I flash my breasts at the red tourist trolley that passes back and forth everyday, up and down Commercial Street. The tour guide announces things on her loudspeaker all day long in a thick Boston accent. The passengers are all old people who stare at and photograph all the things the guide points to and describes, including me. All the "townies" hate this thing because it clogs traffic and takes up the entire girth of the street. So Josh and I insult it as much as possible with nudity and water, with water guns, hoses. and profanity. Sometimes we just yell at it. It's a showstopper.

I have a little black Agnés B. bag that I wear on my back that says *Lolita* on it in white script. I carry my books and journal in it. Everyone is up in arms about the statement I'm making by wearing the bag. But I'm wearing it as a literary reference—because I love the book—not because I'm trying to embody the coquettish male myth of female virginity and pre-pubescence. Everyone knows, if someone tries to fuck with me, I'll kill them. That makes the Lolita bag even more confusing and infuriating. Guys insist that I'm cock-teasing them with the bag. But I'm trying to show that I *read*, that I'm not just *being read*. The cloth bag is cinched together tightly at the top like a secret, so every time I want to read something or write some-thing, I have to uncinch the neck of the sack. And I'm basically the same way. The bag looks like a little medieval pouch with hid-den arcane stones in it. When I wear it I look like a cross between a hipster, wearing all black (black engineer boots even in summer, even on the beach), and one of those lone traveler cartoon char-acters. Bugs Bunny with all his belongings scrunched up in a sin-gle polka-dotted bag on a stick.

Josh says he loves hearing my big black boots stomp down the hall to his little room on Young's Court everyday. I think back then I had a straddle in my walk. It gets him excited before he even opens the door. Most of the time I just walk right in. There are no formalities. No hang-ups. He thinks I'm so sexy and butch in my boots. So strong. He says *I* fuck *him* in the relationship, not the other way around. He says its never been that way before. I keep him up all night, starting things over and over again between us, or when he thinks it's finally all over. He laughs because he's so exhausted, but complies anyway. He's a Scorpio and I'm an Aries, but sexually, I'm the "Scorpio." He is eating granola out of a bag on the couch one morning while I talk to him from his bed. He's wearing a second-hand, white terry-cloth robe that he got at *Ruthie's*, the sec-ond-hand store in town. He's laughing because he is so deliri-ously tired. The sun is always coming up while we're still awake. Only I get to go to sleep;

he has to go to work at 7am. He teaches me about health food. He only buys organic shampoo. The brand he uses has a deep, earthy smell I'll never forget. He almost never sleeps and always goes to work a satisfied, beautiful wreck. He always looks beautiful. He calls me a Rotweiller puppy because I'm brown all over. Kissing me goodbye on the way out. He doesn't wear socks with his "cooking" sneakers. I find the idea of bits of food on his bare feet disgusting. Everything stinks in a good way. He loves all my stories and journal entries, which I often read out loud to him. I write long, poetic diary entries about the movies I watch. For a short time we are best friends.

I go to the movies then talk about it with anyone who wants to talk about it. It's always a disappointment to talk about what people think when I get older. I sit for hours, until 2 am, at Café Express, which is the only movie theater in town (and a next-door neighbor) and write in my journal, alone. Hoping to be found.

I walk through the 1 am Spiritus rush (crowd) (John Waters and Cookie Mueller wrote about this back in the 70s, when I'm sure the crowd was even better), to my house on Pleasant Street every night and the drag queens talk about how pretty I am. Sometimes, they even summon me. Pull me aside to tell me. *Come over here.* It feels kind of sexual. Like they're going to kiss me or take me to bed. They're standing by the water. It's always nearby. Many of them are my friends. Sometimes we become friends via the things they tell me. Or the things I tell them. Most of the time I love being with them. And even later, when I realize that gay men can be sexist and fucked up too, I still appreciate the friendships I had with them. And most of the time, I still think they treat women better than straight men do. But ambivalence can do that.

New York City, August, 1998.

SITTING IN AN ICY VAULT. Stewing even without the flame.

Moisture can be livid too. Feeling heavy about my breasts, which are themselves laden. Not mine per say. I'm not just attached to my own private tits, but to the public projections of tits, which are mine too. Which vary in sizes. Milk, blood, water, tissue, cyclic, endless supply and retain. Waiting for the horror movie *The Beyond* to start at the Angelika movie theater. I am burning in the frozen time of air conditioning. I've been struggling with the demons of having breasts lately. The hell of bodies. I think it has to do with shame, but the shame is complicated. Not always reconcilable regardless of theoretical intervention or respite. I can't always *just* love what I'm supposed to love—my body—no matter how enlightened I am. There's a whole world out there I need to bring along. It's my personal weight in the form of social luggage. The shame comes from the fact that I dread having anything attached to me, exposed, because it all gets ripped apart. Anything that hangs from me, off of me. Anything that protrudes. I want to decide who gets to see, who gets to touch, who gets to want my body. It's a daily task and my breasts play a large role in my overexposure. Breasts being just one example. The size of breasts equals the size of Reaction. This is a nuisance for the single reason that I don't want to be responsible for carrying anything obviously degraded while looking for uncertain and imperceptible preservation. I'm in an empty parking lot waiting to be encountered. I'm a building that resists cataclysm for better structural pursuit. More can live here, more will. I am walking around with my anatomy riding across my back as if it were the Brooklyn Bridge. What does it mean to assist in access? Travel fare? If it weren't for me, it would be harder for you to get things. I can offer a good example: I'm walking to the movie theater tonight. I'm wearing a long blue Commé de Garçon skirt and a white shabby Chinese tank top. I'm waiting for the light to change so that I can cross the street. I don't always do this. Sometimes I go ahead without the right signals. It's hot and everything has gold smudge and blink crawling around it like a spider. Greene Street is empty apart from four boys who, out of nowhere, come racing down the street on their bikes. It's like a bad '80s movie with bicycle gangs. *The Karate Kid*, or something in that fabulist vicinity. Of course, nothing *I* want comes of nowhere.

I stand frozen because I am not in the fucking mood to anticipate the bicycle gang's direction or the game I can feel coming. I wait for them to pass. To go away. I'm nervous, charred, but I carry grudges well and look well chilled. I know they want to intimidate me with their speed and outnumbering, basic machinery. Also their dicks. I avoid trying to choose an exit. Streets don't work that way. They are always negotiated. Blocked and open. Let them disappear.

One of the boys, 15 or 16, rides up really close and rocky like a kiss or a sailboat in a storm, and cups my left breast and grabs it, twists it like a key, pushes it in hard like a car cigarette lighter, or tries to rip it off, like the superfluous part of a tree he wanted to hear snap, but that bends, bows instead 'cause it's a tit and tits are polite. Too much fluid to crack and no one ever takes their broken branches with them. Wind is more or less like men appearing unannounced. The shame is overexposure and no worth and insisting on worth. The boy continued to ride on with me in his hand like caught insects that boys learn to like so much. I punched his jaw. He announced his victory to the company. Tissue, blood, water, milk, all in his pinch like salt and the way it usually doesn't feel like it wants to be let go. What did he get unless I make something of it? What did he ride away with unless I give it away like eggs in a basket? He wasn't looking for a trade anyway. My tit is like a stamp of admission into some club. Rubber Ducky that lets out water when you squeeze it. Only he didn't get any kind of pleasure squeal from me. You got into the club, now go through and dance. I yelled back, "Fuck You!" But sounded far away. My tits in the way. In the air. In the world.

Croatia, The Island of Ráb, 1999:

AM ON AN ISLAND, in its only park. It looks fake, but isn't. The good news is that other writers have been here. Nabakov spent his childhood summers on Ráb. So I try to figure out why. Ever-woods grow out of the salt. Buy some bleached postcards of donkeys that are thirty years old. Humorously send them to friends in Prague and Berlin and say nice, compensatory things about how great it is to spend time alone. Be damned if I seem overcome. Sit alone while writing. In the evenings, creep along wall that separates New Town from Old Town. Do it for nearly three days. An experiment in how much loneliness is actually bearable. Feel unincorporated. Snailing, not walking, low, through small twist of town, along wall, a rodent, wailing. Not out loud, built in. Find one empty street. Old white stone. Have hat on, it drips down over face. Eyes. Have pimples from Dead Sea Clay facemask that made everything pop out. Also, no longer eat ice cream, haven't in years because of problem with ovaries and what they "can't handle," according to Chinese doctor, who is the only one who even has a theory.

While crawling around the wall first night, stumbled into stone courtyard used for out-door screenings of American movies. Blockbusters. Go see John Carpenters' *Vampires* starring James Woods, who dyed hair back to brown again (killing vampires requires a similar kind of colorful virility), something a female actor could never get away with doing—looking old, looking young, then looking old again. While watching, hide in the dark, in hat. Courtyard filled with teenagers and mosquitoes. Feel it's appropriate that am watching movie about vampires when acting like one. Is vampire narrative really about shame? *"Only come out at night. We only come out night,"* informs the Smashing Pumpkins song. Skin is crawling. The dark is not dark enough, need the hat too. Then feel paranoid that must look bizarre with straw beach hat on in the dark. No sun, *what do you need straw hat for?* Must be some other reason. Some fucked up reason.

9:30pm: The walls are half-broken in courtyard due to time. Lots of it. Couples smoke cigarettes while watching the film. Want to ask for one too, but am wary of drawing attention. Couples cheer when vampires get impaled. Watch vampires and feel even more alone. The whole "point" is to kill vampires. Movie says it's okay to fuck (female) vampires, just not love them. Started off in twilight. Found a theater on the first night while climbing up a narrow side street to avoid lights and crowd. Cinematic vampires have always been fine with street lanterns or candles. Caverns. Like Lestat in New Orleans in Anne Rice's vampire books. Followed street cats that sleep on the walls and under the blue lamps. On Donjá Street, saw light, a low blue flame, flickering and out of proportion to loud sound of American movie. Dwarfed old town. Dwarfed small walls. Dwarfs everything. See small glass booth built into the stonewall where movie tickets are sold. Booth had red wooden sign that flashed, "Kino." Next to the sign was tiny blue shutter, which was closed. Movie had already started, so decided to come back the next night and the night after that. Hear voices of audience inside the wall. Don't know yet that everything inside is medieval stone and the sea beyond. Dream movie theater, dream location, dream little Kino sign. Dream world. Only wish could see dream movie too. Bell towers and stars. Ocean on other side of the wall. Dark. Can hear the waves lapping on the walk back home. Too embarrassed to do anything else. To turn back. Thrill of stupid movie in a beautiful place. Can't wait to watch one. Otherwise, these kinds of movies seem so dire in a normal context. Eat almonds for protein, and dinner, get them from the big outdoor market during the day. Barely costs anything. Wasps hang out in trashcans. Makes me afraid to throw anything in. The market is the old heart of every place. There are no lights.

2000:

I CAME TO LONDON for Kathy Acker, who said she felt better here. Thinking words will give me everything I want. She was in my mind even before the flight, and so was Dickens, or the streets he wrote, which she then rewrote, which became many movies, and not something I needed to read. I tried to track them down, in spirit. All my travel comes too late or goes out like a light. So this will have to be imagined. Remembered.

On my birthday you bought me a handful of eucalyptus and held my eucalyptus. I was buying it for myself years before you came along and bought it for me. It's nice to have someone acknowledge that by giving you a break from relentlessly pursuing your own desires all the time. Now I have what I like because someone else knows what I like. We ran into a man I fucked, or almost did, or couldn't, or wouldn't, when I first got here and after years of purposeful nothing, and he wished me a happy birthday and said, "Congratulations on the wedding." He hardly made it through the sentence before I was harked back to a time that included knowing that sentences are unreliable strategies (policies) and castaways that I need to dream about and get stranded on like an island in order to understand.

It's stunning how things take. It was sweet and sick. Working-class nourishment and dialect at Portobello Market, everywhere, four days a week (*"What would you like love?"* Sometimes means fuck you). I could buy any vegetable and/or fruit (cooking apples) almost every day.

I felt your eyes bashfully slip behind the aromatic shrubbery as he said, "Congratulations" to us. Your cheeks blushed and the flowers were a fan for your composure. You are so Victorian. English, after all. You were eavesdropping on how I gave up waiting and he was the guy I gave up waiting for. Before you, I had a lapse, got fed up, and took it out on someone. Sometimes there's a nice way to do it. There's always something to conceal and England's good at that, and I like the subliminal mess more than the laden one. The water, which is my sludge, starts to pour out. I think it's your doing, and claim that love is the perfect desert. And will love do away with it the next time I spread out? We walk down the market like a promenade, rolled out and bright like the fruit or a carpet. Like the street weddings in Mexico. One time you walked behind me and held onto my pinstriped pant loop like a key chain. Flirting. I could never lose you. I lost you all the time and you told me to play with the windows if I wanted to get back in. I feel bone dry and still have wet eyes. We are on display, displaying what our display is, which is ourselves, and what we managed to get by being with each other. I feel like I'm in a nineteenth century French novel (*Au Bonheur des Dames*) on the look out for a cathedral of window display. This is when things in the consumer world really got lucky and started to bloat. I had no idea how much I would love you or how much I wanted to. I still don't know the difference. There still isn't a difference. Everything is in the intention. All reality is plan and contextualization. I made sure it all happened on my birthday to seal the odds with you. To stamp safety on finders keepers. When it comes to people there's nothing to do but trade and love your imports. Fiercely prefer them over the exports. I've got sadness stuffed in me like taxidermy.

I came to London to walk it off. Shake it off. Jump through, jump rope.

Kathy Acker said, "I write to get it out of me. I don't write it to remember it." When any body asks me what I write about, they don't know what they want me to say and it sounds like I don't know either. I don't sound like I know what I'm thinking about when it comes to writing it down, but I'm doing the same thing she is. I want to be a microscope over this shit and a needle too. I'm self-censoring to give other people an easier ride with me. I get quieter every year. I sound like less than I am.

South-East London, 2002

TWENTY MINUTES ONE WAY to the mall and car park where we do our shopping at Tescos, open, we find out 6 months later, 24 hrs. Easy to buy things on 8 quid. Easy to hate everything and run out of alternatives. Count change almost daily. Makes you crazy. I say, "It's still money." I prepare it for exchange, coffee, converting many coins into fewer coins. Silver for gold. Otherwise it's embarrassing. Benson & Hedges always on sale and gold too. Then, walk back home for 20 minutes with four bags of heavy groceries. On the way there, and on the way back, usually hear shouted insults about what am wearing from boys on bicycles in car park. A hangout. They're ready to kill. They're ready to kill for not liking something. They're ready to slur, ride up, lap it up, break something they don't know. *Where are you from? Love.* Originally? *Bitch.* My origins are canine, and anyway, origins are not original. Village mentality, don't feel like in city at all. Easy to be different. Feel like that's good news, but also understand the reality of facing intolerance. Good idea clashes with bad choice, like wearing a weird hat. Looks good on paper but bad walking on pavement. Wear the crazy hat and things explode, like walking into party with a costume on, only without permission to dress up. Every ritual needs consensus. Every party. Have none. Had fantasy of London Street culture and style from movies like *Darling* and *Performance*. Powis Square was just around the corner from where we used to live in West London. I used to stand outside the famous townhouse waiting for James Fox to walk out. Or fuck James Fox, I wanted to go back in time to when maybe I could have afforded to live in a house on Powis Square like Mike Jagger's Turner. Maybe everything boils down to movie-culture and no style. Or a fantasy of it. It's raining, it's cold, gray, really need to stop for other things on walk, like stamps and dry cleaning, coconut milk, but can't because haven't got hands left or energy. Use hands for energy and for getting things on walk. Will have to do the walk again... forgot spring onions. Only call them that now, no longer scallions. Also say *cheers* for goodbye and thank you. Had no idea was such a fucking mimic. Want badly to rearrange words or trade them. Shuffle identity by flipping the switch on words. Only have washing machine, no dryer, so will have to make a third walk to drop off laundry at launde[rette] for drying, and then fourth one for pick-up. Laundry's dry, but it's raining on walk back, so laundry is half-wet again. Am sick of draping wet laundry all over radiator, furniture, and bicycles in flat. Like a ghost house. Like no one's there. Amazing how quickly home can become a ghost house, always on the verge. Border. Does ghost mean layer upon layer, covered, sheathed in Victorian? Eventually, when move out, and flat is empty, prophecy of loss is finally fulfilled. Just a few more final touches. Laundry makes this clear. Other things too. Ghost is premonition. Say flat now. Like it better than Apart-ment. The word APART is there. In it. Prefer not to say that, especially when living with someone. When married. In it. Need to bring multiple bags. Also walked the other way, down Evelyn Road, then up Deptford High Street. At least look forward to getting to the café and market. Took grassy route, along train tracks where things grow—where once looked at studio for work— to go to Hayle's café for coffee. Almost time to sit in the garden outside. Makes walk legible. Café garden has tombstone recipe for lemon icing. Death is sweet. Three soy lattés, two were free. Eventually every single one will be. No one else gets that kind of treatment. No one else gets things for free. No one wants to ever have me charged. In life have people looking out for me. Should see that more clearly and be thankful. In life have no life span. Spend time thinking about what goes into making things last. What goes out of them. Gave you ultimatum in the cemetery. The fact that there is so much death around seems to make no difference to you. You don't act

desperate. You don't feel threatened. You don't care. Marriage is falling apart. A surprise of new tulips came out of the graves. Or out of spring. *Interview with a Vampire* was filmed in Deptford Church, which is now closed unless sufficient funds are raised for renovations. Just want to see inside to see if church interior matches the vampire "theater" in movie. Two years go by and never get a single glimpse inside. Try looking on multiple occasions. Movies are religious experiences. The whole thing is a horror movie, and as the main character, am used to the terror that I feel. Every time I walk through the cemetery, bad news. People get impression that am looking for a way out of misery or want to give that impression themselves. Visits to café are anticipated and looked forward to. I meet you there and bring an enthusiasm that is stunning considering we live together. Can't read or write when there. Talk for hours everyday. Easy to take things for granted, like when never spoke to anyone.

For years. Not in London, back home. Never write anymore. Then do, finish, apply for fellowship, and finally secure romantic future by doing so. But first have to lose the life already have with you. Had maps in the form of applications spread out on the floor next to you like a plan. Ghost. Old ghost. Current ghost. At moment, only write about what have found. The life now have. Maybe know things won't last. Maybe this is an experiment. To see if it can work. To see what happens if it doesn't. To see if can get back up again. Maybe know this, but only years later. We sit in the garden in two months. Mood is always better when he's in the garden. Talk about plants, names of plants, like names of dog breeds. Coffee cups collect. Friends work here, so always try to keep tables neat and bring empty cups to dishwasher, who is also friend. We both share discomfort in being served. Prefer to do things ourselves. Dishwasher gets facts all wrong when talks to people about me months later. Says the city killed us. The one we go to later. After London. Back home. We live in different ones now. Walking's better in May. Clothes get shorter. Pull them down over arms because am never satisfied with my limbs. Rummage through charity shops for great find. Garden and sun to look forward to. You get brown, are already brown. Redundant. I run out across street to buy chicken stock, veggie patty from Caribbean food shop, spring onions at the bodega while you wait. And return as though I've really been gone.

16

Reading is a Nightmare

1. On Wednesday I go to San Francisco to read my book. I can do that anywhere. It's not location-specific. But I'm alone, and when I'm alone, I travel in small ways in order to make things feel more exciting. Reading is what I do most of the time, so instead of doing something else entirely, I modify the environment in which I read. I don't stop reading. I like to spice it up, throw new situations in for flavor—noise, crowds, woods, libraries, trains, rooms, cars, couch, bed. It makes the reading feel bigger than it is, go further than it does. Bigger than the form of the book-as-object, or the book-as-subject. When I read I look like some silent-film star posing with my book. The book relies on me to express itself. Some people just don't look good holding a book, the way that some people look like fake smokers. I'm not a fan of realism, but Winona Ryder is a very phony smoker—though she really does smoke. In her movies she always smokes and she always performs smoking as badly as she performs everything else, like intelligence, despair, longing, passion. Fake readers are a turn-off. But real ones, the ones that look like they can't live without it, are sexy. I feel pretty justified in saying my version of sexy isn't as trite as some other, more embellished, version, since there's no aggressive promotional campaign behind trying to make people think that readers are sexy.

2. I don't go anywhere special in San Francisco. I never do. I don't sight-see, I don't go to bars to drink. I don't drink. The Golden Gate Bridge is much too high and just reminds me of all the people who jump off it. I learn places by doing what I do—I read, go to the movies, drink coffee, think, talk to myself, look at the ocean on a pair of train-tracks. There is nothing special about what I do. It's more how I do it (intensely) and why. Also what I don't do is just as significant, if not more. It's good to be isolated and almost no one is that different on a daily basis. Almost no one can stand being alone, not when you carry around what people think everywhere you go. I've learned this through my solitude. When you're alone, you're closer to the way things are, then when you're surrounded. Company is kind of like a soundproof room. It doesn't bother anyone. Morrissey said this in 1984—an important year to talk about the merits of alienation.

3. On the outside, the only things that show are the faces I've been told I make when I read. I laugh. Like the trapeze artist from Kafka's circus series, I contort myself into a book acrobat. I look heavily invested. It looks both nerdy and sexy. I'm changing the face of reading. Sometimes I feel myself make faces at what I read, about what I read, and if I'm alone doing it, I don't mind. I even like that I'm intellectually emotive. The way I wince and flinch at the things that go right to my head. The way I squirm and shudder. The way a book goes right through me like a ghost. My reactions to the books I read are a natural reflex, a side-effect. Like a tennis player's groans when they hit the ball over the net. I think, *I'm doing something when I read. I'm going somewhere. I'm moving.* Going over the line is always hard. But when I read in public, I feel self-conscious. Like instead of reading alone, I should be talking to someone, or making faces at a *real* person, not some character in a book. I like thinking that a book is a portal. I like thinking I've dropped off the face of the earth while reading all about it.

4. I like to read things over and over. Not an entire book, but parts of it. Some pages. And some sentences over and over. I underline passages with a black pen and try to imagine ways to include them in something else. My everyday life. Something I say to someone, something I think while someone is saying something to me, something I can inscribe into another book to give to someone else, something I can memorize and recite on special occasions. The way the poets used to. They performed their work, or other people's work, the way that people who could play an instrument would play a waltz or Chopin at a dinner party in a Chekhov story. Words were a skill. Something you show-off. People liked to watch you say something. Sometimes I walk while I read, or read while I walk. It makes me feel like I'm combining a daredevil sport with something geeky. That is, something physical with something physically, but not mentally, static. Or that what I'm doing gives me so much pleasure, I can't stop doing it. I don't want to. Not even to look where I'm going. Not even to see if I'm being looked at. I've only fallen once that way. Actual extreme sports are a problem because they're hard on the biorhythms. Though people never even think of them, biorhythms are more important than just the mind, or just the body, or both. They're what make a roller coaster ride or sailing on a ship stay in your body like a hangover for days even after you've gotten off whatever you were on. You feel like you're on things when you're not. Biorhythms are the body's photograph.

5. This is what men sometimes say to me when they see me read in public:

What's the matter with you? You're such a pretty girl, what are you doing reading all the time? Smile. You should smile. Why are you so serious? Are you depressed? You should be having fun, not reading. Don't read that book, read my dick instead. I can give you more to mull over than that book can. God, you look so serious. What's the matter with you!? You should look where you're going bitch. You should put that book away, or you might get hit by a car.

6. Contrary to popular belief, I think a lot of guys like me because I read so much. I mean honestly, how many times in your life have you seen a young, attractive (some people say even more than attractive) woman walking down the street while she's reading? Not many. Maybe not ever except for me. I've been to more than 30 countries, and I've only ever seen one other woman reading while walking down the street. It was breathtaking. I saw her in LA—a double-whammy. What the hell was she doing walking? I thought she was my twin, that I'd imagined her, or that I was looking at a reflection of myself, the way that maybe a twin imagines their twin. I wanted to stop her and ask her what she was reading. I felt like she'd touched my skin. I've seen women read street maps on the street, but never a whole book. And never something as morally big as Dostoevsky, or a writer with difficult sentence structure like Henry James. I can read big things like that and find my way around a city without looking. I can pay attention to what's around me while drowning it all out. I think guys find that kind of combo, or any combo, fascinating. They're so used to binaries. We all are. Tits but no brains, brains but no tits, strength but no brains, brains but no strength, strength but no beauty, beauty but no strength. Strength but no fun. I think a lot of guys can tell how strong I am by the way I can take charge of a book and a city at the same time. And that turns them on.

7. Reading can get you killed. After I'm done reading in San Francisco, I leave the café on Valencia and get back on the train—the Bart, then Amtrak—where I read for another two hours. I take it as

far as I can. Until I'm tired, and there's no more room, and the words go right out from under me. "Jim," the conductor, wants to know what I'm reading right after he asks me if he can see my ticket, but looks offended when I tell him, *Western Attitudes Towards Death: From The Middle Ages to The Present.* He either thinks I'm a witch or unhappy or both. Considering the time-span, the book is tiny, the size of my palm. I guess when it comes to death, not much has changed in the last nine hundred years. We're still dying. When I get home, exhausted, I read until I fall asleep. While I read, I start dreaming. Reading is a kind of dreaming, so by the time I fall asleep at night, I know what to expect and how to get there. The transition is smooth. I can't come up with things unless I dream, and when I read, I am constantly reminded of what I can't invent, imagine, or explain. It's scary to always be face to face with your own endless limitations. Limitations I, or someone else, could write an entire book about. Reading is a nightmare. Instead of giving me things, sometimes it just takes more away. I don't think reading is as easy as everyone thinks it is. You can't just love it or just hate it. You can't just do it and then forget about it, like in high school, when you'd read a book for English class, second period, *The Glass Menagerie*, and then when class was dismissed, so was the book. Goodbye. Once the book was done, you were done.

8. On Thursday, my friend Norma calls. The first thing Norma asks me is what I did the day before. I tell her honestly—without the exaggeration that *norma*-lly accompanies these kinds of statements:

I read all day.
For *school*?
No, not for school. I'm not *in* school.
God, the life of a writer is *so glamorous*. I wish I could just read and do nothing all day.

Is that what you think Norma? That I do *nothing* all day?

Norma, who is prone to watching movies all day, said:

No, of course not. Why would you think that I think that?

9. As usual, a comment about a subject is somehow separate from the actual subject. People think that you're paranoid when you come to conclusions about what they say to you. The message is, *nothing is personal.* I don't think anyone really takes reading seriously, and when they do, it's because they're readers themselves. But even then, they treat it purely as an act of pleasure, which it isn't. Or isn't all the time. *Oh, how I love to read...* They associate reading with: two weeks on the beach, seven hours on a plane, fifteen minutes on the toilet, twenty minutes before bed—in between time. The time when you're losing time and coping with it by shoving some reading into the dead-space. The lost space. The non-space. Reading is like performing taxidermy. You stuff things into the black belly of an owl or a cat. Into the animal abyss, which is basically the intestinal track. The guts. It's hard to find your way around the colon and still think straight. The colon is the organ that most resembles the tissue of the brain. So that when you're in a bad mood, it affects the way you shit, and when you can't shit, it affects the way you think. During these times, people read when they'd normally be doing something else. Sometimes people read on the toilet while shitting, or feel the urge to shit while reading. Half the time, it really doesn't matter what you read, *People Magazine, The New York Times, The Da Vinci Code*, a cookbook, a manual, the Bible, or even an old love letter. Most people are utilitarian and read everything that way. They think reading choices are arbitrary—that what you like, and what you read, is the same thing, which of course it is. If you like Reagan and baseball, you'll probably really appreciate historically patriotic accounts of War. Any war. Maybe the more recent the war the deeper and more enthusiastic the appreciation. People like things that hit close

to home. I think you can judge a book by its cover, or at least a person by the books they read. Sometimes though, you can confuse a D.H. Lawrence book cover with a Harlequin Romance novel. It happens. In the '70s, printed editions of *Women in Love* or *Lady Chatterley's Lover,* could deceptively come across as overt lesbian fiction or an *Emmanuelle* film-poster. The colors are so peachy cream and dream-like. In them, ecstasy is a fantasy and women everywhere are enjoying their fantasies.

10. On the ride home, the train moves around the ocean the whole time. It's a water line. There is metal everywhere that sparkles, and both the water and the hardware pick up the sun and pick up on each other. Both seem endless and huge and full of blue and white shadows that resemble photographed bees taking off of a flower as if it were a landing strip. On the way, there is a 19th Century brick sugar factory that puffs sweet smoke into the sky and left over wood from old docks and bridges. There are cranes, and the silvery industrial Carquinez Bridge. There is wood everywhere rotting in the sea, and people think the area is an aquatic ghetto. Like the old POP Pier in Santa Monica in the late '60s and early '70s. That's what I hear people say when they look out the window. Two college boys describe the place as a salty hell hole and watch dvds on their portable dvd players. They can't sit still, can't stand being on the train, or looking at something that doesn't tell them how they should see it. I get resentful and glower. I think it's Eden and fantasize about having a bridge for a bed and diving off it in the mornings for a swim. I wish I had a water porch. That my house was on the Louisiana bayou. That my carpet was Spanish moss or lichen or seaweed or an alligator camouflaged as leaves. I can't tell the difference between land and water, metal and wood. I love the view, its decay, and take the train twice a week just to face it, ride beside it. As if the water through the window, on the side of my

face, is a long tear or blue eye shadow liquefying around me. The train undulates, traverses like a snake in the marsh grass.

11. Self-interrogation on the train: *Is being alone, like reading, my hobby too? Instead of being with someone (not reading with them) all the time, am I just spinning solitary waste? Are relationships a form of recycling? Rather than the decadence and single use of doing something alone, I would be splitting everything down the middle and reusing it. Would that make everything better? The virtue would come out of being divided and shared.*

12. In the movies, reading usually represents a parallel world or a parallel identity—you're dead and you're not-dead, you're human and more-than-human, you're animal and repressed-animal, etc. It connects the people doing it to what's happening in the movie or in the spiritual realm. The book is the link to the preternatural world that is just around the corner, or through a wall, a revolving wall of books, but cannot be seen, like in the movie *Phantasm*. The Phantasm's gatekeeper/graverobber is a giant mortician called "Tall Man," who drives around in a black hearse and lives in a phantasmagoric white mansion. The Tall Man's real name is Angus Scrimm, which also appropriately means, "a firm fabric used for theater curtains." Tall Man spends as much time behind Mikey's bedroom wall, the center of dreams, as he does in the town cemetery—the center for death. This both here-and-there points to the fact that horror can do just as well out in the open and does. Horror in the bedroom, or through the bedroom, is a more obvious premise, being that beds are typically associated with privacy, sex, and the oneiric. But I think it's harder to be afraid in public.

13. In horror movies or ghost movies, it's clear that reading becomes a plot device, a way to know things in the movie, and to literally get

access to the power you need to overcome a beyond-human situation. This is especially true in monster movies, in which old men who like to read, and terrified single women who are being stalked, visit an occult friend or an occult bookshop, or are shown reading in armchairs with books on werewolves or vampires, or both, right before they are about to overcome the monster. Many movies reference the occult—*Salem's Lot, Rosemary's Baby, The Exorcist, Don't Look Now, The Evil Dead, Hellraiser, The Omen, Suspiria*, and *The Howling*. In *Jaws*, sitting with a glass of wine after dinner, sheathed in a fish-tank blue—blue light and red wine connect the two main elements in the film, which are blood and water—Roy Scheider looks at old photos of sharks, mostly Great Whites, attacking various things—boats, people, seals. When he says, "Nobody knows how long they live," the shark enters the realm of the occult. He means, no body knows how to kill these things, no body knows if they're immortal, or how they got started, and by not knowing these things, the shark gets lumped in with the vampires and werewolves of the world. All three bite and require special killing devices. As pseudo-gods that are often difficult to get rid of, celebrities also fit into the supernatural category. The modern meaning of the term *celebrity* actually derives from "the fall of the gods, and the rise of democratic governments and secular societies." Jaws isn't the only thing that Roy can't rid of. You can't get rid of a lot of things, so I wonder if that makes them part of the occult too? Both the ocean and murder have been around forever. Does that mean you're slipping into spectral territory every time you go for a swim?

14. I watch *Jaws* at least three times a year. I like the weird melancholy effect it has on me. It's both stupid and deep. It doesn't make me afraid of the water, sharks, or politicians. It's very clear on men. And it's the only movie that makes me feel like a bite has been taken out of my life. In Moby Dick, Melville sees the whale as void, and

says, "*I saw the opening maw of hell.*" But instead of missing a limb, or a cause, part of my memory's been chewed off. I get jealous of the centuries a shark has had at its disposal—all that access to space and time and water and speed. All that privacy. *Jaws* reminds me of what I love, and badly makes me wish for what I would do if it came up again. It's a kind of sand and water and glow that spells red-light alert. Over the years, I've read a lot of behind-the-scenes movie trivia about *Jaws*, accompanied by captioned photos that read: "*Woods Hole experts load the shark's head with red paint, squid and dynamite,*" and "*2000 watts under sea water.*" Through reading I find out that on the *Jaws* set, "*Things had been going so badly they had given rise to all sorts of rumors—that the movie would be called off; that troubleshooters had arrived to straighten the operation out; that the Mafia was involved, or that the film would be completed in Hollywood.*" But all this just makes me love/hate the movie even more. I study pictures of the metal shark's disembodied head and open mouth, propped up and operated by an underwater "*mammoth rig of construction steel covered with rubberized ocean-bottom green paint.*" Both the rigs and the three mechanical sharks came from California. The rig looks like an aquatic rollercoaster. Again, just like remnants of POP Pier's amusement park. They called that particular shark the triple S shark because it stood for Sea Sled Shark. They had to clean its face and reinstall its teeth between takes for all the close-ups. And a little Panaflex camera was used underwater for scenes from the shark's point of view. A compact, hand-held camera, the Panaflex could fit into anything, even a shark's mouth, and cost $2,400 a week to rent. *Jaws* may be the first wide-screen Panavision movie made with a hand-held camera and meant more to the crew than any real person or character in the film. Once, during a third-act scene where the Orca boat was supposed to sink, the camerman, Michael Chapman, panicked and strapped a lifejacket to the camera so that it wouldn't drown and die.

It turns out that it took the crew weeks to load the shark for its death scene, failing over and over to make it look real, that boats like the "Orca" were sunk over and over again. I read that make-up artists used Max Factor spray cans for blood, and that there were "a dozen gallon tins filled with red paint and squid labeled "blood & guts,"" just like Kathy Acker's novel. Footprints were swept off of sand dunes for each take, marbles were thrown against the surface of the sea to make it look like bullets were hitting the water in the final crows nest shoot-out between Roy and the shark, hot coffee was poured onto live crabs to get them to move all over Christy's severed arm, and Oak Bluffs harbor was dubbed Shark City. Apparently Roy felt upstaged by the shark from the beginning, which led to "creative differences." After being eaten several times, Robert Shaw needed a film double so he could flee the country for tax evasion from the IRS. A few years before *Jaws* was filmed in Edgartown, one evening in July Senator Edward Kennedy swam in between two islands where sharks forage after dark without getting eaten. Originally, Verna Fields, who edited *Jaws*, and introduced George Lucas to Steven Spielberg, was asked to be the producer on *Close Encounters of the Third Kind*. But once *Jaws* came out, Spielberg got jealous of all the credit she was getting for its success, and killed her off in more ways than one. She disappeared from a lot of things and *Jaws* is the last movie she ever edited. And when the Bombay press in India asked Julia Phillips, the producer of *Close Encounters*, *Taxi Driver*, and *The Sting*, how Steven Spielberg "got the girl in the beginning of *Jaws* to go this way and that way so violently in the water? Judging by the parentheses she puts her answer in, in *You'll Never Eat Lunch in This Town Again*, Phillips writes, but doesn't say, "Fearless stunt-woman, ten men, ten harnesses, pushpullpushpull, lacerations and bruises for years to come, don't ask." Somehow, knowing all these things helps me sleep at night. "*After 10 hours they made 140 seconds of the movie.*" I think of money being wasted on so little. "The Yacht

Club couldn't get over the huge sums of money spent to make money." "Four hundred people will stampede…chased by a shark…then destroy each other in panic!" "No wonder they all go nuts in Hollywood." And the people watching do too.

15. Apart from sleeping pills, there are two major sleeping aids that everyone uses, or has used at some point to recede—reading and watching TV. Both work unconsciously on you in minutes. I've had friends and boyfriends who have said, "I'm gonna go and read for awhile," and minutes later were fast asleep. I wonder if they knew they wanted to go to sleep and got a book out as a lullaby. Or if they couldn't fall asleep and thought reading would help. Or does reading just bore some people? Maybe dreaming is another kind of reading—your own brain a page-turner. I used to like it when Peter would fall asleep with his face buried in a book as though the book had eaten him, instead of the other way around. It was like I'd caught Peter in a book-kiss and that excited me and moved me. When I see someone sleeping like that, I leave them that way and turn off the lights. I want to give them some personal space because reading is a private love affair.

16. On the train home, the book, *Ghosts in The Medieval Ages*, makes me wonder: What's the difference between being unconscious and being asleep? Is there a difference? Does unconscious mean you're dead and sub-conscious mean you're under something else, a spell, out of view, like a ball that's rolled under the bed? When something or someone knocks you out, are you dreaming during that time or just temporarily dead? Both books and movies attempt to address a lot of these kinds of things. They like to point out different nightmares, digging into them the way a therapy session digs into a person—teasing the nightmare out.

17. All my life, books have turned me on more than movies have. Especially book-sex versus movie-sex. I feel like getting off on a movie is obvious, but getting off on a book isn't. Sometimes during or after a story, I jerk off. I stop reading in the middle of some passage or sentence and just do it. Just to feel closer to the book. Usually I'm bed when this happens. I get really excited by certain words, by certain things being said in a certain way, by people thinking about something in a way that really appeals to me. It's a breath of fresh air, the way that a guy who doesn't sound like most guys is a breath of fresh air. For example, the *Brokeback Mountain* story turned me on more than *Brokeback Mountain* the movie did. I can feel words light up in my cunt. At the thought of a thought. The fact that I can only see it the way that I see it is the best part. I'm not sharing the image I'm seeing. I do that all day long, but with a book, the tables get turned and, like taxes, you get back everything you lost. A book image isn't final. I mean there isn't just one copy to go around for everyone. And it doesn't show up in the same way to everyone, the way a movie-image or a TV-image or a photographic-image does. Reading is a one-of-a-kind process. There's a lot of variation in reading and a lot of me in what I'm picturing. We might all *feel* differently about seeing the same thing, but ultimately we do *all* see what we're seeing. Unfortunately, Winona Ryder is basically Winona Ryder to everyone. She's who she is. She isn't Isabella Rossellini or Uma Thurman to one person, and Brooke Shields or Bob Hope to another. The face I see in a book will never be the face someone else reading the same thing will see.

18. When I lived in London I had an English friend named John. He used to come see me whenever he was in town. I was writing my graduate thesis on the ways in which promotional constructs are mostly shaped by language, not images. In other words, people

talking about things until they're drilled into your head. It was summer. John would visit from Amsterdam, where he normally lived, and pop in to see if I was home. When he was in the neighborhood, we'd go out for coffee. We'd talk a lot. Sometimes when I'd tell him I was busy writing, he'd ask me when I was going to get to a *real* job, which was a really shitty thing to say, considering it was writing that had saved John. It was as if what I was doing wasn't real, and doing it meant I wasn't either. Maybe I'm not. People think because reading and writing are something everyone does in some capacity, or has had to do at some point in their lives, it's not specialized, it's not work. That's why people like fast writers who write a lot of fast books all the time. Book after book—like a Stephen King or a Joyce Carol Oates. Writers, who like any good, productive American, don't turn back, don't look back, and who never get depressed enough to stop. A writing machine, so that writing gets incorporated into any other industrious, mechanical system of labor and produces clear-cut results. I spent a long time feeling pissed off with people who said that I wasn't really doing anything by being a writer. Years. Maybe I'm still pissed off about it. Writing is no picnic, no piña colada. In "Dare to be Lazy," Roland Barthes points out that the Latin adjective of *piger* means slow. Whereas, in Greek, the word for lazy is *argos*. Barthes thinks argos is much more deprecating because it literally means one "who doesn't work." Simple as that. Nada. The Greek don't mince their words. It's really great when you don't have a come back for something and then one just pops up through reading. And if you hadn't been reading and writing to begin with, you'd never learn how to defend yourself. If you believe in them, books have that kind of fairy godmother quality. And when you come across those kinds of things, it's as if ideas are protest spells you can cast on people to get back at them.

19. Barthes said:

1. He often struggled to get things done.
2. When this would happen, laziness was a thing "that imposed itself on him and not the other way around."
3. He took naps until four or five in the afternoon.
4. He'd relax and take orders from his body.
5. This was just a period, an experiment, in his life. Not the norm.
6. This experiment only took place in the country during the summer and consisted of standard diversions—drinking a cup of coffee, getting a glass of water, peeing.
7. If the diversion came from *outside*, he'd get very irritated.
8. Mentions Flaubert's concept of "marinating." Marinating consists of throwing yourself onto a couch or bed—"your thoughts whirl around, you're a bit depressed"— an intellectual damsel in distress act.
9. It takes courage to terminate the marinade. To perk back up from such deflation.
10. He says he never liked sports and, at the time of the interview in *Le Monde*, was too old to play.
11. He asks himself, and others like him: "So what do you want someone like me to do if he decides to do nothing?

(The following passage is Barthes' response to his own question. Throughout, I'm going to interrupt him and step-in during his explanation just to poke around a little, since time has passed. It's a book after, all and I'm reading it. He's in italics, I'm not).

Read? But that's my work. Write? Again, work. That's why I'm fond of painting. (but Roland, painting *is* work for some people—to each his/her own.). *It's an absolutely gratuitous activity, corporal, aesthetic after, all* (by 1979, Conceptual Art had been around for a long time, you should know better than to say that), *and truly restful at the same time, real laziness, because there's no pride or narcissism involved* (most male artists are megalomaniacs), *since I'm just an amateur* (people thought Punk Rock was amateur). *It's all the same to me whether I paint well or badly. What else? Toward the end of his life, in Switzerland, Rousseau, made lace. One could raise the question of knitting, without too much irony. Knitting is the very gesture of a certain idleness* (Victorian women didn't have much choice in the matter), *except if one is caught up in the desire to finish a piece of work* (so, does lazy mean *incomplete?*). *But conventions forbid men to knit* (so you see my point). *Things were not always like that. 50 or a 100 years ago, men commonly did crewelwork, but that's no longer possible these days* (you make it sound like paradise)... *I even wonder if there is such a thing as idleness in the modern age?* (maybe worse than idleness is the co-option of all space—material, symbolic, cognitive.).

12. Idleness can be both the most banal and the most thoughtful thing you can do.
13. He quotes Schopenhauer, who said: "The social representation of boredom is Sunday."

20. I never feel bored on Sundays. I feel like I should be dead and people should be reading about me. On Sundays people read the Bible. In church or at home. There isn't anything that we don't have to read in order to know what it is or how it's done—a recipe, a tax return, an obituary, a manual. When Peter and I used to have sex, I'd ask him to talk to me, to read my turn-ons out loud from the

records that existed on the subject—the past and the things I'd told him. Also, the oral records, which are the original testimonies. I'd ask him to spell out what we were doing in my ear like a narration on sex. *Read me*, I'd order Peter. *It's the only chance I get.* In our relationship, I was famous. A story. At least my desire was. Peter blew it in my ear like a fan from his wrist. Peter was great at telling me stories about what I liked and how much he liked what I liked, and on and on. And as soon as I heard the story out loud, I swear I liked it even more. I looked so good on paper. Our pleasures fused and became part of the same chapter. I'd think: I had no idea I was so open, so dirty, so pliable, so adventurous, so radioactive, so apparent, so interested. I talked back to Peter, only not so much about what he liked, more about what I thought about what he said I did. If he requested something about his own tastes, I was equally happy to oblige. I went crazy when he said he couldn't take anymore of something I was saying or doing. It made me say it even more. The text anchoring the image. We were a bunch of word freaks because language is so sexy. It was like watching the news program, or a *60 Minutes* segment on how great our sex was. What happened between us, what I found out, was always news to me.

17

ACTRESS

I shall awaken memories of love and crime and death...

— *The Mummy,* (1932)

LIKE A CELEBRITY, sometimes Carrie talked about her flaws and sometimes she didn't. Like everyone, she wanted people to know she was fallible and infallible. And like everyone, she had to pick and choose. Carrie sat in a red leather chair that was high, like a wheelchair, or a director's chair. Everyone is an oratory cripple on canvas or leather. She talked as though she was giving an interview just after a touch-up, a close-up, and kept her anger on a palette she was discouraged from sampling. Anger is not a good color, Carrie told herself. Chinese medicine sticks it in the liver, which is sunny or chemical or green. In Medieval times when jaundiced, people ordered you to go home and drink some olive oil with a pill. The liver should never look like tanned skin. Carrots make membrane appearances as well and people are like straws. No body wants to get stuck watching yellow. But flames are nice. A series of blues put Carrie to sleep. *Hill Street Blues*, Dario Argento's early blue films, and *Blue Steele*, where Jamie Lee Curtis is perfect as both sexes. An egg before it adjusts. Carrie had heard it confirmed by Jamie's brother himself, just before he overdosed on a hill, that Jamie had been born two.

Carrie never turned into fire. There were no fire extinguishers in Hollywood. She learned the attitude toward subversion was like the attitude towards smoking—you shouldn't even start. Look at what happened to Norma Desmond. Look. Her close-up was ruined by clouds that verged on architecture.

Sometimes celebrities talk about their plastic surgery, screening their surgical shark bite fresh from the water like an oyster pearl. And sometimes they hide until everything changes shape again. Carrie thought celebrities were the new monster, as monsters have always been in fashion. She thought that someone should really make a horror film about how closely related celebrities are for example to the *Phantom of the Opera* at least once a year. Like before the Oscars. Nosferatu, was a shape changer too, and avoided death by vaporizing himself, sinking into rooms in the form of scanty vermin, or stroking the air with Chiropteran wings. Bats wrap themselves around themselves, one arm across their breast, noticed Carrie, both in *Dracula* films and nature programs. They're so loyal to their cause, they're like soldiers taking a pledge of allegiance while hanging themselves. But bats have a dandy quality too, as does Dracula himself. Or Oscar Wilde.

Celebrities are shape changers just like the undead, with their reruns and revolving doors: their movies, their performances, their costumes for all shows, off screen and on a screen. Character on character, like toast. Promotion about how this and that went and looked, and endless pictorials from circa all the way through circa, and counting. Dracula blocked breakfast for fear of being charred. His centuries like yeast.

"You want to survive and stay alive, but you want to look young doing it," said Brian, Carrie's agent. "That's what I'm here for. You should have a look at *The Mummy*. Have you ever seen that movie Carrie?"

"No," said Carrie defensively. "Why?"

"Because *The Mummy*, Im-Ho-Tep, is the first human restoration project. Even before Dr. Frankenstein stitched up his monster. Everyone pitched in. Dr. Frankenstein had the whole culture behind him. The country will support any length you might go to make yourself better Carrie. It will give you an idea about what you might look like while you're wrapped up in a vortex. A beehive. They're gray too. But buzzing with life inside. Like London. Have you every been there? It might be helpful. Oh, and the producer of *Sarcophagus* is the grandson of Karl Freund. What do you think Dr. Frankenstein was?

"What was he?

"He was the first plastic surgeon. This has been going for a long time Carrie. You're part of a long tradition. But it all worked out for the monster, didn't it?"

"*Which* monster?"

"*Frankenstein*'s monster. All monsters. He got married. Somebody loved him. Somebody beautiful."

Carrie rented the movies that Brian had mentioned and went home. She pushed play and cooked up an image like an egg. Things have to get fried in order for them to be as hot as everyone thinks they are. Frankenstein's monster included. Being looked at was a tragedy. Not being looked at was a tragedy. No one ever gets it right. What is being looked at, if it's done badly? If the looks that are put upon you cause everyone else dread? While Frankenstein was getting started in 1931, and names were showing up, Carrie started making the comparison: Monsters make you turn away. Monsters have you coming back for more. Maybe horror films gradually disappeared because horror no longer needs a separate category, thought Carrie. Nicole Kidman made Carrie just as tense when she thought about all the blood Nicole had lost to look the way she looked in *The Stepford Wives*, compared to the way she looked in *Days of Thunder*. A feral garden, now a sewing kit. The difference is night and day, just like the monster is night and day. Boris Karloff spent just as much time in the makeup chair getting ready for *Frankenstein* as Nicole Kidman, or any other actress, does for any movie she's in. And she's not a monster. *No, she's not a monster*, said Carrie.

Brian was an eclectic and unconventional agent. A werewolf. He only met Carrie at night. A movie buff and an expert on horror special effects and trivia, he thought that as an actress, Carrie should familiarize herself with all kinds of sources and venom. Why just look at the obvious paradigm? In *The Exorcist* Linda Blair did wonders for women and young girls. She showed them what happens to women who don't play by the rules. Women should never be as messy as menstrual blood, Washington DC, or projectile vomit, and are generally much harder to clean. Some religions recognize this and give them a pool to swim in for seven days. It's easy to look sick, but it's just as easy to look well.

Originally, *The Mummy* was based on an Italian alchemist/ hypnotist who claimed to have lived for centuries. Something everyone wants, including Carrie. She looked at the mirror like a sibling, expecting the worst, but sometimes getting something mildly pleasant and familiar instead. Her reflection was like blood, she needed it. She sucked on it. DNA is just like beauty, sequenced. Brian said actors were alchemists because they were transfigurations and highly visible from space. From flesh into gold into stars. Brian's teenage daughter had Brad Pitt tapped to the lens of her telescope, so instead of looking into space, she looked at a movie star. Brian couldn't argue with her. It was true. Carrie turned on the VCR. She pressed play.

Frankenstein: Some time ago…

What happened to the monster? He wasn't a monster but become one through craft. The monster could be invisible and seen at the same time. Like Liza Minelli, whose cardboard image lives in the basement in *The King of Comedy*. She belongs to Rupert Pupkin's celebrity nightmare. Rupert goes downstairs every night and does fake interviews with her. And Scorsese, who's dating Liza in real life, thinks this is hysterical. Liza got stuck in her red sequence dress for twenty years and left her mind. Without the red shoes, she couldn't go home like her mother. Carrie wondered if Liza unconsciously wore the red dresses because she was lost.

Carrie finished watching the film. It was 3 in the morning and her solitude was so spacious it felt like a castle. Brian had lied about the black and white monster. About monsters having prospects. To be successful, monsters must always be present-tense, up on the times. Part of a zeitgeist. They have to swallow and regurgitate the immediate fears of the culture, thought Carrie. And maybe existence wasn't that important after all. Once you're dead, you're dead. People want to stay alive more than anything. No one cares what happens after that. Not even Henry Frankenstein, who became ambivalent as soon as he got what he wanted. A lot of people are like that thought Carrie. There is no happy ending for the monster. Dr. Frankenstein retracted his experiment like a witness statement and the monster was revolved around a torched windmill like a ferris wheel he couldn't get off of. It took the mob less than five minutes to do the job, torch the body, get the ride, while Henry Frankenstein waited in bed much longer, was waited on hand and foot. Recovering. Carrie thought Henry was a bad father who was less than pleased with his son's teenage outbursts. The veins gummy in his head. Henry's fiancée, Elizabeth, never knew what hit her. Like *King Kong*, she had a brief run-in with the monster in her boudoir. But instead of an ape arm, the length of a city bridge, or an erection, Frankenstein's monster stumbled through the window full-bodied and inept like a slapstick comedian. Elizabeth's father was a wedding planner. He got what he wanted.

Boris Karloff sat perfectly still under his make-up like a muse for its painter. Brian was wrong. Things didn't end well at all, and the end is never good. It was only in The Bride of Frankenstein that the monster finds his match and flirts on camera. Holds still or poses like a fashion model. Comes up with his own life, walks away from paternal restraint. Maybe Brian forgot to point this out. All the black and white made Carrie fall asleep, as dreams are rarely in color.

Carrie woke up from a nightmare about *The Mummy*. She thought about what procedures the mummy might be concealing under his bandages. The Mummy looked like a pile of dirty sheets. The smell was a dust rag. Brian hadn't told her. Boris Karloff was always the monster. He was the Mummy and he was the rebuilt car engine. Carrie tried to prepare for her film role and for her role in films. She tried to think of a way to make her life, her summer in Los Angeles, bearable. So she made a list:

1. Get Curtains
2. Wrap myself in curtains
3. Get plants
4. Have flowers
5. Let them die
6. Spend time in the dark, *bathtub, movie theaters, freeway at night*
7. Spend time outside during daylight with black sunglasses
8. Get used to spiders
9. Don't look at anyone
10. Don't think about anyone

I want to be alone, said Carrie. In the credits at the end of *Frankenstein*, the monster's name is a question mark. Not Boris Karloff. On the stormy screen, it read: "The Monster = ?" The space was open and could be filled in by anyone. Carrie thought it meant the monster is interchangeable, replaceable, but also unknowable. She was all tied up. In herself, like the Mummy who is waiting to unravel. Who sat in a box while beauty grew into a nightmare. Traveling isn't easy. The wait is terrible. She lay in bed remembering the intimacy of positions. The moon stayed up like a lamp. Carrie was scrolling through images like a rolodex. The camera was good at reminding people how angles are everything. From inside, two people, two actors, look appropriately spaced out, but from the side, it seemed like kissing was inescapable. The imminence was alarming. Lips have nowhere to go but together. Forward can be nice, but forward was also a different face.

Los Angeles has been cruel to monsters. From the beginning Los Angeles had given monsters full reign. Like any monster, stars need makeup. Carrie thought about how Frankenstein's monster was called up like an ignited rotary telephone. It took a while, but the call was made. His suit didn't fit and folded like paper. He had nothing. Since the movie had been made in 1931, when Los Angeles was about to get black with noir instead, exposing a different set of monsters, Carrie thought Boris Karloff had probably burnt something of his own in that fire. It probably wasn't just the monster that had suffered, but the people who imitated monsters. All those in the company of monsters bear and become monsters. Like Zombie movies, which Carrie thought, were really about conformity. In *Network*, with William Holden and Faye Dunaway, the monster gets up early. He loses his fangs and turns into channels and television stations. The monster is so close you could touch it. He came into your home everyday. He scared you on the hour, every hour. He told you how cold it was. He gave interviews, he interviewed.

"*All the electrical secrets of heaven.*" Carrie had been to Los Angeles three times. But never for her career. She had once eaten an ice cream sundae that came with a plastic palm tree and matched the color of stucco and a few sweaters. The life-size palm tree was also in the window, but she ate through it. The second time she visited, she insisted on walking instead of driving, and then couldn't find her way back to her hotel, so she booked into a new one and bought new clothes. Her ticket and passport were in her pocket the entire time. Carrie barely knew what she looked like at that point. At eleven and sixteen. It was a refuge. Children, girls, don't have that luxury anymore, she thought. Now they're on the outside right away. Like the dusty bookshelf, the mirror is full of dirty things to teach. What happened to not knowing you were in a room? Your body, small, in a room. The body being a rocket ship that takes off and burns you on the way up.

She didn't think about new faces, she thought about new people. It was only when she arrived for the movies, did she get her map of Hollywood. And Hollywood got one of her. But she didn't have to go to Hollywood to get that. It all looked the same wherever you were. In Hollywood, every star has been in every house. Has been seen from every house. Juliet is now a cinephile standing on her balcony, reciting her lines and facing the moon, facing the moon, which like a film icon, changes every day. Romeo replaced by Romeo, Romeo, Romeo.

Carrie learned that in the 1970s directors had had a decade of balls thrown for them, like the one that haunts the *Shining* and Jack Torrance, who is recycled from the roaring twenties into the cold coma of the '80s. When things don't work out, everyone is grumpy. The balls had no frills this time around and took place on the California beach. In the 1970s, it wouldn't have been agents telling Carrie what to do. It would've been directors. On Nicholas Beach, Margot Kidder and her friend, Jenny Salt, found a cheap 1960s A-line house to live in, but the rest of the sand was blank, surrounding them like an island. Donald Sutherland, Margot's once-Canadian boyfriend, told her about the house, *it costs $400 a month Margot. You gotta see it!* Before she ended up naked in the trash, Margot was poor enough to live like a queen in the dunes. Carrie saw some super-8 footage of the water they lived on and thought it looked just like the beach during the end credits of *Jaws*, where Roy Scheider and Richard Dreyfuss wash up underneath the names on the screen, like garbage or seashells. Or Bond spies. Paul Schrader came in like a cloud over the water. He was cruel to his brother and kept a gun beside him at all times. Brian De Palma brought Martin Scorsese, Martin Scorsese brought Harvey Keitel, who Margot thought was weird. One good review, the right pool of words, kept *Mean Streets* indoors for an entire year. Paul Schrader said, "film criticism was part of the movement, not the enemy." No one would ever want Carrie to criticize films, but that's what she really wanted to do. Steven Spielberg never let his brain turn to mush so that he could turn other people's into it instead. The minerals made him lucid. He watched the sea bank and gave it to the movies. Gave it to a shark. Margot Kidder was always naked on the beach. She never meant to end up as an urban accomplice to *Superman*, hanging off his neck like a tie—an Eve to a Super-hero Adam. He was superficial, she was superficial. Originally, Margot wanted something completely different. She was trying to demonstrate what that difference was on shore. She had ideals. But in the end, Carrie thought it wasn't that different, and that's why the end is always the same. Brian De Palma was shy about Margot. He moved closer through film. In *Sisters*, their first date, he made her into a complicated sibling duo and then tore them apart. It made sense since women are so torn about things. Before the separation surgery was even performed in the film, Brian had everyone imagine what it would feel like by using red walls. It was the best relationship he'd ever had. Film was his property, his right. And films are closets for things that need to be put away, like in the movie *Rosemary's Baby*—one long closet with fake towels and fake sheets and doomed utility.

On new year's eve, 1979, Carrie read that Joan Tewkesbury, a writer and director, was watching television, when *Entertainment Tonight* announced a new system for film review called box office scores. Just like football scores, the monitor, where the numbers would flash, was huge and full of paper like a racetrack. The news ruined Joan's night and her arc. She turned off the light and sat in the obscurity. "We're over," she said.

For Halloween Brian told Carrie, "You should carve some new breasts and glow a jagged smile." Carrie knocked on doors, and people changed her and dropped candy into her body bag. It wasn't that her costume was better than everyone else's, it was that it was the same, and on tight. William Holden shed his in Norma Desmond's pool and played it back like a surveillance recording. In movies, everyone is spied on. Did she want be spied on, worried Carrie? No, considered. She felt relieved by her answer. The difference was big.

Brian showed up. He had a key. Carrie said she didn't want to go through with it. There were videos everywhere. She had spent hours, days, watching. Deliberating. Brian was shocked. He thought all the movies would seal the deal. His hair was wet—he had been in some kind of water. His pool, his shower, his thoughts.

"What do you mean Carrie? I'm trying to physically indoctrinate you by incasing you in a history of images. All these films...you're not alone. Faces are human suffering. You think you're the only one?"

"No, I don't."

"Well, then. Did you watch *Frankenstein* like I told you to?"

"Yes I did."

"*And*? Isn't it great?"

"He *dies*. Miserably. He is tortured with his own phobia."

"We're all tortured by that."

"Why do I have to be part of a tradition, why can't I turn my back on it?"

"And be ugly?"

"And be beautiful. Left alone. I want to be alone."

"What are you fucking Greta Garbo? You think all this darkness in your room is going to save you? Why are your curtains always drawn?"

"Movie theaters are always dark. I'm trying to be authentic. I don't want to know about you. About things like you. People don't drop out because they're losers. They drop out because they can't fucking stand it. Where did you get the idea that the monster was rescued?"

"What monster?"

"Yeah, exactly. *What* monster? You tell *me* Brian. I also watched *Targets*. Brian. The monster dealt with his own monstrosity. Karloff finally reveals himself and gets to tell his story. I never knew he was such an Englishman."

"What story? I don't think you have what it takes Carrie. All this is undefeated nerves."

"Nerves are intuition, Brian. Warning signals. My spine isn't the world's fucking ladder. I want to watch movies, but I don't want to be in them. And I won't be the monster for them either. You can't make me into death."

"What are you talking about? Is this because your auditions fell apart this week? You still have *Sarcaphogus*."

"I want a life span. I don't want to be on some life support machine that could be turned off at any moment by a publicist, or you. I start off bleeding and being pelted with corks. Everyone wants me to shut up and die. But look at what I can do with a gymnasium and a fire hose Brian. I flipped cars outside the high school prom. I don't know what you wanted me to get out of watching that one, but it was very educational. Was it for my namesake?"

"What are you talking about? What gymnasium? Is this when we played basketball?"

"Carrie. Carrie. Sissy Spacek. What was it like for her to work with Brian De Palma? A lot of people, women, hate him."

"I don't like to gossip Carrie. I have to go."

"Women aren't gossip, they're news Brian. *News*. 'All the electrical secrets of heaven.'"

"What does that mean? You writing poetry now, Carrie? You're depressing."

"IT'S A LINE FROM *Frankenstein*. They're the magic words that ignite the science. The spell, so to speak. *All the electrical secrets of heaven*. Dr. Frankenstein abused and underestimated his power. Or the monster's power. Or power in general. He discarded it. You think he's a romantic, promoting life, but he isn't. He can't handle anything but death. He's morose. Whereas the monster has seams. He's fiery and his passion is used against him. Henry is work obsessed. He's a businessman. You want me to know that being an actress is a business that creates you? I already know that. It stopped being art a long time ago Brian. Brian. Maybe when it first learned to talk. But the sound ruined everything."

BRIAN WAS LOSING weight. His face looked like a skull. His face was a skull. The death underneath, and the work on top. Brian already had his cell phone in his hand. Emergency exits were at the tip of people's fingers now, thought Carrie. He called someone and walked out the door. He didn't walk out the door and call someone. Downstairs. He worried about thunder. Carrie whispered, "a man after his own image."

Carrie announced her news and slept on it like she'd never slept before. Good decisions are like deep rest. Holidays. She went on a permanent hiatus. She talked images down, slowing their heartbeat. She learned to love movies as a critic and became one. She wrote and thought this about *The Mummy* and *Frankenstein*:

On Being A Monster:

Watching movies can kill you if you don't stand up the right way. Being in them kills you too. I know, I tried. But talking about movies, thinking about them, learning to write about them, might be the only way to endure the rays of celluloid. The stalking, the windmill blaze. Like sunblock as a precaution against not having an ozone layer. It's what Garbo was trying to do with, "I want to be alone." Or, I want to be in the shade. How did cruising ever become optional? In William Friedkin's Cruising, *Al Pacino is sent on a mission to find out, but then turns into a monster and kills things. Or was the monster all along. Men. Maybe. I don't know, maybe he kissed things too. First. Men. People rave about a movie or a book the way they rave about a face. One that's been edited like a movie or a book. Catching on maniacally, the plot gets so easy, it's used over and over again like cooking grease. With the right machinery, you can make anything. We're still in the industrial age for that reason alone. Not yet cyberpunk, or cybereal because of the categorical reticence and creationist plots. We still think constructions are natural growths and treat them like a sublime mountain that's always been there. But even mountains come and go. Move like sets. They haven't always been there and they won't always be. It takes every fashion model hours to get ready, but you think she got out of bed and walked right into your magazine. You don't think about how she's squeezed herself in there, like you squeeze yourself in there. You don't even know she's buying bread beside you, she's that similar. But still, you're willing to give her everything you will ever believe about beauty. Boris Karloff and his monsters visages were written about like any fashion model or actor. The look is poured over. "Heroes and monsters were also subject to scrutiny and adoration in fan magazines," writes Rhona J. Berenstein. According to film scholars, Karloff was always featured in the popular fan magazine* Photoplay. *In one article in particular entitled, "Meet The Monster!" fans were "introduced to the man behind the mask" and "here is an actor who has to suffer in order to become a monster that makes others suffer."*

In other words, there is no difference between Boris Karloff and Robert De Niro, who eats his roles like rat poison, trying to die like vermin. Vermin burrow just like actors burrow. Or Demi Moore, who broke all her bones just to fix them all up again for Charlie's Angels 2. *Sometimes people want to know about monstrosity and sometimes they don't. Sometimes people talk about the plastic surgery they've had and sometimes they don't. Like, how long it took for Boris Karloff to get ready, the chemical sheets on him before he could say even a word. No one wanted to see him without his getup in tact and he knew this and talked about it in the movie* Targets *as though it were a documentary about the disadvantages of horror. No one wants to see anyone they see on film without their get up in tact. Unless their getup isn't intact.*

Two years ago, I quit my job. I was a screen temp. An actress. My breakthrough role was a monster flick that came at the height of my beauty. I would never be as young again or have the chance to play it. My agent turned my apartment into a film library of choices and initially, like everyone, I chose to see the image as intimidating. It scrutinized me, not the other way around. No matter which way you look, or which way the camera points, or which way you point yourself, it's all horror if you believe in monsters. Or, it's all monsters if you believe in horror. I was supposed to make my grand entrance in a stone coffin—a sarcophagus. And it's true that life is something you can take death breaks from. But I didn't want to start off on a death break. It's the wrong foot. It's a bad way to do things in Hollywood, where they always want you dead from the get go. Boris Karloff was in between masks all the time and so are a host of other monsters, I discovered. In Targets, *you were able to clear a lot of things up for yourself Boris. You took full advantage of what films have to offer us in the right hands. You finally told us what you were afraid of, and that is the ways in which horror changes, and can always horrify the horrifier. If you're in the middle of it, do see you it? That monsters are afraid of monsters. The monsters are afraid of themselves.*

18

PROVERBIAL[*]

I got you in my camera
I got you in my camera
A second of your life
Ruined for life

— *The Sex Pistols,* (1932)

BECAUSE YOU TOOK A PHOTOGRAPH of me, I came to life. Before that, no one even knew I existed. But after the photograph, every-one went out and sparked into action. Went out and turned into my hair color, bone structure, my outward rejoice. *I say: "I think most human beings have cruel eyes."* After they read about my internal dynamic, everyone spent their Sunday afternoon com-forting me even though I wasn't there. They'd heard something bad had happened from magazines. My hue, ass, waist, style tips was on their laps, piled up high on their coffee tables. I never even looked like this. And the dream wasn't mine until it was given to me.

---

* All italicized passages in this piece are from *Good Morning, Midnight,* by Jean Rhys.

Because you said my name in the newspaper, the newspaper wrote about my name. Because you told people I was beautiful, people went around thinking I was beautiful. It didn't take much for people not to notice me but notice what other people said about me. *My life, which seems so simple and monotonous, is really a complicated affair of cafés where they like me and cafés where they don't, streets that are friendly, streets that aren't, rooms where I might be happy, rooms where I never shall be, looking-glasses I look nice in, looking-glasses I don't, dresses that will be lucky, dresses that won't, and so on.*

Because you said I had a nice body on TV, my body was included in a television program about the "The World's Best Bodies." They spent hours trying to make my body look beautiful. It wasn't easy. They had to make sure my body was one of the best before they could include me on the list, but it was the list that made that happen They shoved my beauty at people like a fist. They smothered people in my beauty. They gagged people with my beauty. They dragged through people with my beauty like a fish-hook. They depressed women with my beauty. Women are depressed you can see it in their bones. You can see their bones. Even if I wasn't beautiful, there was no one around with the nerve to say it. The camera clicked, and you felt you owed me. For a moment I escape myself.

Because you told a fashion journalist I look like a model, they wrote an article and said I looked like a model. Word of mouth is a powerful way to spread a myth, they say. Writing something about someone is a sure way to spread this virus in a paragraph. Last night and today—it makes a pretty good sentence. Someone wrote something and you got sick. My beauty doesn't budge, but yours does. *I know all about myself now, I know. You've told me so often. You haven't left me one rag of illusion to clothe myself in. But by God, I know what you are too, and I wouldn't trade places.* It's being said and you're saying it. It's a velvet curtain tampering with your view. It's a solid pyramid, and soon I'll be at the bottom again.

Nobody stares at me, which I think is a good sign (1938).
Nobody stares at me, which I think is a bad sign (2003).

Because people say I am six feet tall, I am six feet tall. My height is a story told to intimidate other women. No one really knows how big I am. If I walked by, and was really only a midget, they'd still think I was enormous. It's the size of language making me this big. Making this illusion. I'm not proof of myself, myths are. I'm not beautiful, but the insistence that I'm beautiful is. I'm not the happiest woman alive, the profile on my happiness is.

I think I saw a blonde ponytail swing by. Hit me in the face, block my view. Clear a path. I think I saw a crowd of people gather around the blonde scene like a car crash. Coming to its rescue. I think the blonde ponytail on your head is the modern day equivalent of a tail on a mythological beast, rushed through the dark forest, pulling things in. The Pied Piper's music made all the children accumulate and stay there like humidity. *Blond cendré, madame, is the most difficult of colors. It is very, very rarely, madame, that hair can be successfully dyed blond cendré. It's even harder on the hair than dyeing it platinum blonde. First it must be bleached, that is to say, its own color must be taken out of it*—and then it must be dyed, that is to say, another color must be imposed on it. If being blonde is cultural work, then my work is done and your work is just beginning.

I think it blew past the lens of a camera. I think it became a roadblock, a photograph, a record, a magazine issue, a fashion layout, a purchase, an emulation, a season, a conversation, an imitation, a neurosis, a whispered worry amongst feminists and psychologists. *Today I must be very careful, today I have left my armor at home.* I think it became a contemporary disease. I think I saw dark roots successfully vanish during an appointment. And when the job got done, no one even remembered that you once had dark hair. Dark anything. I think everyone gave you permission to change, to disappear. I think everyone on television said it was acceptable. *Those voices like uniforms... Those voices that they brandish like weapons.* I think I saw the world mask things well, enough to convince most people that it had never been any different. I think everyone spent most of their time pretending and lying, lying and pretending, pretending they weren't lying. I think all the lying and pretending is well lit. I think the scars are like your funny bone, tucked behind the ears, easily hurt, pulled into the hairline, ready to ache, ha, ha.

I think most of them went on to do nothing, but these days the past is all you need. I think beauty and motherhood is more than enough. I think a man once photographed you in the Canary Islands and then became your husband. He took a photograph of you when you were fifteen, and then he wanted to keep looking at you. *And whether prince or prostitute, he always did his best...* I think I heard that he didn't notice you until you stood in front of his lens. I think I heard that he didn't have anything to say about what you looked like until he was looking at a photograph of you. No one had to ask what he saw in you, it was obvious. It was a job. You get paid for things like that. He gets paid to look at you in certain way.

I think there is nothing wrong with being devalued because everything is devalued. I think there is nothing wrong with not being taken seriously because nothing is taken seriously, so you don't stick out in a crowd. Except when you stick out in a crowd because that's what everyone writes, says, you do: stop traffic, kill people, steal breath but in a good way, break legs that are too short anyway, look-perfect, all the time, the most beautiful woman in the world, and they've never seen you. Except there are a lot of women being accused of being the most beautiful woman in the world, so it kind of defeats the purpose.

Venus is dead; Apollo is dead; even Jesus is dead.
All that is left in the world is an enormous machine,
made of white steel.

I think you make neighborhoods fashionable, lucrative, skim milk the only logical choice. I think I lost my apartment because you could afford it and needed a lot of space. I think a fashion degree is a waste of time because didn't you get a job designing socks for Burberry simply because you got paid to wear a lot of their rain-coats in magazines? I think you made meals out of saying you ate them. I think you're starving because you can afford it. I think you said you have an enormous appetite now even though you weighed more before. I think two women on TV complained about how ill you looked, and then praised you for your beauty, and then coveted you for your radiance. I think I was in bed when I heard you got a million dollars to write a book you didn't write and no one read. I think people spend a lot of time defending you when you are the person who needs the least amount of defending. I think when I say that you're stupid everyone comes to your rescue, and when I explain that wisdom and knowledge is something you have to work for and dedicate yourself to, like anything else, everyone says that it's not your job to be smart. I think I went to go work at a pro-gressive art gallery and theater to get some peace and quiet, but all the women who worked there kept getting together for tea to talk about how you were the ultimate fashion model because you were the perfect combination of beauty and brains. I think I went home and never went back because I thought that of all the brilliant women who could be praised for that combination, the beauty and brains combination, it certainly shouldn't be a model and it cer-tainly shouldn't be happening in an "alternative" space.

I think that magazines claim you have flawless skin naturally, but I saw you off the page, and your skin was red and broken. I think I went out and bought something you never even had. I think I want to look like something you never looked like. A computer adds most of the intangible touches. I think I would look good in that position, that light, that color, that way. I think people told me I should be a model, have I ever thought of being model, look like a model, be a model. I could have made a lot of money, but my time has passed. Old hats now. I think you said that at 27, my best years were behind me. I think people decide your beauty for you.

I think I read that you would binge and vomit all night long even though you were the funniest woman in the world. And instead of helping you, women kept saying that you had stumbled upon something brilliant. A great remedy, trick, discovery. Something they wished they could do and then maybe even did. They didn't say. I think I read that by the time you were married to the funniest man in the world, your body just couldn't take it anymore and you got cancer and finally wore down to nothing and couldn't eat because your intestines were tied shut. I think I'm convinced you got cancer and died because of what you did to your body all those years. There was comedy but it was a nightmare. Your guts were miserable.

I think I heard men refer to only models when talking about beauty. I think I heard people refer only to beauty when talking about women. I think I heard people only talk about women who had been opened up when discussing who they considered beautiful. I think people think as long as it's obvious, it doesn't matter whether it's real. I think you drop out of being in the movies until you get a makeover and return. Like the repressed, you make desperate comebacks. I think you have made it impossible for people to expect anything accept bigger tits and a tighter face from you. I think you'll drop out again for a touch-up. *It's the extrovert, prancing around, dying for a bit of fun—that's the person you've got to be wary of.* I think you gave an interview about being sober and then I heard you went to parties all coked-up. I think you had a baby, so that made it unlikely that you were still doing all those drugs. I think you had the baby to have an alibi and so that you'd have something to be other than be a model.

I think you dated her because everyone else wanted to. But no one was angry because they saw you as a good fill-in. If you were fucking her, then so were they. I think I read that you weren't even fucking, that you just wanted everyone to think you were. *When she looks at herself in the glass, naked, she's as proud as Lucifer. In the romantic tradition, and very generous.* I think you wanted to get in on all the action. I think your face is collapsing and something in this society is so disfigured that you never have to think you are. I think I heard a rumor that your husband requires you to be this way. I think I heard the media say you were a strong woman, but I seemed to think that you missed your chance in this case. I think *20/20* did a piece on you saying that you were happy because you took pride in filling your mansion with beautiful things. *That's my idea of luxury—to have the sheets changed every day and twice on Sundays. That's my idea of the power of money.* I think I saw your eye twitching, but it wasn't moving. I think *20/20* did a piece on you when you died of a drug overdose. I think they bragged that you have the best marriage in Hollywood. I think you were married to someone else six months later. I think everyone knows that you are gay, but you still show up with a heterosexual armrest. I think someone on the red carpet asked you what her name was and you responded by saying that you were proud of the ensemble cast in *The Usual Suspects.* I think it was reported that you got on like a house on fire, but really, you wanted to kill each other and the movie was nearly canceled. I think you were the star of your own show and because the camera was almost always on you, you got nervous and reduced yourself to nothing, hoping the camera wouldn't see you. And then when the show got canceled, you met a man twice your age, and stopped acting altogether. I think now you eat again and show up mainly as a smiling accomplice to his achievements.

I think everyone knows that you've molested hundreds of children but they send you more children anyway. I think everyone says you look great for your age, but any part of your age, which could show up in your skin, was eliminated years ago. I think people are saying that now is a great time to be Black, Latino, Asian, a woman, in this country, even though black women in the media wear straight blonde wigs, blue contact lenses, shake their booties at the camera, lick their finger, look like ultimately they're fucking you, or would. I think women wear bikinis on stage because otherwise they wouldn't be on stage, and you are anything but dark skinned and down with your old block. I think they said you were hometown chums, the most famous friendship in Hollywood, an-Oscar-winning-screenplay-writing-team, but really you haven't spoken to each other in years, except when a premiere for one of your movies is nearing and you are expected to be seen supporting each other's careers.

I think it doesn't matter how you treat women in this country because you have learned that you will still be elected to be governor no matter what you've done. I think you said you love women even though you also say they aren't capable of anything, and didn't you kill one of your wives in the '70s? I think you got paid, or agreed to let someone pay you, to keep your mouth shut, hold your cheating husband's hand while the cameras were rolling. I think I thought you were dead because you were so good at being silent. I think everyone thought you were noble, an example. I think you would rather be married to a rich rapist then not married and poor. I think you've signed more contracts than any of us will ever know. *From your heaven you have to go back to hell.*

I think you buy things because you're told to. Try on clothes and purchase them even though they don't feel comfortable, even though they don't look good on you. I think six months later you haven't got the faintest idea why you bought those things because you don't know what you like. I think most of your closet ends up in a high-class charity shop, with a heavy price tag despite the sweat stains. *She says: "Walk up and down the room in it. See whether you feel happy in it. See whether you'll get accustomed to it."* I think the rise of make-up stores in your area makes you think you have more opportunities to look your best, rather then thinking that the rise of so many make-up stores means the only available opportunity is for you to be looked at.

I think I was sitting on a bus when I heard 3 people talking. I think one of them asked what celebrity the other one found attractive? I think they were playing the "Name Your Beauty" game. I think one of them had to defend the celebrity they selected to the other two. I think I thought it was pointless to discuss what famous person someone finds attractive because the selection has already been made for you. I think if you nod your head in approval to somebody else's choices, all you are actually doing is agreeing. I think it's meaningless to take pride in something in which all you've done is subscribe.

I think you are often heard saying that you won't apologize for your wealth, but you want the paparazzi to apologize for the lengths they go to accumulate theirs. I think you go right ahead with your bag of bones shtick and your punched-by-a-needle-upper-lip because if A-list Hollywood men keep showing up at your door, the mutilation must be working and no one's complaining. I think you could have tried to achieve something real, but you wanted a million dollars in a day, so you ate a spider the size of your face on national television without flinching. I think actresses are punished for aging by being forgotten and ignored

(What the devil is she doing here, that old woman? What is she doing here, the stranger, the alien, the old one?), but instead of choosing a profession that would allow them to be valued, they choose to devalue themselves for their profession. I think I have often wondered why women don't exit Hollywood altogether, and then Hollywood would be left with no women to exit.

Never mind…One day, quite suddenly, when you're not expecting it, I'll take a hammer from the folds of my dark cloak and crack your little skull like an eggshell. Crack it will go, the egg-shell; out they will stream, the blood, the brains. One day, one day…One day the fierce wolf that walks by my side will spring on you and rip your abominable guts out. One day, one day…Now, gently, quietly, quietly.

The film shows no signs of stopping. My film-mind. ("For God's sake watch out for your film-mind…") I think when both of you won your Oscars two years ago, it was like killing two birds with one stone. Everyone felt relieved and the tears you spilled was the reason you are currently the most desirable black woman in white Hollywood. I think you asked her a question on TV about whether she had cheated on her boyfriend and expected her to give you an honest answer. I think you forgot what you were dealing with because you wanted everyone else to forget too. I think we need to see you doing it first, if we're going to know how to follow. I think the myth of "turn-off-the-television-if-you-don't-want-to-know" is a myth. I think you can turn off the television, but you'll just end running into some body else's.

I think it doesn't matter if you're a cliché, as long as you're a cliché in demand. I think he has already been married to three other clichés who look just like you, but who's counting? I think he makes sure that he gets the same thing every time and that way it never feels like anything has changed. It never feels like he has ever changed. It never feels like he will ever have to change. I think he has a right to age, but a cliché never does. *But, my dear good lady,*

Théodore's has been crawling with kindly Anglo-Saxons for the last fifteen years to my certain knowledge, and probably much longer than that... Why get in a state about it?

I think you used to be the highest paid model in the world. I think you said you wouldn't even get out of bed for less than 10,000 dollars, and now you're pulling your eyes up with knives just to stay in the game. I think many people were outraged by that statement for the wrong reasons. I think you didn't want to get out of bed because you didn't have a reason to unless a carrot was being dangled in front of your face. I think a magician paid you millions of dollars to have your blonde hair on his shoulder, a sense of generic possession, but whenever I saw you, you were not with the magician. I think you became ugly, but people have been invested in your beauty for so long, that it doesn't matter what you look like anymore. *It's all right. Tomorrow I'll be pretty again, tomorrow I'll be happy again, tomorrow, tomorrow...* I think what you do says a lot about your character, but we live in a country where we are constantly being told that it says nothing. I think you do things that are impossible to conceive of, and yet I am the only one who can't conceive of it.

I agree with everything. A queen, a princess—that's something. I do not speak.

19

Who's Afraid of Virginia Woolf's Nose?

(The Reception Climate)

Everyone recognizes her with delight, since everyone has already seen the original on the screen.

— *Siegfried Kracauer*

WHILE LOOKING GLORIA THOUGHT, *the easiest thing to say is that someone is beautiful.* Already everyone agrees and is saying it, so you don't have to go out on any limb. What's hard is to not like something everyone likes. Gloria hadn't seen anyone try, but that just proved her point. On TV no one was trying, in the movies no one had tried for years, and around her everyone was afraid to try. Didn't give trying any thought. The other day, by the sound of things, because things sounded the same, she thought she was at Cannes or a film premiere, but it was just a neighborhood bar. Acclaim for far away was scenting the social like incense. And a few weeks before that, Gloria's friend Joyce asked her what she thought of Catherine Zeta-Jones and got angry when Gloria had only bad things to say.

"Is she a personal friend of yours?" Asked Gloria.
"No, but everyone thinks she's gorgeous."
"Well, if everyone thinks she's gorgeous, then why do you need my vote?"

Joyce continued the redundant survey with someone else. Redundant because it was a survey that got Joyce hooked in the first place. The room chimed in psychically. Conversations are like séances.

Brad Pitt absorbed approval like a sponge. She watched *Entertainment Tonight* use him to give everyone a bath. She watched showbiz get dirtier and dirtier as the years went by. And yet everyone still thought it was the way to get clean. The TV flared up and scheduled bath-time like the consummate babysitter.

Liking things is a chore. Listening is a chore. It's not easy to scrub away. It's not easy to get rid of your skin in favor of other skins.

It was true, Hitchcock had done his share of cattle branding and was blonde repetitive just like Peter Bogdanovich, but at the end of the day, Tippi Hedren stopped making Hitchcock's movies. Stopped taking Hitchcock's calls.

Gloria waited for something to come that be would interesting to scrutinize. Whatever happened to Sunday afternoons with Bela Lugosi or Ingrid Bergman, when at least you could watch their films without having to listen to what everyone thought of their faces.

Before you heard anything about them, remembered Gloria, first there were just films.

Now all you did was hear things first. Now you were just told. Who knows what the details of Bergman's body were? No one ever saw a layout, except maybe her lovers. But even lovers don't always get up close or spot things. Gloria thought most lovers are like bad doctors. They miss all the signs while they pull you apart like curtains. Beauty, America liked to point out, was about being able to look at a face without wanting to push through into another one. Some faces are turnpikes, the Holland Tunnel, While others are like the Hamptons, expensive and popular.

It used to be that bodies were only prone to forensics and computers if they were dead. Now you can't tell the difference between shows like *CSI Miami* and *America's Next Top Model*. They were both basically doing the same thing. Testing the limits of how much death a life can take.

Gloria didn't want to walk through the crowded parts of New York City anymore for fear that she'd be walking into a laboratory. *When I watch films, should I stop thinking about whether the men who make them are good?* Gloria was amazed at how different people were from their stories.

At a coffee shop, Gloria insisted, "Marilyn Monroe was different."

"Why? She was from the 1950s. That means things *weren't* different. They're the same, and any potential for further exploitation was only impeded by a lack of technology," said Joyce.

"I didn't say they were better," insisted Gloria. "I said she was a particular kind of symbol, for a particular kind of thing. Now everyone's the same kind of symbol for one kind of thing. Marilyn paid the price, just like Judy Garland paid the price, reaped the rewards right into her grave."

Marilyn's nightstand was photographed like a mausoleum of death—night lamp at night, night pills shining like stars. She saw it every time Marilyn's death was under review.

"But Marilyn didn't have her nipples poking through a see through teddy in the supermarket next to a rack of gum and some Tylenol. It's that kind of shit that gives me a headache. She got chewed up like gum, but it didn't happen at a check out line. It happened over a period of time. It happened with presidents. Now everyone's a president."

Gloria remembered how in the movie *Klute*, the female character Bree Daniels, a prostitute, had an autographed picture of John F. Kennedy hanging on a wall, above her bed. In an interview that Gloria had read while sitting in an anonymous bookstore, Jane Fonda said that it was her choice, not Bree's, to use Kennedy's autographed picture in the movie. She wanted viewers to think that Bree had been JFK's special client. That he was a fan of hers, not the other way around. Jane's biography, also at the bookstore, said it was 1970 and Jane was "getting people into trouble." She was bringing risks onto film sets like dirty laundry or a private diary. After Pakula finished shooting *Klute* in New York City, Jane kept wearing Bree Daniels' shaggy haircut. In the movie she wore it as a prostitute. In real life, she marched in anti-war demonstrations with it, accepted an Oscar, went to Vietnam. In the movie and in real life, she fucked Donald Sutherland.

"So that makes it better?" asked Joyce. I think it makes it worse because they were so invested in Marilyn and it still didn't make any difference."

Joyce liked Gloria, but thought she was too serious. Gloria could laugh with Joyce, but Joyce could not be serious with Gloria. Not everyone's a cocktail, able to mix something sweet with something astringent. It's how people are, capable of easy things, not capable of hard things. Gloria was full of hard things to say.

"If *you* weren't so beautiful, I wouldn't take you seriously," said Joyce like a man. "You could have made a fortune, but instead you choose to make yourself miserable."

Gloria flinched. When people, women, misunderstood her on such a high note, she wanted to stop talking altogether. Stop showing her face.

"I don't do that Joyce. That's done for me. I'm trying to swim in the pond without getting diarrhea. Anyway, you should only take beauty seriously if the person who's beautiful goes against their *job* as beautiful. The best thing I ever did was use my beauty as a backdrop instead of a platform. I'm not going to walk around administering it like a vaccine."

"Maybe I'm just used to the dirty water," said Joyce, who treated the conversation like she could take it or leave it.

Both Marilyn Monroe and Judy Garland had their names removed like tumors. Before they did anything else. They were like

immigrants, who always have to sacrifice something to get something in return. Who starts off with their names? Stars are woven
into the fabric of life by everybody, one stitch at a time. And, anyway, people have such a limited vocabulary when it comes to stars,
thought Gloria. They get called the same thing over and over again.
Everyday. If you chant something, it becomes part of you. The
sounds you make. *Most beautiful woman in the world, most beautiful women in the world, beautiful.* Everyone is the most beautiful.
Gloria watched beauty get cancelled out like an algebraic equation.

It was harder to like something everyone wasn't pressuring you
to consent to. Before the 1990s, people didn't have to see every
female nook and cranny unwrapped and dissected, week after week,
while waiting to buy butter. That's how coveting makes its excessive
way into things like food, and that's why bodies and food stick
together. Gloria knew how mercurial self-esteem was. You need
something cold to freeze it. If it moves, it's no good. You slip on it,
you get loose in it. The real job of a celebrity was to seem stable. If
they budge, it's because a producer pushed them. Gloria wondered:
If I didn't look, or stopped looking, would I be free?

If the media was a zodiac, like, "Born In The Year of The
Media," Gloria was lucky because she was born right on the cusp.
In 1973, she had had a quieter time with the TV and countless flu's
that left her impaired. She was moved onto the living room couch,
sick in front of everyone, and didn't know if what she saw was real
or a fever. She still doesn't know. Like, was there a show about a
father and his two kids, a son and a daughter, who ran around in the
'70s surrounded by dinosaurs? They wore plaid and Clarks and
flared jeans? There was limited vegetation? They hid in caves? Did
Plato's cave have anything to do with it? With reflections? Was this
before human beings happened or after they ended?

Gloria mainly watched old and new movies when she was little,
and rarely heard a peep of praise about who was in them. If you

wanted that, you had to go out and look for it. The supermarket magazine aisle, a celebrity biography. Thirty years ago, brainwashing took more motivation. Now it melts in your mouth like a lozenge. Gloria didn't remember anyone popping in to tell her how beautiful Brooke Shields was. She'd have to pop in herself to find out, not the other way around. She could have just as easily never heard a thing. She was interested, immersed, but only to see why other people were. By extension, the way extension cords can start off in one room and plug into another. Gloria thought Siegfried Kracauer was a visionary prophet for writing *The Mass Ornament*. This in particular: "Nobody would notice the figure at all if the crowd of spectators, who have an aesthetic relation to the ornament and do not represent anyone, were not sitting in front of it." He would have thought the 21st Century is just like the 1920s. Crammed, full of extras, lumps and clusters, and pattern and expense accounts. He said, you can't have one without the other. You need a kaleidoscope. You need photocopies. He would of thought the 21st Century is like nut butter. Clogged, and may contain traces of other nuts. The peanut oil sitting at the top like a murky film. Film *is* murky, thought Gloria, as she read *The Mass Ornament* on the subway going Uptown to work. Film glazes over things, keeps them smooth and quiet, and if you stir it, it seeps right into everything. Everyone. Dario Argento made his films red & blue because he understood that films were like veins. Everything goes through them. Your ideas, my ideas, nightmares.

Once, in a library at night, Gloria read part of Andy Warhol's diary. In it, he described Brooke Shields as the perfect doll, the closest thing to mass production. Up until that point, Gloria had thought artists didn't like what everyone liked. But Andy got rid of the difference. *Maybe artists can't protect you either.*

For their 10th anniversary, *Access Hollywood*'s Nancy O'Dell, herself named "One of the 20 Hottest Stars Right Now," opened with a section called, "Support The Stars Bumper Stickers" for people to stick on their cars. It was just like the "Support The Troops" stickers, only less pressing and stars are always near by. Though both soldiers and stars are on TV during times of crisis, the country is just as crazy about soldiers and stars when things are quiet. On the program, a fan of Jennifer Aniston's exclaimed, "I love her and I think it would be *so* cool to drive around with a sticker that says that. That I'm there for her. Especially while she's going through *such* a difficult time with her divorce."

They've got banners, what do they need stickers for? Gloria snapped. Cheers and applause. Even when she turned the volume on the TV down, the subtitles read, "*Cheers and applause.*" Gloria turned the TV off and walked to bed thinking, *even if you're deaf you can hear.*

On Monday, while drinking coffee at her local café, Gloria thought about how when a restaurant opens, no one ever wants only a few people to like the food. Maybe in Europe, but not in America where intimacy is a self-help term. Everyone has to like all the food. That's how you know a restaurant is successful. The waiter asked Gloria what she would like and where she was from. Both questions were taken like orders. She told him, but named only the city. She remembered how on her recent vacation in Lisbon she spent thirty days walking. Two days into her stay, she met a filmmaking couple. They talked about documentaries, anti-abortion laws in Portugal, and the food they loved. She drank espresso with them by a fountain and a garden, Praça de Flores, across the street from where she was staying, and they listened to her intently. They said, "You should try the risotto with shrimp and mussels, or fresh fish with its head still on. It comes with parsley and lemon."

José and Sina told Gloria that the best place to eat in Lisbon didn't even have a name. It was in the Bairro Alto, half way up a hill. On Rua do Norte Street, No 73. Walking in Lisbon was hard work. The slippery tiled hills strained Gloria's calves. There were seven hills and Gloria could only wear sneakers, otherwise she would have slid down.

"But it's not always open," said José, "so, you'll have to investigate."

"What time do you usually eat there?" Gloria asked them, intrigued. She loved being told about things most people didn't know. She liked anything that was outcast. She wanted to be on the periphery, instead of through the center. She liked receiving things word of mouth and wanted to eat rice dishes like secrets.

"Oh, whenever it's open," said Sina.

There was no desperation. Gloria wasn't used to doing things without it. No one cooked with desperation and no one ate with it. That's also probably when no one ever got fat. She went to the name-less restaurant everyday. No. 73 didn't have any lights on. It was black, like the street name. The shutter door was black too. And everyday it was closed. Gloria went at lunch and dinner to check. On the fifth day, the restaurant was finally open, and there was a crowd of around twenty people outside waiting to get in. Smoking and leaning against the pink walls. Some couples reclined across the street on the sidewalk like they were in a living room. Gloria sat down on the dark slope and smoked a cigarette. She studied the anarchy sym-bols and love poems scratched into the walls. The street tipped over like a scale and she could see the Tagus River at the bottom. This was the awful part of being alone. Not being alone itself, but aloneness in relation to *other* people who think there's something wrong with being alone. Most people don't like people who spend all their time alone. She didn't mind being alone except when people screened her solitude like a movie. Spying on her like an unconventional plot, both entertained and confused. Female aloneness by choice was so rare, it was almost a separate genre, a fantasy, science fiction. There was always some suspension of belief and some degree of sexual apocalypse involved. If she could get laid, why wasn't she? If she could fuck, why wasn't she fucking? Gloria walked around like a monk in modern apparel with everything bouncing off her. Being alone was the opposite of being an actress. No one has anything you do on record. No one wants to imitate you. She was like a tree that falls in the forest. If she was beautiful, but no one said so, or had her, did her beauty really exist? Was she important, but buried like treasure? Gloria lived her days undocumented, unphotographed, documenting, photographing. She liked being alone, *alone*. Alone while everyone wondered why she was alone was where it all crumbled.

"Are you alone?" everyone asked her when she traveled. "Why?"

Because being with people leads to that, Gloria always wanted to say, or sometimes said.

Gloria wanted someone and something to stick. She was alone, then she wasn't. Then something would happen, and she'd be alone again. There was never any middle ground. There was never any transition. It was either complete consolidation or complete deficit. Each time Gloria thought she could get rid of it completely. Never be alone again. Like the time she was in the blue room in London. Whenever Gloria would stay at her friend Louise's house, Louise would put her in her roommates Fred's room. Fred always slept at his girlfriend Mia's apartment on the weekends. Gloria didn't know if Fred knew that she was sleeping there when he wasn't. She asked Louise if Fred knew over and over again, but Louise would just tell her it didn't matter. Fred's room was like a blue box. There was a window, a camera on a tripod, and clothes. Gloria slept in Lousie's orange tee shirt with the windows open, the rain spewing into the duvet. She liked all the elements of sadness at play in Fred's room— the color, the size, the gray sky, the rain. The blue duvet. She wondered if sadness made the blue room blue. If Fred ever felt blue in his room and if the room had anything to do with it.

What Gloria didn't know was that her husband Ben, whom she hadn't met yet, had slept in the blue room three years before she did. When instead of Louise, Janus and Anna, who were from Denmark, lived there. Whenever Ben would get drunk and couldn't walk home, he'd sleep in the blue room, though she didn't know if it was blue when Ben had slept in it. She liked to imagine that because they had both slept there before they met, they had slept in it together. That they were together all along, in a cinematic diegesis, and the cobalt was just a period, an emotional style. Part of their nervous system. Gloria met Ben through Louise. Ben lived around the corner from Louise and Gloria never even knew it. In Fred's blue room, Gloria imagined finding someone. Discovering them underneath the blue blanket. She wrapped the blue walls around herself like a temper, her solitude pinching like saline. The wait was a hospital, and the delay was held in static on a radio station. When she was little, Gloria thought that because of their blue-black color, their beaten tone, horseshoe crabs were the heartache of the sea. They were always left behind on the sand after the tide had retreated, black and shiny like polished boots. Gloria went to Lisbon because she was alone again.

Inside the unnamed restaurant, there were only five tables and the light was on everywhere. Inside the restaurant was the opposite of outside the restaurant. The waiter asked her if wouldn't mind sharing a table. "With a couple," she asked him? Gloria never wanted to seem alone or reliant. She worried that the couple would feel obligated to talk to her and then she'd feel obligated to free them of that obligation. She just wanted to be on her own, no questions asked. When Gloria was alone, she could think about what everyone around her was saying. But maybe no one wanted to feel her eavesdropping. As with everything else in Lisbon, when it was open, she wrote emails in a small cyber café called "Luna" that served espresso, fruit salad, and let her smoke. What the waiter should have asked Gloria was, *do you think they would mind sharing a table with you?* Above all, Gloria tried to stay out of everyone's way. Out of harm's way.

At Simons in New York, the waiter said, "That's all you're going to tell me?" he grinned and moved closer to the table like it was his bed.

"That's all you would understand."

"That's not very nice," he said.

"Neither is being treated like a cliché," snapped Gloria. Tough as nails, soft as damp wood.

She lowered her head. He walked away thinking Gloria was somewhere between sexy and paranoid. She felt him complain about her as "the woman with the dark hair who never talks to anyone," in the kitchen like it was part of her order. Gloria came in a lot, only ordered mint tea or coffee, and always read a book. Simons was the kind of place you only went to spot or be spotted, but Gloria went there anyway, to look at what people were spotting, so she could think about it or write it down. She hadn't yet, but it was all material that she cared about greatly and turned like doorknobs on a door. Walking inside. But sometimes she didn't have the heart to go anywhere.

When the movie *The Hours* came out people were afraid of Virginia Woolf's nose. Many had never seen or read the real Virginia, but from what the adaptation revealed, it didn't look pretty. Science has a saying about symmetry, and Virginia's ugliness was put together like a bad science project. This was good, said *The New York Times*, *The Post*, and *The New Yorker*. It made it so much sadder. So much truer. But female intelligence is female trouble. Is trouble period. And genius is suicide.

The screen said if Virginia was good and gloomy, she couldn't also be pretty. Gloria thought Virginia wouldn't have dragged herself through sleep, against the mileage of England's current if she could have had it all. In the movie, they hung an elephant trunk on her face, a piece of ham, and then slammed into it. In the press, Nicole Kidman said it was a compliment, an honor, to wear the nose. Instead of looking beautiful, Nicole could look ugly and miserable. Could really be free. It was freeing to be free of beauty. She liked having literary misery pinned to her face. Either way, those characteristics had to be worn somehow. So Nicole slipped into Virginia like a Halloween costume. Gloria didn't know what the nose was made of, but it was made to look significant. She also didn't know who invented the nose, but it was there forever now. Boris Karloff was also hosed down with chemicals and treated with colors that nearly killed him.

Everyone in the theater believed what they saw about Virginia because no one was interested in looking at old pictures to see the difference if they could look at new ones. But Gloria knew that the pictures revealed a patrician nose—"*aristocratic, blue-blooded, gentle*"—*not* a special effects disaster. The message was being mixed. Gloria thought both descriptions were alienating. The one above described a WASP. *Gentle* was good, Virginia did look gentle, but the rest of the definitions were there to push people away. The other, the nose, was there to make everyone feel better about not being an crazy, ugly artist. Gloria thought it had to be important that Hollywood made a special point of ruining and trashing a perfectly good nose. A nose that was better than Nicole's because it wasn't sweet and subservient, it wasn't masquerading its feelings all the time and cut up into little pieces people could swallow.

Gloria had looked at the famous black and white photograph of Virginia in her white dress, sitting sideways, with her hair in a perfect circle, many times. The first time she saw it was in a Women's Literature Course she took in college. First she read, *A Room of One's Own*, then *To The Lighthouse*. She saw *Orlando* one summer in Provincetown. She saw it with her parents, in the only theater there, when she was fourteen. Then she read it in college in the woods and wrote a paper on it. About doubles and androgyny. About ambiguity. She said Virginia and Orlando were changelings. Nicole was just a creepy birthday clown. When the computer ate her first draft, Gloria wondered if the campus computer lab had a thing against feminist term papers.

The photograph of Virginia was romantic and intelligent. It made Gloria sad because the world turned a beautiful woman into something ugly. There was no way she could be anything but One thing. An "and" would have killed the whole thing. But everywhere Gloria looked, she saw people being labeled important because they were "beautiful." Virgina Woolf was the best kind of beauty—"a serious goddess," Gloria told Joyce, who had never seen or read Virginia. "Not a Hollywood car accident." Gloria wasn't just being paranoid. Even before the movie came out, she had heard about the "nose-in-progress." It was everywhere. On the news, in magazines, *how brave Nicole Kidman was to play someone so ugly. How did she get so brave? What's it like being ugly?* They never once treated beauty subjectively. They never once imagined that an actress could be ugly and a writer beautiful.

"The problem is, Gloria told Joyce, "is that Virginia's ugliness, or more specifically, her ugly *nose*, which for people always sabotages the entire face, has simply been invented. There was nothing wrong with her nose. Maybe somewhere, someone in the world didn't like it, sure, but it certainly wasn't the focus of anything. In fact, she was considered very beautiful during her time. So why create a facial blight that didn't exist? Why feature it as a prominent physical "problem"? And why upstage Virginia's talent and genius with a rubber prop?"

"Because a woman who is beautiful would, or rather should, never choose to write and be serious, *painfully* serious, if she could ride on the coattails of her beauty instead," said Joyce. Joyce knew what the problem with most things was. The problem was she just didn't care.

"That's exactly what it is!" Gloria yelled. Excited that she wasn't going to have to convince Joyce of anything that day. Instead they could just go on from there.

"She went against the grain," said Gloria, both angry and hopeful. "The grain of her beauty and appearance. And Hollywood wants to punish her for that even 64 years later. Even though Hollywood and literature are really miles apart, Hollywood still gets to be everyone's fucking disciplinarian."

Joyce hadn't read anything by Virginia, but she had seen the movie *The Hours* and read Michael Cunningham's book. Gloria had read it in 1999, a few years before the movie came out. She was sick in bed and read four books in a row, one of which was *Alias Olympia: A Woman's Search for Manet's Notorious Model and Her Own Desire*. Gloria would fall asleep, covered in books, in between books. Then, when Gloria was better, and back to work again, she kept reading more books, walking down the street reading, as though her fever had never ended. She didn't want to let go of the feeling of protection that books gave her. The light was so bright, but books were able to shade her. She could hold them, look into them, take as much time as she wanted. Ignore people. *It's hard to ignore people. If I let go, I won't be nearly as concerned.*

On her walk home, Gloria thought about what Joyce had said. About Virginia's face on film. She thought being famous was like being prehistoric. People survive on screen the way cockroaches survive in households. There are TV's in households too, she thought. Actresses and fashion models are reassuring because they make everyone believe that women just want to be seen all the time. Gloria remembered how when Bree Daniels' therapist asks her what she wants, Bree says, "What I would really like to do is be faceless and bodyless, and be left alone." Greta Garbo had said that too. And so had Gloria. When you're on film, everyone just continues watching regardless of what time it is because film is permanent. Women will look into anything for a reflection, thought Gloria. Cracks were always meant to be bad. But maybe they weren't. Maybe people had been avoiding the wrong thing. *If I didn't look, would I be free?*

In *Klute*, no one in the room was beautiful until it was declared. And even then, it was shaky. No one is sure of anything, not even of decisions. In *Klute*, there is a scene in the beginning, where Bree Daniels is at a model casting for a commercial. She is sitting in a long row of women. The women in the room are stacked in a row against a wall, like photographs or paintings before they've been hung up. They're all sitting down, waiting. Three judges, two men and a woman—the woman the loudest—walk past them, appraise them, dish out the dirt, insult them. They pause, then start to walk again. Just like they're looking at paintings. Mainly bad paintings, or paintings they don't like or understand. Most of the art is bad, but the taste is bad too. Some women are worth looking at for a moment. Talking about for a second. But in the end, they're all dismissed. Compliments and insults are handed out and then retracted like flyers.

"There is very little difference between a compliment and an insult," Gloria informed Joyce.

Between a flaw and perfection. Both have the same impact. For a moment, one of the models in the movie thought she was beautiful because they looked at her the longest. But when they decided she wasn't beautiful, she stopped thinking it too. Beauty is a road show and moves around a lot, from town to town, so you have to be willing to tour. *It's like a job, people lose beauty all the time.* Successful, then unsuccessful. Gloria liked movies because she liked things that were revealed in the dark. She was in the dark when Bree Daniels' psychiatrist asked, "Bree, what's the difference between going out on a call as a model, or as an actress, or as a call girl?"

People said, "It's so good to see someone like Sarah Jessica Parker get to be on TV in *Sex and The City.*" But Gloria would rather not see anyone get inflated. Even if they start out "ugly," the outcome is the same. "She's untypical. An underdog. An unlikely icon." An underdog is no longer an underdog, explained Gloria, when they're on TV and worshipped by millions of women. And anyway, it wasn't just what the underdog got excluded from that mattered, it was what the underdog refused to be a part of.

Gloria is tall. Has dark eyes and dark skin. Fits some mandatory categories and fails others. Sometimes she fits completely and sometimes she doesn't fit at all. It all depends on the city, the country, the neighborhood, the village, the suburb, the year, the weather, the context. The century. It really depends on who's doing the fitting. The tailoring. The pining. People have been taught all their lives to see something one way or the other. Beauty as a final destination takes a lifetime to land on. But with the right tools and talk, it can be shifted, moved around, undone in minutes. Then there's also highlighting some other person's version of something, instead of your own. It gets complicated and seasonal like grapevines. It may have to do with ad libbing, or just the right sparks.

Gloria has been stopped and asked if she is a model many times, or ever wanted to be one. Do you? Some people find it hard to believe that any one would look at Gloria twice. Gloria wondered: *Does beauty mean being looked at all the time by everyone?* Sometimes she gets ignored while shopping for food at places like the *Gourmet Garage*, where everyone is too busy to take note of what works and what doesn't. Who works and who doesn't. Where the narrowness of each aisle and shelf, translates to the narrowness of vision and desire. If people want to sample fresh bread and olives, do they really want to sample faces too? If they go out on a limb with victuals, take chances with contents—their guts—do you think they really want to change themes? See differently?

Most people don't eat food for nourishment or taste or well-being, or repair. And they rarely consume beauty for those reasons either. Everyone is sloppy about everything.

Gloria gets told she dresses brilliantly. Where did she get that? Where did she find it?

I see you around all the time, and I love the way you dress. Gloria tells herself and others, "*Now is the easiest time to be different.*" If she wanted to, she could march right into these things, take them to the heart. Take them to the bank. But she marches away. Swats it like a fly.

ACKNOWLEDGEMENTS

To Wesley Savage, who took me to California, allowed to me write uninterrupted, and gave me many gardens to cultivate. I'll always be grateful. To my sweet & remarkable parents, who are always there to talk to me. To Chris Kraus and Hedi El Kholti, for letting me pursue them, and for giving me and my manuscript a chance before it was even a manuscript. To Marilyn Minter for giving my book its beautiful "face." To Andrew Berardini for his editorial help. And finally to Brian Pera, whose readership and support alone, made the book worth doing. And to all the Hollywood ghosts, who through literature have somewhere to go.

ABOUT THE AUTHOR

Masha Tupitsyn was born and raised in New York City. In 2004, she worked as an assistant literary editor at *BOMB Magazine*. She has received numerous fellowships and awards, and most recently, her story, "Houses (Or The Uncanny Glows in The Dark)" was a 2005 finalist for the Panliterary Award for Fiction, sponsored by *Drunken Boat* Magazine. Her fiction and film criticism has been published or is forthcoming in *Bookforum*, *Fence*, *Five Fingers Review*, *Unpleasant Event Schedule*, *Me Three*, *Monkey Bicycle*, and *Nth Position*.